DELUXE UFO TOUR COMPANY

"The truth is out there. So stay home."

James Wharton

Deluxe UFO Tour Company

James Wharton

Published by Desert Wells Publishing

Second Edition

Copyright © 2015 James Wharton

1

Eddie's Wake

Cousin Eddie died. The call came Friday morning just minutes after our terminally ecstatic boss, Lisa Tomorrowoski, announced the parent company had decided to downsize our advertising agency. That double dose of bad news left me trying to balance my loss of income with the $834.00 last minute airfare for a flight from Detroit to Kansas City for Eddie's Saturday funeral. They didn't balance.

Eddie and I were never close. We were in school together, but when we reached seventh grade, my family moved away from our hometown of Elberta, Kansas. Since then, I'd only seen him at infrequent family reunions. I always tried to avoid him.

Mother said I was uncharitable, but being around Eddie was distressing. He had what some people refer to as a lazy eye, except he had two of them. When I talked with Eddie, his eyes would sort of point off to the left and stare past me as if he were talking to someone behind me. Now and again I would turn around and look, but there was never anyone there. Sometimes, he laughed as if whoever wasn't there had told a joke. And now he's dead.

But my biggest worry was the probability of losing my job. You noticed I upgraded the threat of losing my job from possibility to probability. That's because that's how those things always go. "There is a chance, though only a slight one," Lisa said, "that you will be laid off." She told me I shouldn't be concerned. "I'm not at all worried about the downsizing, Stan," she said. Of course, she wasn't. She was the daughter of the company's CEO and there was no way she would be one of the unwashed masses getting their walking papers.

But today was Saturday and I was trying to look on the bright side of things. I'd started reading a motivational book on the airplane this morning and decided these events were the best things that ever happened to me. That's what the book said to do. No matter how bad things get, just look at them like they're the best things that ever happened. The glass of wine I drank had reinforced that conclusion.

As I pulled my car into the parking lot of Elberta, Kansas' only funeral home, I was dreading going inside. I didn't like seeing Eddie even when he was alive. At least he wouldn't be in a conversational mode. But Aunt Virginia, Eddie's mother, would also be in there. It was Aunt Virginia who called me yesterday morning. She was a perennially talkative woman who soaked herself in perfume every morning. One hug from her and I would be haunted by her scent the rest of the day. I forced myself to open the car door and walk to building's entrance.

Once inside, I went directly to the parlor and looked toward the far end of the room where Eddie was displayed. Because of the large crowd, I only caught a glimpse of him. "Oh my god!" I blurted, obviously shocked. Everyone turned and looked at me. "Shush," a familiar voice scolded, and then came the inevitable slap across the back of my head. I could tell by the whack on my head it was Aunt Virginia. It was her signature greeting. She had spotted me and immediately scurried across the room to let me know I was late and they were just about to start the eulogy.

I forced a smile. "It's nice to see you, Auntie. What happened to Eddie?"

Aunt Virginia ignored my question. "You know you're late, Stanley," she said. "Do you want to go up and visit poor Eddie?"

"No, thank you, Auntie. I'll wait for a while."

"You remember Eddie's friend, Calvin, don't you? I didn't. She pointed at someone in the crowd, but I wasn't sure who. You met him two family reunions ago. He's going to deliver the eulogy. Oh, let's find a chair. He's about to start." A portly, red-faced man with a reddish-gray beard walked to the front of the room and everyone became very quiet.

Calvin shifted nervously, cleared his throat then gazed sternly at the crowd. "You people come here today to see poor Eddie and sit there all couch potatoey and self-righteous, but this is my third day here at the funeral home and I'm sad. So it's okay if I have a drink or several. For them that don't know me, my name is Calvin Dupo, with a long "u" and long "o." I always think it's important to pronounce a person's name right, don't you? You musta come out from the city, huh?" He was looking right at me. "You a long lost relation or that preevert third cousin nobody ever talks about? Just kiddin." No one laughed, but several people stared suspiciously in my direction.

"You might a heard a me cause I'm the assistant manager at Big Marge's Grain Elevator here in Elberta in this great state of Kansas. Yeah, the same Calvin Dupo who won the three-state award for excellence in elevator grain dust control. And you know how important grain dust is cause that stuff explodes. Big Marge's first grain elevator exploded and blew her through the office window and all her clothes come off too. That was a scary event, not to mention the actual explosion. Now she's deaf in her left ear and squints kind of odd unless you speak to her from a exact thirty-seven degree angle from the direction her head is pointed." He waved at Big Marge sitting somewhere in the mass of people.

"I'm drinkin' cause I'm in a state of grief, not meaning Kansas, but extreme mourning. As said, for three days I been here at the funeral home viewing my best friend Eddie. I know you all are curious about how he died. It was tragic. He got sucked into a hay baler and come out the other end all mixed in with that big, rectangular hay bale there. Only his head was stickin' out the end of the bale. I mean, you go through one of them hay balers you don't come out the other end lookin' like you're ready for the Senior Prom. Anyways, there ain't a coffin in the state big enough to hold Eddie and his hay bale body so he has to be displayed layin' across them two saw horses.

It was me that stuck them four broomsticks into the hay bale so Eddie would have arms and legs and look more natural. I bought the broomsticks and also them shoes of Eddie's over at the Dollar Deals Depot. We call it the 'Triple D' for short. You can get a real nice pair of shoes for a dollar. That don't include tax, of course. Damn, they tax you on everything don't they? Anyway, I rigged some blocks to hold the shoes in place so they'd stick upright and pointed at the ceiling. It wouldn't look right with Eddie in his hay bale body lyin' on his back and his shoes pointed toward the floor. That helped a lot and is somewhat artistic don't you think? I also do chain saw art sculptures of large fish if you're ever in the market.

Then Eddie's wife Kay with a long 'a,' she put that pair of white work gloves on the ends of Eddie's broomstick arms. He always loved them white work gloves. He wore a new pair to work every week. You can buy them over at the 'Triple D' too. The funeral director agrees that Eddie looks much better.

And you know what else is real nice? After the funeral, Kay is going to put some broomsticks with white gloves up in her front yard to make it look like they're wavin' to passersby. Eddie was always so friendly, you know. That's a nice touch don't you think? Kay says she will put a new pair of white gloves on them broomsticks every

Monday, the same as Eddie used to do."

Calvin raised his hands as if to calm the crowd. "Don't worry. We ain't using them broomstick arms in Eddie's hay bale body. I mean, if we took off his broomstick arms and white glove hands, how could he drink a beer in the afterlife? Nope Kay and me got class. We purchased some extra broomsticks." Calvin stopped and pulled a large white handkerchief out of his pocket and wiped his eyes and blew his nose. It was a touching gesture.

"Speakin' of Eddie bein' friendly, although I really shouldn't say nothin' about this, Eddie was sometimes a little too friendly. One time I saw him and Bradley Furscomb in the barn. They didn't know I was there. Well, they was puttin' their hands all over each other. They was puttin' their hands in places that I don't even put my own hands on my own body. I'm liberal minded, myself, don't you know. I don't object if someone is attracted to a person of a similar sex. My philosophy has always been, to each his own said the lady as she kissed the cow. You can't get much more liberal than that now, can you? But it's just not my cup of tea; although I also think you should always keep your options open, not that many were ever presented to me by either sex.

You woulda' liked Eddie if you knew him good, though he was at varied times a son of a bitch, but not like quotidianly, just here and there. I wish he never died, but not because I don't care too much for dead people or that he still owes me ten dollars. So maybe I am a little intoxicated but that don't affect nothin'. Think about it. If your best friend went through a hay baler, would you not imbibriate as well? Yeah, I would think you would. So don't stare at me in that demeanotory manner. Besides I don't like dead people so much. Or did I already say that?

Sit down, Big Marge," Calvin abruptly yelled. A large woman had abruptly stood up and begun strolling toward Eddie. "You're walkin' around with that far off look in your eye, Marge." He looked back at the audience and whispered. "That usually means she wants to have sex with one of her employees, but not this time I don't think. One time she surprised the aforementioned Bradley Furscomb in the seed dryer. Oh God was that a sight when someone accidentally switched on the spinner and dryer and there was seed and nakedness flyin' everywhere and screamin' and cursin' like hell. They almost put that embarrassing happenin' in *Today's Soybeaner* magazine but exercised their sense of propietnous and opted not to.

6

On a procedural note, after the funeral, I arranged with the Mug Shot Tavern to give you Happy Hour prices on beer. It will not apply to premium beer however because the owner is a former convicted murderer but now an ex-convict who has some serious anti-social inclinations. He don't discount premium beer cause it was so hard to get when he was in solitary confinement. Anyway I guess that makes it pretty easy to see where the Mug Shot got its name, don't it?

But, other than havin' a bale of hay for a body, Eddie looks real good. Oh yeah, the undertaker tried to change that odd expression on Eddie's face but it kept coming back. Those of us who was friends of Eddie had saw that look many times before. We knew from that look the last words poor Eddie said just before he went through the hay baler were, 'Oh Shit!'

And you know, the funniest thing, in the last few days every time us friends of Eddie greet each other, like in 'Hey, how you doin?' we burst out laughing and remember Eddie with his hay bale body. 'Hey, how you doin'?' Get it?

Now when the service is over, we will have the six pall bearers stick their hay picks into the bale and carry Eddie to the cemetery. It's just down the street so you can all walk behind them. Well, it's been real good talkin' with you. And remember, like us friends of Eddie always say, 'Hey, you take care now.' Get it?"

2

Laid Off

I stayed in Elberta Saturday night and flew back to Detroit Sunday afternoon. I was glad to be back at work on Monday, though I was naturally concerned about what the day would bring. Management is always so considerate when they announce looming catastrophes. They informed us of the probable loss of our jobs on Friday morning so we would have the rest of the day and the weekend to worry about it. And Monday morning the bad news came quickly.

First we had to listen to Lisa Tomorrowoski tell us how hard she fought to save our jobs. Then she told us about her own fate. Even though her only job experience had been as a sales girl at the make-up counter of a large department store, the company figured she was a "high-pot," which was short for high potential employee. It meant something totally different to those of us who weren't included in that classification.

Her CEO father gave her a six-figure salary and put her in charge of the entire office. It made a lot of infinitely more qualified people, including me, very unhappy. Lisa told me the bad news before the rest of the office. "I'm sorry, Stan," she said, as she executed a ravenous chomp on her fourth jelly donut. "We've got to make some changes. Our agency isn't producing its share of profit for the company. Things are more competitive in the automotive industry every day. There are new manufacturers in China, India, and Korea. It's harder for the American manufacturers to make money and they're cutting back. And you know where they always start. They cut back on advertising. So there you are."

"Where are I?" It was a grammatically incorrect, but one is always shocked to lose one's job.

"There, Stan. You're right there." That made no sense, but neither did the rest of the conversation.

"Thanks for letting me know." I wasn't sure I should be thanking someone for putting me out of my job, but how should a person react when that happens? For some reason, I began reflecting on the box of jelly donuts on her desk. She brought in a half dozen every day, but never shared, and never seemed to gain weight. Yet, she definitely seemed much shorter than when she first began working at the office. I didn't pursue that.

I decided to protest the injustice of being one of those let go. "I'm your top producer at the Detroit office. I've generated more profit for the agency than your next two account managers combined. I picked up three accounts in the last six months. I just got the company's Top Producer award at the annual dinner two weeks ago." I pointed at the plaque hanging on the Trophy Wall across the hall from the glass window of Lisa's office. "Top Producer of the Year-Stanley Henry Ian Thompson," the dark wooden plaque proclaimed in gold letters. Lisa stared at the plaque as she spoke. "Didn't anyone ever tell you not to use so many 'I's' when you're talking. It makes you sound self-centered. And do you know what your initials spell, Stan?"

I nodded and forced a weak smile. "Yes," I said. "I changed my name. It's just Stanley Henry Thompson now."

The reason I deleted Ian was because the four initials of my original name spelled an unpleasant expletive and I was tired of people discovering that embarrassing fact and asking me whether I realized it. Of course I did. I discovered early on my aberrant father was even less interested in having children than my mother and he retaliated against my birth by purposely giving me that profanely sequenced name.

I never realized his evil contrivance until he took me into a saloon one day when I was thirteen years old. "Hey everybody, meet my son, Shit," he blurted after his second beer. The only consolation was that he was a lousy drinker and after his third Pabst, I managed to filch one and then another. By his fifth beer, he was so blitzed I easily swiped a third beer and got drunk enough myself to actually laugh at his crude exposé of my initials. The bartender was laughing so hard he served me a fourth beer. "You deserve this kid," he said. Then I threw up.

I asked the personnel department to change my file to reflect my new name without Ian six months ago. They never did.

Lisa was still staring at the "Trophy Wall." It was her suggestion that created this motivator for the worker bees. For that brilliant idea, Lisa got a "Great Idea Letter" from Corporate, another innovative motivator from senior and even more incompetent management. She enlarged her "Great Idea Letter" so it was nearly twice the size of the

Trophy Wall and stuck it up next to it. Her "absolutely brilliant" idea to install a trophy wall was much more valuable to senior management than actual profit generating performance.

As I sat in Lisa's office I was assessing my life, which had changed so greatly this year. My wife fell in love with someone else and divorced me. I was happy for her, but without her substantially larger income, I couldn't make the mortgage payments and the house was foreclosed. That was okay too, because I never wanted a house that big to begin with. Being positive, I again reflected those might have been the two best things that ever happened to me. Losing my wife and the house were sort of a relief. And as far as the job went, that was also a burden of which I was relieved. I was beginning to enjoy my new carefree status.

Lisa was now staring blankly, her eyeballs darting in every direction. It was her signal the conversation was over. She concluded with, "You know what's wrong with you, Stan? You're too nice a guy for your own good. Now get out. I'm busy."

I returned to my office, and a short time later, Lisa announced to the entire staff the agency was closing and everyone needed to clean out their desks and be out of the building within an hour. She concluded by wishing everyone "Good luck" and "Have a nice day, everyone."

Although we were all in shock, some of us maintained our composure and responded to the emergency by carefully developing a comprehensive action plan. We would immediately head for the nearest saloon. Everyone was invited, excluding Lisa, who miraculously survived the downsizing.

Losing one's job was scary, but as I drove toward the appointed meeting place, I again reassured myself this was the best thing that ever happened to me. Sure, I had to find a job. And I had no savings thanks to the massive debt created by my ex-wife's spending. This was a chance for a new beginning. There was nothing to hold me to Detroit, no job, no house, nothing. Oh, there was my one hundred year old Mother and baby brother Albert. Even though Albert was fifty-eight and twenty-one years older than me, Mother always called him the baby of the family. He had never married and lived with Mother all his life. They wouldn't miss me. I was seriously thinking road trip.

As my car rolled into the parking lot of Eddie's Tap Room, I figured I would have one beer and say my good-byes. I didn't really expect any serious conversation would come out of our get-together. I pulled the car into a space and walked toward the building, recognizing most of the cars in the lot.

Everyone was sitting at a large round table and I sat down next to Jean Monaghan who had come with her co-worker Ellen somebody from Creative Support. Having been on the road so much, I didn't really know these women or some of the guys from the office. My only interaction with most of the office staff had been by phone. Jean said "Hi Stan," surprising me that she even knew my name. "Hi Jean," I replied, surprising myself her name was familiar enough that I was comfortable when I said it. Even more amazing, I found myself talking with her for much of the time I was there.

Although my plan was to bid everyone farewell and leave after one obligatory beer, I didn't exactly follow the plan. "I'm not a detail man," my ex-wife often reminded me, although I don't know exactly how many times because I'm not a detail man. The point is, beer after beer magically appeared in my right hand. The left one was filled with peanuts, a detail of which I was aware.

All in all it was a pleasant evening with the exception of Bernie LaFave accidentally traumatizing himself with a sixth Manhattan. We first noticed his condition when he retracted his body into full fetal position while remaining upright in his chair at the end of the table. His eyes were fixed on his drink and the six cherries floating on top. "He keeps track of the number of drinks he has by counting the cherries," someone explained. "He doesn't drink a lot, but when he does, he drinks a lot."

It was eleven o'clock at night, and Jean, who drank very little, drove me home in her car and her friend followed driving mine. We reached my house and Jean pulled the car into the driveway. I was intoxicated, but still coherent and polite enough to remember to turn toward her to tell her thanks for the lift. However, as I looked into her eyes, the words just wouldn't come and it became an awkward moment. But she smiled then leaned over and kissed me. "See you around, Stan," she said. I got out of her car and waved goodbye. Although it was the slightest of kisses, just a quick touch of our lips, the thought of it stayed with me.

As I walked through the front door of my foreclosed home I stared at the empty rooms. My ex-wife had taken all the furniture when she left. "Goodbye Stan," I remember her yelling from the driveway two months earlier. She got into her new love's car and as

I watched them speeding down the street there was a grinding noise as the new love missed a gear. "At least I can drive a stick shift," I called after them. Mrs. Rominski scowled at me from across the street. I cheerily waved to her. "Yes! It will be a good day, Mrs. Rominski." She smiled ever so slightly.

3

Abduction

Pounding on my front door jolted me from a deep sleep. I pressed the palm of my left hand against my forehead thinking it would somehow make my splitting beer headache disappear. It didn't. Bleary eyed, I glanced at the clock sitting on my suitcase performing double duty as a nightstand. It was seventeen a.m. No, that can't be right. I looked again. It was three-seventeen a.m.

"Stanley!" I heard an all too familiar voice scream. "Stanley, wake up! Something horrible has happened."

What horrible thing could have happened that had not already befallen me? I briefly reflected. I pulled the pillow over my head, trying to ignore the frantic knocking and forget the bad stuff in my life. Then I smiled. "It's a new day. I'm free. No responsibilities."

"Stanleeee!" the voice hollered, melodically drawing out the last syllable like the falsetto wailing of a cat having sex. That was sure to waken the neighborhood and prompt Mrs. Rominski across the street to call the Humane Society or 911. She always called one of them if she heard an odd noise. Sometimes she called both, "just to be on the safe side," she once told me.

"Stan! Stanleeee!" came the ever more urgent yells, now sounding more like the yowls of a coyote giving birth. These noises would certainly be assessed as odd by Mrs. Rominski. I estimated I would hear police car sirens in about two minutes. Of course, that would set off the inevitable howling of every dog in a fifty mile radius as they mistook the police sirens for the alpha male leader of the mystical wolf pack of every canine's fantasy. "Big-dog's coming," they would bark to each other. "You better howl and yelp like hell to let him know you're on his side."

"All right, all right," I called, figuring I better answer the door before Homeland Security raised the national threat level to "High." Do they still do that?

"Oh my head," I mumbled to the alarm clock. There was nothing else in my bedroom to mumble to. I pulled myself out of bed and started walking toward the living room. I knew precisely who was making all the noise. It was my ex-wife's new partner, the woman who had caused her to abandon me along with her unpaid credit card charges and the big house we couldn't afford.

I pulled open the door to face the distraught Latisha Wimberly. I was less than overjoyed about seeing her as she stood before me sobbing hysterically at three o'clock in the morning. She was not my favorite person. I suppose I resented her because she was all the things I was not. Of course, that didn't include her being black, female and a lesbian. I mean, I'm okay being a Caucasian, male, heterosexual. No, really. I am.

But Latisha is also smart, assertive, and decisive. That's where she had me. Not being assertive and decisive is what bothered me most, and evidently, also my ex-wife Nancy Nussbaum, who was now Latisha's partner. In my estimation, which is less than objective, I was smart enough but my problem was that I was always trying to make people happy. I was indecisive, and instead of making a conclusive decision and making some people unhappy, I waffled and compromised trying to keep everyone happy. I did that over and over knowing that it never worked and everyone ended up unhappy anyway.

Latisha charged through the door and threw herself against me. I found myself unenthusiastically putting my arms around her. Whatever problem could she be facing at this ungodly hour? Her body was shaking in genuine distress and I immediately forgot about my envy of her strong personality and was truly sorry she was suffering so much, whatever the cause.

"Latisha, what's wrong?" I asked sympathetically.

Still shivering, she looked up at me. "She's been abducted, Stan. They took her less than an hour ago. I called the police and they sent two officers out but all they did was laugh at me and said they would write a report."

"You mean the police took Nancy?" I replied, finding it difficult to speak my ex-wife's name in view of the ruinous financial situation in which she left me.

"No," she answered sharply, "of course not."

"Then who took her?"

"For god's sake," she replied, "the flying saucer men took her. She's been abducted by space men."

"What?" I gasped, in obvious irritation. "You got me up at three in the morning to tell me my ex-wife who is now your wife was abducted by a UFO?"

14

"Yes, Stan."

"That's the best news I've ever heard. It's the dream of every divorced person to have his or her ex-spouse abducted by a UFO. There is a god!" I happily proclaimed. The tone of my voice imparted not only my irritation at being awakened at this uncivilized hour, but my disbelief of her ridiculous story. "I hope she didn't leave you with a big stack of credit card bills."

"Stanley!" she said firmly, "this is hardly the time for sarcasm."

"Latisha, would you please leave?" I said, assuming she and Nancy must have quarreled. "I really need to get my sleep. The bank takes possession of my house tomorrow and I have to be up early for my garage sale." I'm probably the only person on earth who would have a garage sale on a Tuesday, but so what.

My plan was to sell the few pieces of junk my wife left me and take the rest to Goodwill or some other charity. I wanted to leave the house nice and clean for the bank, although I really didn't know why.

"Stop it," Latisha demanded. "I'm deadly serious. Stop talking to me like I'm an idiot. Nancy was abducted by beings from outer space. They took her from our house and into a space ship hovering above our back yard. The UFO shot away at tremendous speed and disappeared."

Latisha is an intelligent, serious woman, I reflected. Why is she talking so crazy?

The overwrought Latisha interrupted my thoughts. "Will you please help me? I honestly didn't want to come to you because Nancy is your ex, but you're my only hope. You can't dislike us so much that you won't help in such a horrible emergency like this."

My head was pounding and my stomach rebelling against yesterday's beer and peanuts.

"Latisha, give me a minute to think. Yeah, I'll help," I immediately replied, again falling into my habitual blunder of helping someone by jumping from the odd frying pan into the bizarre fire.

"You gave that one a lot of thought, Stan," I scolded myself. "You did it again. You got yourself involved in helping someone in a crazy situation. But this one is the craziest ever. Run Stan! Run out of the house. Get in your old truck and drive away now!" That notion lingered in my aching head.

Obviously, another of my faults is my inability to recognize the warning signs of life's really bad situations. I always help the downtrodden and the underdog. And there are way too many of them to begin with, I concluded, as I had so many times before. But, I keep trying to help these troubled people even though I think a lot of them are nuts. But they're drawn to me. I'm a magnet for the moonstruck. It's like I have a sign on my forehead that says, "If you're crazy, let's talk."

And, I was beginning to think Latisha was crazy. "Look, I've heard some wacky stories but this one takes the cake. I don't believe in UFO's and the like. Whatever happened has to be something other than a visit by a UFO. We've got to sort out the facts before we can begin looking for Nancy. Sit down and I'll get you some tea and we can talk about it."

Our conversation didn't last long. Latisha continued to insist that beings from a UFO abducted Nancy and I didn't believe a word she was saying. However, something she said made me wonder. It was after I said, "I just don't believe in little green men." She looked at me solemnly and said, "They weren't green, Stan."

Her sincere tone shocked me into an epiphany of sorts. I believe she could tell by my changed demeanor that I was beginning to believe her story, at least to the extent that something very strange had occurred when Nancy was taken.

"Do you remember anything else?" I asked. That I intended to help seemed to calm her. She thought for a moment, slowly regaining her composure.

"Yes, I do," she answered. "It was dark but they didn't use flashlights or anything. That made it hard for me to see them because there were no lights on in the house. There were three men. They had to be men because they were so large. They were frightening and I was scared to death, but Nancy didn't seem to be at all afraid. And you know what is so weird? When they walked out of the room, Nancy was at the front of the group, almost as if she was leading them. That doesn't make any sense, does it?"

"No, it really doesn't. Is there anything else?"

She paused to think about it. "Nancy stopped at the bedroom door and turned to me. 'I'll be back, Latisha,' she said. Then she walked out with the three men following. I heard them go through the back door so I jumped out of bed and peeked through the window. The space ship was hovering about forty feet off the ground. A circular beam of light like a transparent blue tube came out the bottom of the ship and extended to the ground and surrounded the four of them. It was then I noticed the men were wearing Oriental style red robes and had their hair in long black, single pigtails. And they were wearing swords. The three men and Nancy then shot upward through the blue tube of light and into the ship. I know it sounds crazy but that's exactly what happened."

"It sounds bizarre. If I didn't know you better, I'd say you had a bad dream."

"Oh, wait a minute." Latisha said. "After they were gone I turned on the bedroom light and grabbed my phone to call 911. As I was talking to the 911 operator, I noticed something lying on the floor."

Latisha reached into her pocket. "Here it is." She handed me a book of matches. "One of them must have dropped this."

I looked at the black matchbook cover with the bright pink heart and red print. It said, "Get Wild at Club Feral!" Below that it said, "Phoenix, Arizona."

***

The next morning I was up early, suffering from a punishing hangover and Latisha's late night visit. I asked her to spend the night, as she was still very upset about Nancy being abducted. I gave her my bed, the only one in the house, and I slept on the living room floor. Latisha had already left when I woke, apparently slipping quietly out the side door.

We had decided on a plan to find Nancy. Latisha would stay in Detroit and continue working as usual. She wanted to be there doing her normal routine should Nancy return as she promised. I still hadn't bought into the idea that a group of Oriental men wearing red robes and carrying swords flew in on a UFO and kidnapped my ex-wife Nancy. I really liked the thought of it however.

Although I had already planned to leave Detroit because of the poor job market, my original intention was to travel east to Pittsburgh. I never bothered to check out the employment possibilities, but I had a couple of second cousins living there and I thought they might be able to help me find a job.

However, since I promised Latisha I would find Nancy so I had to go in the opposite direction. I would follow up the only lead we had, the matchbook from Club Feral in Phoenix, Arizona. After I finished up with my pitiful garage sale, which netted a grand total of fifty-seven dollars and four cents, I got ready for my road trip to Phoenix.

Besides the fifty-seven dollars from the garage sale, I also had my un-cashed two months' severance pay check. It was about three thousand dollars. My twenty-year-old truck had two hundred thousand miles on it. It ran but I wasn't sure how far it would go. But that's what I would drive on the two thousand mile trip from Detroit.

All I owned would fit into the truck. Luckily it had a cap covering the box. The cap was probably worth more than the truck. There were half a dozen cardboard boxes in all. I had an old sleeping bag I could use to sleep in the back of the truck.

Somebody at the bar mentioned they were hiring in Phoenix and I thought I might kill two birds with one stone. Phoenix might be the answer to my job problems and I might get lucky and find Nancy. Not being a detail man, I never bothered to check out the Phoenix job market either.

As I bent over to get the last box in the bedroom closet, I noticed a piece of folded paper sitting on its top. It was a note from Jean Monaghan. It must have fallen out of my shirt pocket last night. "Stan, please keep in touch. Let me know how your job search is going. Good Luck, Jean." She included her phone number. The note made me happy.

Since I no longer had a house, car, or credit cards, I decided to cut my ties with my one remaining obligation. I laid my cell phone under my truck's right front tire and jumped into the cab and started the engine. As I drove forward, I heard a crunching noise when the tire rolled over the irritating device. I was headed to Phoenix to find my kidnapped ex-wife and a new job, though not necessarily in that order.

4

Radio Therapy

"Are you a loser? Radio Therapy will change you forever!" When that announcement came over the radio I had been driving for several days in my ancient, but so far reliable truck. I was using the time to try and sort out my life. What do I want to do for a living? Where should I live after I go through the motions of trying to find Nancy? I really hated to think about it that way, but how do you find someone who supposedly flew off into space in a flying saucer?

As usual, I had not come to any epiphany on the sad state in which I now found myself. I'm not talking about Nebraska, which I was passing through at the time. What I meant was that I was thirty-seven years old and had to start over with nothing. My life was literally in shambles.

But just as I was about to give up on my self-analysis, salvation appeared. Between the country and western songs and the hog report, something even more interesting than the price of a bushel of corn blared out from my cannibalized, cobbled up radio. The original radio in my old truck had long since given out and a friend of mine visited a boutique junk yard, and for a mere five dollars, picked up the present contraption fastened by a coat hanger to the bottom of my dashboard. I had to reach down below the dash to turn it on and then manually turn the dial to get different stations. That's what I was doing when I stumbled upon the good news that was sure to change my life.

Once again I heard, "Are you a loser? Eliminate those self-destructive thoughts and transform your failed life. Radio Therapy will change your life forever. Dr. Kathleen O'Halloran will show you the way with her award winning Dublin System. Call this 800 number for a free analysis."

Wow, this was exactly what I needed. I pulled into the very next rest stop, which was one hundred and thirty two miles down the road, yet still ten thousand miles from the Nebraska state line, or so it seemed.

I dialed the "800" number and immediately someone answered. My first words were, "Is this really free?"

"Oh yes, it is for sure, Laddie. Tis free for certain sure," the female voice said with a heavy Irish brogue. "I wish you the top of the morning, by the way. Now let me explain how our simple system works, Sonny. We send you a form either on-line or by fax. You follow the directions and complete a self-evaluation and either e-mail or fax it back to us. It comes straight to Dublin and Dr. O'Halloran will personally analyze your form herself. Then we call you back with your free analysis and a Dublin Action Plan, or DAP as we call it."

"Great," I said. "I'm on the road but I'll stop at the next motel and see if you can fax the form to me there. I'll call you back and give you a fax number."

"Oh, to be sure lad," was her very Irish response. "Be sure to ask for Molly when you call in, Laddie."

So I did it. To save money, I had been sleeping in the back of my truck, and that night, I stopped early while there was still enough light for me to fill out my Self-Analysis Survey. I finished just as it got dark. Here is what I faxed in the next day.

To: Dr. Kathleen O'Halloran's Dublin System
Self-Analysis Survey

My original name is Stanley Henry Ian Thompson, but I deleted the Ian. I was born in Detroit, Michigan thirty-seven years ago, just a few years after the Big Three automobile companies began their suicidal, downward plunge. They began laying people off and continued to do so for the next thirty-seven years. That was the first of many omens. I should have left Detroit the day I was born. My naked little body should have stood right up on the delivery table and scowled with my most frightening expression. Then my naked little body should have pointed menacingly at my parents and the doctor.

"Good-bye Mommy. Good-bye to you too, Daddy," I should have said. "And I'm gonna' change my name! And goodbye to you too, doctor. Thank you for bringing me into this micro-world of self-destructing auto companies and begrudging fatherhood."

Then my little body should have dove from the delivery table to the floor, run out the delivery room door and down the hall and out the front door. I should have hailed a cab and said, "Take me to the airport, Bub, and be quick about it! I'm outa here and hookin' up in Aruba!" That's what I should have done.

My failure to flee my hapless Detroit predicament the very first day I came into this world bespeaks of the characteristic that would define the rest of my life. Even though I knew I should leave Detroit my first day on the earth, I didn't. I didn't heed the warning signs. I didn't remove myself from a bad situation. I would wait a full thirty-seven years to run from Detroit, and then only when my wife divorced me and I was instantly bankrupt. And I still haven't learned to run, even when a bad situation is as obvious as a flaming meteor crashing through my kitchen window while I'm having my breakfast pop-tarts. I mean, look at me. I'm headed to Phoenix, Arizona to try to find my evil ex-wife who was supposedly abducted by a UFO. Is that not insane? Anyway, those examples illustrate my problem-very poor judgment.

After continuous self-analysis I realize that I constantly find myself in disastrous situations with deranged people. Maybe it's the Catholic guilt that causes me to want to help nutty people in trouble, which, of course, they always are. I would describe myself this way. I always help people and try to make them happy. Is that so wrong?

Oh yeah, I drink too much beer. At least ten, maybe fifteen of my one hundred and seventy-five pounds is beer enhanced belly, constantly teetering on the edge of my belt and threatening at any moment to spill over and hang like a medicine ball wannabe.

Anyway, choosing to be an automotive advertising guy in Detroit was the absolute worst career choice possible. My agency closed the Detroit office and six years of hard work evaporated quicker than the three pitchers of beer I drank the day it happened. My degree in marketing made me about as marketable as a diarrhea epidemic at a Marathon.

My main goal at this point in life is to be successful at anything although I still have no clue as to what that might be.

Lastly, I'm a very clean person to the point of being a germaphobe."

I was very excited about the whole process. At last there was real help. Being Irish myself, I had the greatest confidence that Dr. O'Halloran's Dublin System would save me. Once I faxed in the self analysis form, I was instructed to call the "800" number after forty-eight hours and give them my personal reference number which was printed on the document's top right hand corner. They would read my free personal analysis straight from the desk of Dr. Kathleen O'Halloran. It was comforting to hear the Irish brogue. It reminded me of my grandmother who spoke with the same quickness and inflections.

I had just crossed over the Arizona state line and I was increasingly impatient for the forty-eight hour time limit to pass. After what seemed like forever, it finally happened. I could now call in and get my free Dublin System analysis.

Finding a place to stop and call was another matter. Crossing into Arizona from New Mexico is like going from a remote desert area with no towns into a remote desert area with no towns. I found myself desperately scouring every highway exit for anyplace that might have a phone. I regretted running over my cell phone when I left Detroit. Its thousand pieces probably still lay in my driveway, rather the bank's driveway, as they now owned the house. I was getting desperate. I had to know what Dr. O'Halloran would prescribe for me.

Finally, a genuine tourist trap a la true 1950's garishness and landscape blighting repulsiveness came into view. This unlikely aggregation of homogenous trash was being sold instead of buried in the local landfill. I didn't realize pink flamingos were native to the Arizona desert. More importantly, does this place have a phone?

I pulled off the highway and drove along the side road lined with life-size dinosaur statues. I noticed some strange looking desert birds standing on the road watching me drive by. Those are different looking birds, I thought. But, aren't they all? The building itself was a whitewashed cinder block structure with a beautiful display of hubcaps, each one a different style and from a different brand of car. Apparently these hubcaps had been picked up along the highway, or more likely, picked from cars parked in motel parking lots.

As I entered the building a very heavy man wearing blue jean overalls and proudly displaying his long gray beard asked me if I wanted to see the reptile display. It only cost a dollar. I told him I would, but I first needed to make a phone call if he would be so kind to let me use his phone. My attempt to get on his good side by promising to see the reptiles worked. Hardly able to contain my excitement I dialed Dr. Kathleen O'Halloran's number.

"Dr. O'Halloran's Dublin System," a female voice answered. "May I help you?"

There it was again, that Irish accent. I loved it. Truly, salvation was at hand.

"Yes, I'm calling in for my free analysis. Here is my personal reference number." Nearly overcome with excitement, I read it off.

"Ah, you be Mr. Thompson, I see. Top of the mornin' to ya, Mr.

Thompson." It was nearly three p.m. in Arizona, nowhere close to morning, but that was okay. I wasn't a detail man. "Good noos, Mr. Thompson. We have yer free analysis fer ya," she continued, in an even heavier brogue.

But I noticed something a bit different about this lady's brogue. It seemed to have an edge to it, an underlying accent and a sort of conclusive melodic loop at the end of her sentences. But I was so anxious to hear Dr. O'Halloran's analysis I didn't think further about it. And here it was.

"Dr. O'Halloran says you've got a severe self-esteem problem. Also, you don't know how to remove yourself from negative situations such as where you get involved with crazy people. And, what you said about the day you were born, oh Lord, I'm crossing myself as I speak. The Almighty brings you into this world and the first thing you want to do is stand up on the delivery table and start threatening people. Oh Laddie, you've got severe anger management issues. Forgive him, Lord!

And then you said your unclothed little body should have gotten on an airplane and hooked-up in Aruba. You should have been gettin' your blasphemous wee carcass to the confessional instead.

And have you not considered how thoughtless ya are?" she continued. "Let's say you do get on the airplane. Although doctor sponged you down right after you were born, you were only an hour old and hadn't taken a shower yet. You couldn't even reach the knobs to turn the on shower. And you presume your nude little body wouldn't have a B. O. issue. The poor fella' sitting next to ya' on the airplane might have something to say about that. And you'd be puking all over yourself and your seat besides.

Here in Dublin, we don't tolerate such behavior. The Irish airlines would never let a person aboard if they have a stench about them. Of course, they do allow naked people to take a seat if they showered beforehand.

And you've also got escapism tendencies. You want to run away from your problems. You're in great need of Dr. O'Halloran's help, Lad.

And what about these UFO's? Are you daft, Boy? Nobody here in Dublin believes in UFO's. Although, I confess I do remember seein' somethin' strange flyin' along the River Liffey late one evenin' after I left Dooley's Pub. Actually, it resembled a flyin' cup more than a flyin' saucer. It was probably Sean McDermott throwing a beer mug across the lane. But, you must realize, boy, I had quaffed more than one brew that evenin.' Oh, fer sure I did. But, enough about me. I'm bettin' you believe in the Tooth Fairy too, no doubt.

Shame on you referrin' to your own fayther so disrespectful like. Oh you've got problems indeed, Lad. That's fer sure. And then you complain about yer Catholic guilt. Pox be upon you fer talkin' about Mother Church in that disgraceful manner. And finally lad, you shouldn't be drinkin' so much."

Then there was silence. "That's it?" I said. "That's all Dr. O'Halloran said?"

"Well Laddie, I surely think that is enough, do you not agree?"

Once again, I detected a slight non-Gaelic accent in her Irish brogue. It was a strange inflection like she was asking a question with each word she spoke.

"Yes, I do agree, madam, but I already told you all of that myself on the Self Analysis Survey I filled out. You're telling me exactly what I told you."

"Oh, now just a minute here, sir. This is a professional analysis from Dr. O'Halloran personally. I hardly think you should take credit for her clinical expertise."

Once again, her Irish inflections and singsong pronunciations seemed forced and stilted with an unnatural edge.

"But everything you told me was what I wrote in the Self Analysis Survey that I sent to you."

"Well sir, you obviously also have a problem with authority. You didn't include that important detail in the Self Analysis Survey. How will Dr. O'Halloran tell you what's wrong with you if you don't tell her what's wrong with you?" she asked, obviously irritated. Her twisted logic added to my annoyance with her rasping voice now completely devoid of its Irish brogue.

"Where are you located, Madame?" I asked. "Are you in Dublin?"

The woman on the phone began to cry as she spoke, her Irish brogue mutated to a monotonic chant often identified with call centers in Mumbai. "Oh no sir, I am so sorry. I apologize. I am new to my job. I am in India, sir. It was I who analyzed your Self Analysis Survey."

I couldn't believe it. I was extremely upset yet, in another of my typical overly empathetic plunges, I was more concerned about her anxiety. Why am I more concerned with keeping her happy than I am about my own happiness? Maybe I am too nice a guy.

"Look Madam, Let's just forget this whole thing happened. Don't worry about it, alright? I won't complain or anything. No big deal."

"Oh thank you, sir," she replied. "I am so grateful. Before I hang up, shall I send you Dr. O'Halloran's newest self-improvement DVD's, 'Expunging Your Demons and Forgetting Bad Things?' They only cost $495.00."

"Before I answer that, could you tell me one thing? Is there really a Dr. Kathleen O'Halloran?"

Again there was momentary silence. No doubt mindful that I could still call in and raise a fuss about the phone fraud her company was practicing, she responded to my question in a sort of, "We got a deal-you don't complain about me and I will tell you the truth" type of answer.

Dr. Kathleen O'Halloran, it turned out, was really a twenty-eight year old entrepreneurial male whiz kid from Mumbai, which is where the whole operation was based. That wasn't even close to Dublin. The phony Irish accents were taught to the new trainees before they were assigned to the switchboard to sell Expunging Your Demons.

Most depressing of all, however, was the woman's final comment before she hung up. In a perfect Irish brogue she said, "Sir, you seriously should get some help. You are really fooked up."

5

Reptile Show

It's so hard to have faith in anything anymore. Imagine a huge room full of Indian ladies in Mumbai all speaking on the phone with pretend Irish accents. It was too horrible to contemplate, but I just had.

The nametag on his overalls read: Hector. He'd overheard the entire conversation and could see I was unhappy. "Do you still want to see the reptiles?" he asked hopefully.

"To tell you the truth, I'd rather have a beer." His smile faded and he looked hurt. I felt sorry for him. I told the woeful Hector that I'd check out his reptiles and pulled out my wallet and handed him a dollar bill.

"It only cost another two dollars for the reptile show," he said.

I gave him the extra two bucks and told him I'd watch the reptile show. In view of my present circumstances I had no business spending the time or money to watch a reptile show.

Hector and I were the only people in the place. I wondered how he would do a show for only one person. Then I wondered how he would do a reptile show period.

I followed Hector through a rickety wooden door into the back room and sat down on one of the homemade wooden benches which consisted of two by six boards straddling metal paint buckets. Hector walked to the front of the room and stood next to one of the dozen or so tables holding glass cages that were occupied by various desert creatures. On the wall behind Hector was a large white sign with red letters that read: 'CLASS REPTILIAN: (cold blooded creatures like snakes and lizards).' While it wasn't especially scientific, it was plenty descriptive for me. I don't like snakes, never did.

Hector began to recite an obviously memorized presentation.

"Good afternoon ladies and gentlemen and kiddies," he said in a strained voice. Hector was not a polished public speaker, not that I expected him to be. On the other hand, I was the only person in the audience and could care less what he said or how he said it. I was still fretting about Dr. O'Halloran's magic cure, which turned out to be neither magical nor a cure.

"I'm doing a new script I just wrote," he said, winking at me like only he and I knew that secret and no one else in the non-existent audience had a clue. "Okay kiddies," Hector continued, "always remember to never touch snakes unless you are really sure they aren't poisonous." He took the lid off the glass box nearest him. The snake was barely visible from where I sat but I could hear its buzzing rattle becoming increasingly louder and more frantic as Hector's hand came closer. From the snake's vantage point, looking outward from the cage and seeing a large creature reaching toward him had to be a frightful experience.

"This is a Western Diamondback Rattlesnake kiddies. They are very common but very dangerous. They are responsible for more snakebites every year than any other snake."

I knew very little about snakes, but in my recollection the word "rattlesnake" was always used in conjunction with poison and venom. This was not a good thing to pick up.

Hector was practicing his audience eye contact as he mumbled his prepared script. His hand had stopped just above the snake's head and he turned to warn the nonexistent kids in the audience that, "Only the experts should handle snakes."

As he spoke, he absent-mindedly dropped his hand slightly downward toward the snake. I was certain that any second now he'd turn back toward the now extremely distressed serpent and grab him by the neck.

Intent on mastering his newly written script, however, Hector continued to ramble on. "Remember kiddies, never touch snakes unless mommy…. Shit! Ouch," he screamed. "Damn it all!" The rattler had bitten him on his right hand index finger.

Hector quickly tried to put the lid back on the glass box but it fell into the cage and landed on the snake. This further infuriated the snake and it bit Hector on the base of his left hand as he reached to get the lid out of the snake's cage.

"Ouch! Damn you!" he screamed. "Oh my God, I never got bit twice before. I'm gonna die. Damn it all. I'm too young to die. Don't let me die, God!"

Hector started running around in circles. "I'm gonna' die. I'm gonna' die," he screamed.

Reluctantly, I decided to take control of the emergency. I soon realized that was a mistake. But what else could I do? The poor guy was going to die if I didn't do something.

"Hector, do you have some anti-snake medicine around here?" I yelled, as he ran by me for the third time, traveling in a circular pattern to nowhere. "You got some pills or something?"

"No pills. We need anti-venom," he screeched. "You gotta get me over to Gallup, pronto."

I had seen enough Western movies to know that "pronto" meant fast. I began to curse under my breath. Gallup was in New Mexico and over forty miles east. I had passed by it an hour ago. I had prayed every mile that my old truck wouldn't give out and I didn't like the idea of backtracking eighty miles round-trip.

He looked like he was going into shock.

I can't let the poor devil die. I figured I'd better get him into my truck before he passed out. I could never pick him up and carry his three hundred pounds from the building to my truck.

I pushed Hector toward the front door and grabbed an Indian blanket from a display stand as we rushed by. I thought I read somewhere that people going into shock needed to be kept warm. I twisted the inside lock on Hector's front door and pulled it shut. Hector was screaming louder now.

"Take it easy, Hector. You're going to get your blood flowing faster and the poison will spread a lot quicker."

"Oh my God, the blood!" he screamed. "I forgot about the blood. Hurry mister! Get me to Gallup or I'll be dead by sundown!"

It seems like everybody in the west chooses either "high noon," whatever the hell time that is, or sundown to either kill somebody or die. Apparently, Hector had chosen sundown as the time of his demise. Now I want to make it very clear that I am not a priest, nor do I hold any similar spiritual office. So why this very large man decided he should burden me with his last confession, well, I just can't answer that. But, he began what for me was a most discomforting, yet memorable, last confession. This commenced after he screamed several more ominous announcements that he would be dead by sundown. I had already accepted that morbid timeline and moved on, but he was not nearly as calm about his imminent passing.

"Oh God, I don't want to die!" he wailed. "Save me God!" And then he began to bargain with God. "Please God, let me live and I will go to church every day for the rest of my life," he promised. "Please don't let me die. I'll be a good boy, I promise. Please Lord."

It seemed that he had accepted he was a goner as his appeals for survival mutated into contrite outbursts of confession and desperate pleas for forgiveness of his sins. But then he started bargaining again. "Oh God, I'm so sorry I've lived such a sinful life. I've drunk too much. I've fornicated. I've cursed. I've cheated people. Oh please Lord, let me live and I promise I'll never be intimate with the sheep again. It's only happened one time this month. I promise. Oh yeah, it was three times. Sorry God, I forgot about that. But, I'm a really good man at heart, God. I shouldn't be dying. Please don't let it happen."

I had gotten directions from Hector when we first started out because I'd figured he would probably pass out before we made it to the hospital. About half way to Gallup, I looked over at him. He had stopped ranting and praying, and thank God, confessing his sins. His body had slumped a little and his head rested on the back of the truck's ripped vinyl seat. His face was flushed and he'd begun to sweat. His eyes were closed and he was breathing heavily. I figured the end was near.

Twenty minutes later, I saw the sign for Exit 20. "We're almost there, I murmured, remembering Hector's instructions to go past the airport exit and get off at Exit 20."

Hector had passed out and his breathing had slowed. He'd begun to snore, loudly and mournfully, befitting a man who was about to die.

Is this some kind of death rattle? Is he already dead?

I pulled my twenty year old truck masquerading as an ambulance up to the Emergency Room doorway. I immediately jumped out and ran inside. "There's a dying man in my truck," I yelled. "He got bitten twice by a rattlesnake and he's in a coma." The coma was my own diagnosis, but that's what I thought a person would look like if they were in a coma so that's what I screamed at the admitting nurse.

Immediately, two people, a doctor and a nurse, ran out the door toward the truck. A third person with a gurney quickly followed. The doctor pulled the passenger side door open and Hector fell outward toward them. Luckily, they caught him before his large body traveled too far and the three of them somehow managed to move Hector onto the gurney. They quickly wheeled the unconscious victim inside the Emergency Room patient area. One of them came out and asked me what kind of snake had bitten him and I told them it was a Western Diamondback Rattler, which is how Hector had described it.

I waited anxiously for Hector's prognosis, but I figured his self-diagnosis of imminent death was probably right on the money. Twenty minutes later, the doctor, the one who had rushed out to the truck to attend to Hector, walked out of the Emergency Room and headed in my direction. By the look on the doctor's face, I was quite sure poor Hector was dead. I assumed Hector was well liked around these parts and would surely be missed now that he had departed.

As the doctor approached, I stood up and mustered the most solemn expression I could manage and braced myself for the inevitably dire news.

"Get that idiot out of this hospital this instant," the doctor snarled.

I was shocked when I heard those hurtful words hurled at the deceased in such a disrespectful manner. Then, in what was a most unusual move for me, I decided to take a stand. I would defend the honor of this poor man who was killed while trying to make an honest living, regardless of that sheep thing.

"Doctor, first of all, I don't know what to do with his body. Don't you people have procedures for things like that?"

I never got as far as defending Hector's honor because the doctor cut me off. "That nitwit's not dead. He's too dumb to die."

"But I saw him get bitten twice by the rattlesnake, Doctor."

"He got bitten twice all right, but they were 'dry bites.'"

"What does that mean?"

"It means the snake's as dumb as Hector. The snake didn't deliver any venom into Hector's body. A 'dry bite' is a snakebite without any venom. What we have here," the doctor continued, "is the world's dumbest snake biting the world's dumbest man. Hell, the snake probably died."

"Hector's alive. That's good news."

"It depends on your point of view," countered the doctor. "This is the third time in six weeks that idiot has come to the Emergency Room with a snakebite. This is a busy hospital. We don't have time for Hector's nonsense. Ever since he opened up his reptile garden he's had nothing but trouble. Hector doesn't know how to handle snakes. One of these days he is going to end up dead if he's not more careful. We'll release him in a few minutes and you can take him back to his place of business."

"I was sure he had gone into a coma in my truck, doctor," I said, as he turned to leave.

"He just fell asleep. We hauled his three hundred pound carcass all the way into the Emergency Room before he woke up."

A short while later they pushed Hector into the waiting room in a wheel chair. He jumped out of the chair and said, "Let's go."

We got back to Hector's place in less than hour. He invited me to stay overnight with him in his little house next door to the business. That was the first break I'd had in a long time. Understandably, being the calamity that he was, he lived alone. Hector whipped up a substantial dinner of chili and fry bread which turned out to be quite appetizing, although Hector's dinner manners were not. The next morning we were up before dawn and I got an early start.

6

Raging Rhonda, Sumo Wrestler

It was Thursday afternoon when I pulled into Phoenix and checked into the Regal Court Motel. Of the five days on the road, except for my stop at Hector's, I slept in the back of my truck. I didn't want to spend my limited money on a motel room, but I needed a good night's sleep and a shower before I began my job hunt the next day. I didn't forget my promise to search for Nancy. Yeah, like the imaginary UFO would fly from Detroit to Phoenix.

There was a bar near the motel, and as it was three-fifteen in the afternoon, that seemed like the proper destination. In a few minutes I was sitting at a table with a beer in my hand. The bar was a newer place and it was big and crowded. I wondered why there were so many people in the place early on a Thursday afternoon. Happy hour had started at three so I had gotten there fifteen minutes late. But it looked like a lot of these people had been there most of the day judging by their various levels of bleary eyes and boisterous behavior.

My waitress Rhonda, a very tall, very heavy blonde wearing a thick coat of paint on her face and a huge but visually painful short skirt, had just brought me a second beer. The pungent odor of her perfume hung in the air like a sinister olfactory hologram. I was thinking to myself, ain't that the way it always is? The waitress is always named Rhonda. And Rhonda wasn't just heavy. I mean, all of us could stand to lose a few pounds. But conservatively, Rhonda had to weigh at least three hundred pounds. However, she moved very quickly and efficiently for a large woman. That was odd.

Some extremely timid older guy walked up to my table and asked if he could join me.

"Yeah, sure. Have a seat," I said, seeing there were no other seats in the bar.

"Thanks," he said. "I'm Herby Titsmore. Do you live around here?"

"No, I just got into town. I came out here to get a job. I heard that they were hiring big time in Phoenix."

"Who told you that, man?" Herby asked, with a look of shock on his face.

"A buddy of mine," I answered, with a similar look of shock on my face. Fear began to trickle into my consciousness, slowly at first, then more rapidly, eventually increasing to a crashing deluge. My ex-wife always told me one of my many weaknesses was that I never checked the details, the fine print.

Of course she always followed up by reminding me that being a complete loser was my main weakness. Anyway, I never did any official checking on the job market before I came here. I just took my friend's word on that little detail. But, a good marketing guy isn't into the details, I thought, defending my ill-planned venture. But I quickly remembered I was a marketing guy who had just been laid off.

"Your buddy was wrong man, way wrong. There ain't any jobs here. Didn't you see that heavy flow of traffic heading east while you were the only one going west? They were all leaving town to look for a job somewhere else."

Actually, I hadn't noticed a stream of Phoenix escapees traveling east. On the other hand, my mind had been focused on what I was going to do with my out of kilter life. Describing it that way sounded much better than "wreckage."

"Yeah, but I got a guy's name. He's a friend of my other buddy."

"I wish you luck, friend," he said. "You know, your face looks familiar. You remind me of somebody. Anybody ever tell you that you look just like Millard Fillmore?"

I motioned for the waitress to bring me another beer. When the perfumed Rhonda delivered that much needed relief, I immediately ordered another. I wonder if Millard Fillmore liked beer.

"Who is Millard Fillmore?" I asked my new friend Herby.

"He was a president."

"Oh, yeah," I said. "I think I remember hearing his name."

"You know Rhonda is a sumo wrestler," Herby said, completely out of the blue. "She wrestles with the Arizona Ladies Sumo Wrestling Association. Her professional name is 'Raging Rhonda.' She's a big deal," he added, no pun intended, I assumed.

"Oh," I replied, thinking I was again in one of those conversations with a crazy person.

After a gourmet meal of hamburgers, fries and beer eloquently served by my sumo wrestler waitress, I left her and Herby or whatever his name was and drove my old truck two blocks back to the Regal Court Motel. It was after seven o'clock and the bed looked too inviting to ignore.

I had just dozed off when I heard rhythmic thumping, grunting and someone gasping "Oh god, oh god," from the room next door. Then all was quiet. My clock now showed nine o'clock. I had actually slept a few hours.

Once again I must have fallen asleep because the clock showed eleven thirty when the bumping and gasping once again started. "Oh god, oh god," a woman screamed. "Don't stop Herby! Don't ever stop!"

"Herby, please stop," I mumbled. "If you don't stop I'll never get any sleep."

Almost as if he'd heard me, Herby stopped. All was quiet once again. But at about three fifteen in the morning Herby's lust was again surging and his lamb-like bleating for rapturous fulfillment permeated the walls in pitiful squeaks of "Come on baby-face, be nice to daddy," and so on.

But this time, the woman was not interested. "No Herby, not now. I'm tired." There was brief silence. The only part of Herby's reply I heard was "baby."

"No Herby," the woman insisted. "I don't want to. No Herby, damn it. No!"

But Herby was not to be denied. The thumping and grunting started once again. There was no sound from the woman this time however. Herby was grunting away and then I heard a loud cough and what sounded like a growl. Then there was silence.

Suddenly, hysterical screams pierced the wall and directly into my aching head. "Herby! Herby! Herby, are you alright?" And then came, "Oh god, oh god." But these "Oh gods" were not like the "Oh gods" she had screamed before. These "Oh gods" were screams of panic. "Help!" she cried.

I picked up the phone and got an outside line and dialed 911. I figured poor Herby had a heart attack. The woman was wailing now, her deep pitched voice sounding like a cow in labor, not that I had ever witnessed that spectacle. But if ever I were to behold that event, which would only happen after I made every possible effort to avoid it, I'm sure that's how the cow would sound.

The ambulance siren screamed as it rolled toward the hotel, but the wails of the frantic woman in the next room were louder. However, as the ambulance arrived in the motel parking lot, the competition had become an even match. "Oh Herby!" she bawled, "Oh my poor Herby."

I heard the ambulance guys running up the outside stairs to the second floor. Although I didn't need any more grief in my life, I felt obligated to put on my trousers and go outside to see if I could be of any comfort to the woman. Don't ask me why I did that. Whatever help could I be? I was broke, no job, no prospects and my old truck would probably roll over and die that night. I opened my room door and went out on the walkway. Lots of other motel guests were already standing on the balcony outside their rooms and watching.

I walked toward the room next door as the woman's weeping pierced the walls and drifted into the air outside. As I peeked around the doorway and into the room, I was shocked to see none other that my three hundred pound sumo wrestler waitress, Rhonda. She had the bed sheet wrapped around her mountainous body. I was surprised it fit so well. Her red lipstick was gone but her pink cheeks still held the paint.

Rhonda looked much better in the white bed sheet, almost statuesque, like a sculpture of some Greek goddess, albeit a very large Greek goddess. No, don't even think about it, I told myself. Then the next surprise was revealed. The face behind the oxygen mask, the amorous Herby lying on the stretcher, was actually "my Herby" from the bar, the one who had so kindly reminded me of my strong resemblance to Millard Fillmore. His remark had been flattering in a way. No one ever told me I looked like a president before.

Is everything going okay, Rhonda?" I asked.

"Yes." she whimpered.

"Herby's going to be okay," said one of the ambulance guys. "We'll take him to the hospital and they'll check him out. He'll probably be released tomorrow."

"Good," I said. Trying to extricate myself from further involvement, I smiled at Rhonda to bid her goodnight. However, she asked me to stay until they got Herby downstairs and into the ambulance. I cautioned Rhonda that I could only stay a minute as I had a job interview tomorrow and had to get my sleep. That wasn't actually true. I mean, I did need my sleep but all I could do on the job thing was to call the guy whose name my buddy gave me.

As I stood there in the doorway of Regal Court Motel that's when it hit me. Darned if my ex-wife wasn't right, I thought. I drove all this way to make a phone call to some guy I don't even know on the advice of a buddy back east that I don't really know very well either. I could have just called from Detroit rather than driving all the way out here. I'm going to have to get it together.

As I mentally criticized myself for overlooking obvious details, I rationalized that I would have gone to Phoenix anyway to search for my ex-wife Nancy. But I really wouldn't have. I was broke and would never have thrown away my last few thousand dollars on such a ridiculous quest. Abducted by a UFO. Give me a break.

"A penny for your thoughts," Rhonda chortled, broadly smiling while poor Herby, his stretcher and the two ambulance guys squeezed through the doorway.

"Come in and sit down for a minute," Rhonda insisted, pointing to a spot next to her on the bed.

"Okay, but I can only stay for a minute or two. I've got to be ready for my big day tomorrow." Then I changed the subject. "Is this Herby's room?"

"Herby gets this same room for me and him every couple of nights. He lives in a mobile home with his wife and they hate each other. Me and Herby are in love. We're gonna' run off together some day." Then she giggled and moved closer to me, positioning her muscular body like a wall between me and the doorway.

I was getting nervous now, like a cornered animal searching for an escape route. "Well, I better go, Rhonda. Big day tomorrow, you know."

"Please stay," she pleaded, in little girl's tiny voice. Then she stood up.

"Rhonda, I'm right next door if you need anything, but I have to leave." I rose from the bed, which she was now towering over.

As I stood up, my face was only inches from hers. I moved to my left to squeeze between her and the bed. As I did so, in a move so rapid it belied the agility one would expect from a person so large, she threw me onto the bed from which poor Herby had just been carried on a stretcher. Athleticism and quickness were not included in my many failings. She had surprised me with her rapid movement and substantial strength that landed me in the bed on my back. However, I surprised her with my own nimbleness. I leveraged the bounce of my body off the mattress and threw myself to the other side of the bed and jumped to my feet. Less than a second later, Rhonda crashed onto the bed. Thank god I wasn't under her when she landed. I would have followed Herby on another stretcher and ambulance.

"Good night, Rhonda," I said.

"Will I see you tomorrow?" she asked, hesitating because she didn't know my name. "You never told me your name."

"No, I didn't. Take care, Rhonda."

7

My Celestial Third Eye Advocate

The next morning was a rapidly moving blur of unanticipated events, none of them particularly good. After a cup of coffee in the Regal Court Motel lobby, I went back to my room and called the number my friend Brad had given me. Oddly enough, the guy I was supposed to call was also named Stanley. Good omen. We have the same name. That ought to count for something. It didn't. But Brad's name counted for something.

"Who's this?" the voice on the phone asked.

"It's Stanley, Stanley Thompson. I'm a friend of Brad Slater."

"So what the hell do you want?"

"Brad said you were a friend of his and you could help me find a job here in Phoenix."

"Two things, Jack," he replied.

I knew this was not going to be good. First of all, none of my three given names bestowed by my evil father was Jack. Second, Jack, when used in this manner, is usually an indication of something worse to come. Unfortunately, my razor sharp perceptive skills did not disappoint.

"You tell that son of a bitch Brad that he still owes me fifty dollars and as soon as I see him I'm going to kick his ass. If you're a friend of that jerk, I just might come over to where you are and kick your ass too. Where did you say you were calling from?" I hung up. That was fun.

Even more irritating than the just completed phone conversation was the reaffirmation of my ex-wife's wisdom about checking the details. Why didn't I make this phone call from Detroit instead of driving all this way? The situation I found myself in was not pleasant. I was now stuck in a job market as bad as Detroit's.

My cash, while still okay, was a scarce commodity. Of the three thousand dollars I had when I left Detroit, I was now down to around twenty-six hundred. Gas, food, one night at the Regal Court Motel and too much beer had put a dent in my nest egg. I needed to find a job.

Four thuds on my motel room door and Rhonda's shrieking,

"Hey, you in there!" startled me out of my self-reflective moment. I got up from the bed and walked over to open the door.

"Good morning, Rhonda."

"Yeah, hey, good morning ah…hey, what's your name anyway? When's your interview?"

"My name is Stan. There's not going to be any interview. The position was already filled," I lied.

"Jeez, sorry Stan," she said, with not one iota of sympathy. "Hey, listen. Can you take me over to the hospital to see Herby? I don't have no driver's license and he's got a stick shift in that old Dodge and I can't drive a stick."

Ever the helpful person, I agreed to take her to the hospital. I had to check out of the Regal Court Motel anyway even though I had no idea where I was going to spend my next night.

My agreeing to take Rhonda to the hospital, a direct result of my guilt embedding Catholic upbringing, turned out to be yet another misstep in an eternal series of wrong moves. When we arrived, Herby's wife was already there. However, when we went into Herby's room we were not aware of that explosive situation.

We should have known something was wrong when we got to his bedside. He began fidgeting and breathing heavily. I was afraid he was going to have another spell or whatever it was that got him into trouble last night. Finally, he blurted, "My wife's here. You better get out of here now."

The warning came fifteen seconds too late. As we turned to leave the room, standing in the doorway was a monstrous black lady the size of Rhonda. Obviously, Herby preferred plus sized women.

"Lawanda," Herby screamed."

"Lethal Lawanda," Rhonda boomed from behind me.

"Raging Rhonda, so you're the honky bitch that's been bangin' Herby," Lethal Lawanda screamed. "Herby, you been leaving me all them nights for the likes of that pig?" I was to later find out that Raging Rhonda and Lethal Lawanda were mortal enemies and fiercely competing for the Arizona Women's Sumo wrestling championship.

Herby was now breathing even more heavily, his labored gasps sounding like the old steam engine trains used to sound as they chugged up a long hill. Just as I had never seen a cow in labor, I also had never actually seen or heard an old steam engine train huffing and puffing up a long hill. But Herby's frantic inhaling and exhaling sounded like I thought an old train would sound.

Then I realized what I was actually hearing was my own breathing. Herby was completely silent, frozen motionless in bed with a terrified look on his face. He knew what was coming.

Raging Rhonda, taking great exception to Lethal Lawanda's comments, screamed at the top of her lungs and charged forward with her hands outstretched in a strangle position. But Lethal Lawanda was not intimidated and charged forward herself. The two behemoths, six hundred pounds of crazed, feminine sumo wrestling rage, collided next to Herby's bed. Each of them grabbed the other's waistband and proceeded to tug violently. They were both trying to throw each other out of the imaginary sumo circle, the center of which was Herby's bed.

The suddenly recovered Herby leapt from his bed, frantically threw open his locker door and grabbed his clothes. I jumped aside as the thrashing human avalanche advanced in our direction. But Herby didn't move quickly enough, and to his horror, was caught up in the thunderous devastation surging toward him. Down he went, sucked into the vehement roiling and being pummeled mercilessly, screaming for his life. Luckily, four beefy security guards arrived to save the day and Herby.

As they pulled the two women sumo wrestlers apart, Lethal Lawanda screamed, "You go to hell, Herby! I got me a black man who knows how to treat a lady. Besides, I won't have to go to the hospital every time he has sex with me. I'm tired of coming to this place to visit you. I'm throwing your clothes out of the trailer as soon as I get home. I'm not married to your dumb ass anyway. That common law thing don't go in Arizona. We ain't even married you honky little vermin!"

Once things calmed down, the two security guards released Rhonda who was now helping Herby off the floor. Herby's philandering and frequent sex triggered visits to the hospital were a routine in which Lethal Lawanda had no further interest in participating.

Once again, realizing it was long past my time to depart, I tried to ease my way out the door of the hospital room. But I was too slow.

"Stan," Rhonda asked, "where are you going?"

"I have to go find a job Rhonda. I'll see you guys another time." I hoped I would never see either of them again.

"Wait a minute, Stan. You gotta' take me and Herby over to his trailer to get his clothes. Please Stan. Would you do that for us?"

I've always been a sucker for true love, even when it was such a grotesque mismatch as the thirty-six year old sumo wrestling Rhonda and the fifty-one year old balding, sexually voracious, hospital prone Herby.

"All right," I said, already regretting it.

Rhonda got Herby checked out while I went to the parking lot to get my truck. I met the two of them at the main entrance to the hospital where the orderly had delivered Herby via a wheel chair. We drove toward Herby's Royal Palms Mobile Home Plantations and were soon pulling up in front of his residence. We arrived just in time to see Lethal Lawanda throw out the last batch of his underwear.

Herby's clothes and papers were scattered on the ground in front of his former plantation mobile home. Underwear and socks were hanging from a nearby tree and the umbrella of their outside table. Pants and shirts covered the chairs. Rhonda and I got out and picked up Herby's belongings while he sat in my truck recovering by sipping on a warm beer that had rolled out from under the front seat.

Then we started driving to the Regal Court Motel to fetch Herby's truck. On the way, Rhonda and Herby decided to get married. It would not be a common law thing but a real wedding. While I knew that I should be happy for them, my only thought was, here are two dysfunctional people on their way to their next disaster. But I had my own problems. On the other hand, I don't know why I considered my missing ex-wife a problem when I should have been celebrating the poetic justice of her alleged UFO abduction.

Just as we were driving into the Regal Court Motel parking lot, Rhonda and Herby made another decision. They were going to move to Rhonda's hometown, someplace called Empyrean, Arizona. It was another one of those "Oh, Oh!" moments and I should have taken off running the second I heard the name of the town.

I'm always distrustful of words whose meaning is beyond my vocabulary and there are many of them. But this one was way out there. I couldn't even guess what Empyrean meant, and if I had known, I would never have agreed to help them move there from Phoenix. Of course, the two hundred dollars they offered me quickly made up my mind and I said, "Yes," to their proposal.

But it wasn't just the name of the town. I later found out the Empyrean means, "the ultimate paradise," or "highest heavenly sphere," or something like that. At least that's what the dictionary says it's supposed to mean. But to the people of Empyrean, it has a much different meaning, not that either they or I know just what the hell it might be. As usual, I wish I had checked the details before agreeing to get involved with these two mentally off the menu souls.

We were now headed for Rhonda's apartment. Rhonda opted to ride with me, as I didn't know the way. I think she also wanted to make sure I didn't run off and leave them, which I was tempted to do, even if it meant forfeiting the two hundred dollars I could earn. She said she shared a small place with another girl and didn't have much furniture or anything else. She assured me that Herby and I could easily fit all her stuff into our two trucks.

"You'll like Empyrean, Stan. It's a very interesting town." (I was later to find out that was the understatement of the century.) "More Unidentified Flying Objects have landed in Empyrean, Arizona than the rest of the world combined. There are landing sites all over the Empyrean area." She didn't bother to tell me whether she had some kind of official documentation to back up that claim. How and why do I always get involved with the most bizarre of people?

"I was even abducted myself once, Stan," she continued. In fact, that's why I was in Phoenix. I've been in a rehabilitation center for abducted people for the last two years. I just couldn't stay in Empyrean with all that I went through when I was taken. You know what I mean? But I've conquered my fears thanks to Herby's help. I was deeply wounded and now I'm ready to go back to Empyrean. That must be obvious to you, Stan."

"Uh, what must be obvious, Rhonda?"

"For heaven's sake, Stan. It must be obvious to you that I was deeply wounded. That's why I became a sumo wrestler. My Celestial Third Eye Advocate at UFOARI told me that it would happen, that my personality would change. See Stan, the first thing the aliens do when they abduct you is permeate you. They give you a quick shot of radiation and a couple of laser beams to make sure any contagious germs you have are killed. Your personality changes and you become more aggressive and assertive. It's only logical. You must be able to see that."

Although Raging Rhonda's new personality sounded like that of my ex-wife, at this point all I wanted to be able to see was a case of beer for which I would gladly trade my third eye if I had one. Little Herby had helped himself to my last beer, which had been rolling around in my truck for the last six weeks. I could see him in my rear view mirror, sucking on it as he drove behind me in his dilapidated truck as we chugged toward Rhonda's apartment.

"What's a Celestial Third Eye Advocate and UFOARI?" I asked, regretting the question even before the words got out of my mouth.

"Oh Stan, you don't know what a Celestial Third Eye Advocate and UFOARI are?"

My god, if I knew I wouldn't have asked, not that I really cared to know anyway. "No, I don't know what they are Rhonda."

"A Celestial Third Eye Advocate is your own personal mentor who shows you the spiritual path to self-transformation. They help you get through the abduction recovery process. UFOARI is the UFO Abduction Rehabilitation Institute. That's where you go after you've been abducted because an abductee undergoes such a traumatic experience.

I could have stayed in Empyrean because we have lots of celestial third eye advocates there. But because Empyrean was the site of my abduction, I had to go to Phoenix to get far away. That's the only way I could cleanse that part of my brain containing those terrible memories. You understand now, Stan?"

I already understood at the Regal Court Motel. Rhonda was crazy. However, having a sudden and unexplainable urge to participate in Rhonda's insanity, I decided to tell her about my ex-wife, Nancy, who was supposedly abducted. I still didn't buy into this UFO thing, but I thought Rhonda might accidentally say something rational that would help me decide where to look for Nancy.

But as I was about to speak, I suddenly saw the sign. "You're here!!!! Get Wild at Club Feral !!!" I braked hard and turned right into the club's parking lot. Herby almost crashed into the back of my truck but slammed on his brakes just in time, no doubt more interested in not spilling his beer than avoiding a collision.

I told Rhonda to wait in the truck. I had some business I had to attend to and would be inside a few minutes. I waved to Herby signaling I would be right back as he took the last gulp of my last beer.

"Hey Stan! Buy some more beer!" he shouted.

The club was a non-descript aluminum sided building, one of many architecturally toxic structures along the unattractive commercial strip we had been cruising along. I walked through the door of the uninviting joint and the stench of stale beer and disinfectant engulfed me. It took a moment for my eyes to adjust from the bright sunlight to the darkness of the saloon.

As I looked around, I noticed there were only a few customers sitting at the bar and no one at the tables to my right. On the far side of the room was a large, vacant area of floor for dancing and a small, slightly elevated stage jammed with microphones and drums. I went over and took a seat at the end of the bar.

"What'll ya' have, Bub?" an inhospitable voice called from the other end of the bar.

"I just need a little information, if you wouldn't mind."

"What kind of information?" the bartender said, as he walked toward where I sat.

He was eying me suspiciously, wondering who I was and if he should be talking to me.

"I'm trying to find someone," I replied.

"Oh yeah," he replied in a hostile tone. "Who?"

"The man I'm looking for is of Chinese origin, I believe. He wears a red robe and has a long black pigtail. Do you know anyone who looks like that?"

"You from the F.B.I.?" he asked warily.

"No. I'm looking for him on my own."

"We run a straight operation here," he said, his demeanor telegraphing exactly the opposite.

The pungent aroma of marijuana smoke wafted past at that precise moment. My eyes met the bartender's. "The chef's cooking lentils," he said, as he looked downward toward his shoes. Seeing that I didn't believe him, he decided to be cooperative just in case I was a cop. "Yeah, I've seen the guy you're describing," he said, his abrupt pronouncement surprising me. "In fact, I've seen several guys that look like him. They come in here maybe once a month. You never know when they'll be here except that it's always on a Friday night. They throw a lot of money around. The girls love them."

"What are they like?" I prodded.

"They like to have a good time. They dance a lot and buy drinks for everyone. Funny thing is they never drink much. It's really strange. Oh yeah," he added, "and they talk in really high voices. They sound just like little girls. That's so weird because all of them are really big guys. You'd think they would have deep voices."

"You don't know where I might find them?"

"Not a clue, friend," he replied. "Come in here on a Friday night and they might be here. Like I said, they come in once a month, but I never know what Friday night it will be."

I thanked the bartender and walked toward the exit of Club Feral. I hadn't forgotten Herby's order for more beer, but I didn't want him to drink and drive. He was enough of a disaster as it was. The sun momentarily blinded me when I walked out the door. I got back into my truck and we headed for Rhonda's place.

Again, I thought about telling Rhonda that I was searching for my ex-wife who might also be a UFO abductee. However, I still hadn't accepted that it was space aliens who kidnapped her. "Abducted" still sounded too space-like and science fictionish. I'm still thinking, "kidnapped." As we drove into the driveway of Rhonda's apartment complex, I decided to not say anything about the kidnapping.

I was hoping I'd get one last opportunity to escape, politely of course. Maybe I could just beg off because I forgot there was something else I had to do. Rhonda seemed to sense my desire to run because she wouldn't let me out of her sight. We loaded all her stuff into the trucks and set out for the two hundred mile plus drive to Empyrean. Rhonda was riding with Herby now.

8

The Wilkenshavers

I often wonder if I'm crazy or just not very smart. It seems to me that a person could easily decide between those two options. This question always enters my mind when I get involved with very odd people in some hopeless quagmire of life's improbabilities.

As I followed the two delusional souls in the ancient, rusted Dodge pickup rolling past the city limits of Empyrean, Arizona I could only conclude: here I am again. "Oh my god," I mumbled, as I read the faded yellow sign displaying two silver UFO's. "Welcome to Empyrean, Home of the Most UFO Landing Sites on the Planet Earth." Then a sub-heading proclaimed, "They landed here before they crashed at Roswell."

"Not again, Lord! Please not again!"

In a final irony, the last line on the sign proudly heralded the town motto, "I found myself in Empyrean, Arizona."

I certainly did find myself in Empyrean, Arizona. Now how fast can I get out of here?

And there was one other thing. There is probably only one truck in the entire state of Arizona that is rusty. That odd situation is due to the fact that it rarely rains in Arizona, at least in the southern part where we now were. Herby somehow happens to own that one truck, a singular piece of vehicular crap. My god, that he owns the solitary rusty truck in Arizona shrieks of lunacy.

His old Dodge truck was not just a little rusty. Rather, it seems to have stolen all the rust from a thousand out of state rusting jalopies passing through Arizona during the truck's twenty-plus year life span. As I drove along behind Herby, I could see both his right and left rear tires through the rusted flapping fenders of his corroded monstrosity. I halfway expected the truck's rotted passenger door to give way and dump Rhonda into the road at the next bump. I didn't wish to further ponder that possibility.

We drove down Empyrean's main street, oddly enough named Main Street, and were soon at Rhonda's parents' house. A sign on the front wall read, "The Wilkenshavers live here." It was nearly nine p.m. We had stopped at a couple of fast food restaurants along the way, but Rhonda's mother had been holding dinner for us since five o'clock. For some strange reason, she held the dinner even after Rhonda called twice and told her we had already eaten and wouldn't be there for another two or three hours. It turned out to be four hours before we arrived. There was another warning sign. I concluded I had to be crazy.

By concluding I was crazy provided hope that I might return to sanity. By accepting this logic, it can all be figured out. You see, the world works like this. If you believe you are sane, you are a part of the problem. Your thinking that you are sane is annoying as hell to the rest of us who have already concluded that we are crazy, and therefore, much saner than you. We want to institutionalize you and your ilk because you have people like us locked up in the asylums when it is people like you who should really be there. The proof of this argument is that I have followed two terminally dysfunctional people to Empyrean, Arizona, population fifty-six hundred. I concluded I am crazy which means I am actually sane because I know I am crazy. Do you understand now?

I had no way of knowing things were going to get much worse. Why Rhonda's mother would hold their five o'clock dinner until nine PM after her daughter repeatedly told her we had already eaten would make one wonder. The fact that Rhonda called her twice during the drive from Phoenix also makes one wonder. Why does she want Rhonda to eat another dinner?

But it wasn't just a dinner. It was an avalanche of food. What seemed like half a cow, a flock of chickens, a garden full of potatoes, carrots and tomatoes, and a bakery full of pastries would have fed several third world countries. Rhonda's earlier dinner, consisting of two hamburgers, two orders of fries, and a piece of pie had just been a warm-up. Mrs. Wilkenshaver intuitively seemed to know that.

The arrival at Rhonda's house was yet another surprise in day of non-stop dementedness. Well, there were actually several surprises. That Rhonda's parents could not possibly be more opposite was the first surprise. Actually, after the psychotic series of events that had unfolded throughout the day, their incompatibility was more a footnote than a real surprise. Barbara Jean Wilkenshaver, like Rhonda, was quite substantial in girth. She and Rhonda probably wore the same size clothes. And although she was now retired, she had also been a sumo wrestler. In an accidentally perverse moment, I wondered how the two of them would look in pink poodle skirts. That was another thought I didn't wish to further ponder. No, really.

Mr. Wilkenshaver, on the other hand, like Herby Titsmore, was very small, perennially fearful, and demure. No, demure is not the right word. Hibernant, that's the word I'm looking for. Yes, Mr. Wilkenshaver was hibernant. To avoid the unfavorable climate of daily life, Mr. Wilkenshaver's brain simply hibernated each morning, allowing him to go through the day in a sort of hazy detachment.

Of course, his daily consumption of a case of beer also allowed Mr. Wilkenshaver to achieve this cogitative abstractness. Mrs. Wilkenshaver was boisterous, gregarious and fun loving. Mr. Wilkenshaver, like Herby, was quiet and timid, appearing to be in mortal fear of fun or any other pleasure. He never spoke a word. He just nodded and smiled and backed away from us. His given name was "Rock."

This particular name would be deemed appropriate only by someone who believed that a one eared Easter Bunny with webbed feet and a duck's bill was the progeny of an ill-considered threesome between Vincent Van Gogh, Peter Rabbit and a severely intoxicated Marvin the Duck, whoever he is. On the other hand, strange things happen.

Then the mountainous dinner began. There was so much food that even though we were sitting at the huge, extended dining room table, there was also a large quantity of edibles available buffet style on the kitchen table. It was a strange sort of served dinner with Mrs. Wilkenshaver and Rhonda dispensing the initial courses. Once the mother-daughter waitress team loaded down your main plate you were expected to proceed to the kitchen and pile more food onto an extra wide secondary plate. Quite telling as to the importance of food to this household was the fact that what had been the east wall of a much smaller dining room had been knocked out to double its original size and accommodate the greatly extended dining room table.

Since both Herby and I were "normal" eaters, we had already consumed our fill at the fast food place. But now, Mrs. Wilkenshaver expected us to partake of her immense feast. We did eat a little, just to be polite, but our small helpings were no doubt classified as nibbles in Mrs. Wilkenshaver's culinary dictionary.

Rhonda and her mother voraciously shoveled down gargantuan servings with only brief interruptions for conversation. One of these verbal time-outs occurred just after Mrs. Wilkenshaver swallowed an entire baked potato. "Don't Stan look like William Henry Harrison, Honey?" she asked her long suffering spouse, Rock.

He never answered. But Herby jumped into the conversation. "I told him he looks like Millard Fillmore," he chortled.

"I think he looks more like both them presidents than even they do," added Rhonda, assuming the rest of us could make sense of that inane observation. The people I met so far in Arizona seemed to have a fixation on long dead presidents whose names are hardly remembered by the rest of the country's citizens.

Mr.Wilkenshaver, who had met Herby for the first time, looked across the table and asked, "Did you say your name was Herby Titsmore?"

Herby nodded in the affirmative.

"That's an odd name, Rock continued. "How'd you ever get an unusual name like Herby?"

"It was my grandfather's name," Herby replied, as oblivious as Rock to the possibility that "Titsmore" was just maybe a little bit more unusual a name than "Herby."

What I found most odd about Mrs. Wilkenshaver was, in fact, Mrs. Wilkenshaver. Early on in the dinner I was firmly chastised by Mrs. Wilkenshaver for calling her Mrs. Wilkenshaver. "Have you not noticed how I am dressed?" a greatly affronted Mrs. Wilkenshaver asked. Not noticing how Mrs. Wilkenshaver was dressed would be as great an oversight as not noticing a one hundred and fifty car freight train roar through the dining room wall and across the table where we were all seated. No doubt the massive table could handle that unlikely probability as it already held a tonnage of food equal to the freight train's total weight.

Of course I noticed how she was dressed. A three hundred pound woman gyrating through the small brick bungalow the Wilkenshavers called home was impossible to ignore, regardless of how badly one wanted to. Mrs. Wilkenshaver was wearing the outfit of an Indian woman.

It was not, however, a dress like modern Indian women wear every day. It was more of a ceremonial, deer skin, kind of costume like "Indian squaws" wear in the old western movies. The outfit, probably a re-cycled teepee, had every sort of turquoise bead and a thousand fringes attached to it. Mrs. Wilkenshaver advised me in no uncertain terms that she had Indian blood. In fact, her professional wrestling name was "Thunder Squaw."

However, like so many other bizarre situations, this one too would soon be explained. By default, that task would fall to her shy husband, Rock. However, she first laid down the law on how she was to be addressed. Her Indian and thus real name was Desert Chickadee. Everyone in this house must address her as Desert Chickadee, she insisted. Everyone in the entire town of Empyrean called her Desert Chickadee. That got me to wondering, as I so often do, about certain practical aspects of the weird situations in which I often find myself. Do chickadees really inhabit the desert?"

For some reason that I have never understood, I seem to remember the most trivial of facts. Unfortunately, this habit was not a part of my high school and college study regimen. One of these minuscule trivia was that the black-capped chickadee was the state bird of Maine and Massachusetts. I wondered if Mrs. Wilkenshaver's chosen name was a consolidation of desert and black-capped chickadee abbreviated to Desert Chickadee. I also wondered if she knew that the black-capped chickadee's habitat was located three thousand miles to the northeast. Was there such a bird as a desert chickadee? I never wondered seriously enough about these kinds of things to actually research the answer. I just wondered. But then, I thought, who really cares?

"Rock," the seriously misnamed spouse of Desert Chickadee, began to lay out the proof that she had Indian blood. Apparently, Desert Chickadee's Caucasian great grandmother was impregnated by a man claiming to be an Indian chief on his way east to see the Great White Father in Washington, DC. Even though he was clearly traveling west toward California, she did not question his story or the direction of his route. She gave birth to her first, and she hoped, last child.

In a maternal misfire, Desert Chickadee's great grandmother immediately hauled her love child over to the local Indian reservation and demanded that they raise the girl. The Indians protested that the baby did not look like an Indian child, but great grandmother was adamant. "This is an Indian baby. You raise the kid."

But then, much to her dismay, great grandmother gave birth to a second love child, which was to be Desert Chickadee's grandmother. The joy of this mysterious event, mysterious because great grandmother claimed she had not been with a man for several years, was unfortunately short lived. A few months later she was hanged for cattle rustling.

Therefore, Desert Chickadee has Indian blood by virtue of the fact her grandmother's half sister whom her grandmother has never met, is half Indian. Maybe. "So you see, that makes Desert Chickadee an Indian," concluded Rock.

The one advantage to the humongous dinner was that while the two women were gorging themselves, Rock, Herby and I got into the beer. As the feast continued, I was downing as many as I could to fortify myself for whatever might come next. In an hour and a half, I'd passed out.

9

Bud's Rio Malo Saloon

I pulled my body upward as my head rolled around my shoulders like some frantic bobble head trying to figure out exactly what his problem was. Morning had come quickly and I had been awakened by monotone chanting coming from the front yard. When I passed out the night before, I must have been on the couch because that's where I woke up. As I peeked through the slit in the blinds, I could see Desert Chickadee dancing across the front yard rotating like a tilt-a-whirl car spinning wildly as it passed by on its circular ride to nowhere. Oh my god. I'm awake now. The chants, dancing and rotating continued for another half hour. I lay there pondering if this morning's spectacle was a daily routine. I found out later that it was.

Herby meekly entered the room followed by the even meeker Rock Wilkenshaver. They were both hung over, although not as badly as me. I assumed the reason was because my drinking had a clear cut mission, that being to help me escape the madness. But their drinking, on the other hand, also had a mission-to celebrate their toleration of it. Herby paid me the two hundred dollars he and Rhonda had promised. He also paid for my gas and food. My meager nest egg was improving slightly.

I was sitting up now. A broadly smiling Rhonda entered the room. She was dressed in a dark green flannel nightgown with "I Love Art" stitched across the bulging bosom area. She handed me a cup of coffee for which I was grateful, but in truth, I was already thinking of beer to insulate me from the day. I wondered if the "Art" on her nightgown was some deranged former lover or if it referred to painting, ballet and theatre or some other general aesthetic. That's what I need, a general aesthetic. But you have to have surgery to get one of those. Darn, beer will have to do. (I know, I know.)

Once again, I wasn't sure where I would spend the night, although that was at least fifteen hours into the future and why would I want to plan that far ahead. I didn't even know how I was going to spend my day. There was no use going back to Phoenix. Jobs were non-existent. I was half-way contemplating going back to Detroit, but what would I go back to? There were no jobs there either. On the other hand, I had some success in my quest to find

Nancy Nussbaum, my ex-wife. The bartender at Club Feral had provided an important lead. Rhonda abruptly stepped into my thoughts.

"Desert Chickadee says you should stay here with us for a few days, Stan. She senses great stress in your body. She wants you to stay for at least a week. I told her you would. I hope that's okay."

"That's great," I answered. In fact, it really was great. Despite their questionable grasp on reality, they were nice people. I hated to mooch off them for a week but I didn't have anywhere else to go. I would give them some money before I left to at least pay for the food and beer I would consume.

"We should all go downtown," Rhonda suggested. That would turn out to be another one of those all important warning signs that I so regularly failed to recognize. "Sure," I said, beginning to suspect that I had missed something here. My mind couldn't get a handle on just what that might be however.

Desert Chickadee and Rock lived only three short blocks from Main Street and thus "downtown" such as it was. However, we drove anyway with Rock, Desert Chickadee, and Rhonda riding in one car and Herby and me in my truck. In less than a minute we had parked our respective vehicles and were walking through the downtown area. It was a parade of misfits, with Desert Chickadee and Rhonda lumbering along arm in arm, taking up most of the sidewalk as they led the way. They were followed by the ultra-timid, small-bodied Rock Wilkenshaver and Herby Titsmore, who had strangely bonded and were walking along with their arms buddy-like around each other's necks.

I was the end of the parade, stumbling along tortured by curious statistical estimates. I was pondering the fact that Desert Chickadee and Rhonda each weighed more than Rock and Herby combined? Neither man weighed more than one hundred and fifty pounds. Neither woman weighed less than three hundred pounds. I'm not sure that was relevant to anything in particular.

In any other town our five person parade would have qualified as strange however, in view of Empyrean's extreme unconventionality, our strolling sideshow was not even noticed by passersby. There were at least one hundred plus business in town and the attractive little berg was obviously thriving. As we walked past the various buildings, most of which were of brick construction and painted, I began to notice the types of businesses lining Main Street.

There were a dozen or more art galleries and six saloons immediately in view. Ninety percent of the businesses, however, consisted of Vortex Tour Companies, Spiritual Pilgrimages, Psychic Spiritualists, Mystical Energy Spiritualists and so on, a formidable cornucopia of New Age enlightenment and deliverance. There was also a Dollar Deals Depot, which reminded me of the store in Elberta, Kansas where Calvin Dupo bought my deceased Cousin Eddie's shoes. There were a bunch of other random businesses on side streets but we didn't go any further. We had reached our first saloon.

It was quickly decided that the two women would forge (spelled forage, as in searching for food) ahead while the men would go into Bud's Rio Malo Saloon and have a beer. In what was a blatant violation of several laws of physics, the two women turned their sumo wrestler bodies westward in a movement faster than a speeding bullet, as Superman used to be described. They were headed for the bakery.

Once again, some subliminal warning tugged at my brain as we entered Bud's. I never liked the name Bud, other than when it referred to the beer. Bud just seemed to be the moniker for every redneck, hick and river rat I'd ever met. I had an uncle named Bud and I didn't like him either because he was all of those things. But what does Rio Malo mean? It didn't sound good. Bud's Rio Malo sounded much worse. Once again, I was feeling those bad vibes like I was about to do something I would regret.

Rock, showing off by interpreting the only two words of Spanish that he knew, answered before I had a chance to ask. "Rio Malo means bad river," he said.

"What does 'Bud' mean?" I shot back in a smart-alecky quip. It was a misplaced attempt at humor I should never have uttered. Rock was stumped on that one. He looked away with a dejected expression, not sure how to answer. I felt bad about that, but didn't know what to say. I bought him another beer.

Bud owned a gas station too. I had gone out earlier to get some gas so I wouldn't run out when we took our forty three second drive downtown a half hour later. That's what got me on this negative bent. When I pulled up to the pumps there was a cardboard sign hanging on the unleaded one that said, "Gas $6.50." The gas price in the little window of the unleaded pump read $4.50. I filled the tank figuring the $4.50 price in the little window of the pump was the correct one. When I went inside the old concrete building masquerading as a gas station and took out my wallet to pay, the attendant said "That'll be $65.00."

"How much per gallon is that?" I questioned.

"That's $6.50 per gallon friend," the attendant happily chirped.

"Yeah, but the pump says $4.50 per gallon is the price," I chirped back, but not in as chirpy a way as the attendant had chirped.

"The price is $4.50 for locals and $6.50 for everybody else, friend," he chirped back just as merrily as he had chirped before.

I had already concluded that he and I weren't friends and never would be.

"That doesn't seem right. Isn't there some sort of state law that everybody pays the same price?" I wasn't chirping.

"Probably is, I don't know," he popped back, maintaining his chirping tone and irritatingly large grin.

"Who's the manager?" I asked, in a voice hinting of a growl.

"That would be Bud. He owns the gas station and the saloon. You can find him over there at the saloon now if you want to talk to him about it. I wouldn't push him too hard if I were you. He gets real mean when he gets irritated. Come to think of it, he's always real mean. Ha, Ha," he laughed at his own annoying quip.

I wanted to punch him just because he was so happy to relieve me of my $65.00, not to mention the fact that he was just too joyful period. I've never liked people who were too joyful. I mean, joyful is fine, but people who are too joyful, be very careful of them. Their excessive joy, nauseating to the rest of we forlorn miscreants, is caused by one of two things. Either they have a serious hormonal imbalance or they are lying to you. Face it, who is really happy with the status quo? No, these joyful ones, they're not to be trusted.

Take my evil ex-wife for instance. Actually, a UFO full of aliens in red robes and pigtails just did, come to think of it. Anyway, I wouldn't have described her as "joyful" when we got married. But after a few months of marriage, she became one of those "too joyful souls." Of course, that was just about the same time she began the affair with her girlfriend and now partner, Latisha Wimberly. I just realized that. But anyway, it just goes to prove my point about joyful people. So there you have it. Don't ever trust those happy souls. They have a whole separate agenda going on beneath their happy surface.

I'd got ripped off earlier at Bud's gas station and now here I was in Bud's saloon. I had my gas receipt from my earlier purchase and was still thinking I would confront Bud about his gas prices. It took a while for my eyes to adjust from the bright sunlight to the darkness of the saloon. It took even longer for my nose to adjust to the heavy odor of cigarette smoke and spilled beer. My ears adjusted to the jukebox playing country and western music much more quickly. The music put me in a mood to have a beer.

There was a pretty good crowd for ten-thirty Saturday morning. There wasn't a woman in the place. Most of the clientele were dressed western style wearing jeans, cowboy boots and cowboy hats. Sitting at one table in the back of the room were five men, all dressed in black and wearing the same kind of black cowboy hats. That's strange. It looked like an undertaker's convention.

Rock, Herby and I went up to the bar and sat down on the worn stools that were actually quite comfortable. The bartender, whom I assumed was Bud, came toward us from the far end of the bar. He was a big, ugly bruiser of a guy with a vicious smirk on his unshaven face. He stopped just short of where I sat to look me over. I figured this was because he thought I might be from the State Bureau of Standards and Measures, if there was such a department, and was checking on his gas price policy. On the other hand, he's probably just unfriendly.

"What'll ya' have gents?" was the best he would offer for a welcome. But he followed up with an even warmer "and don't tell me I'll have a Bud, Bud. Every stranger that comes in here pulls that one." Charm wasn't one of Bud's strongest qualities. He then charged me $4.50 for a beer while Rock and Herby got off for $1.50 each.

The standing joke in town is that Bud charges "non-locals" the same price for beer as the locals pay for gas, $4.50 per gallon of gas and $4.50 for a beer. How did he know I wasn't a local? Herby wasn't a local either, but he only paid $1.50. Anyway, that made Bud seem even more unfriendly, which was a good trick, because he reeked with resentment from the first second I saw him. I thought I better down the beer and get out of there fast, figuring Bud's next move would be to charge to me $4.50 for parking on Main Street which he probably also owned.

Then I saw the "Happy Hour" sign hanging on the wall next to the bar. The sign advertised "Happy Hour Beer $3.00 for locals and $9.00 for non-locals. Bud doubled drink prices during "Happy

Hour." Rock explained that Bud's philosophy was that if people were going to be happy, they ought to pay for it.

"You from around here?" Bud asked, knowing full well I wasn't.

"No, I'm just visiting." Then I asked, "Where's the river?"

Howls of laughter erupted from all those cowboy clad characters within hearing range of Bud's and my conversation.

"What river do you mean?" Bud asked, in a smart-alecky tone. That set off another round of giggles and snickers.

"You know, the Rio Malo," I said.

The crowd was laughing so hard I thought at least a couple of them would suffer heart attacks, which, with my being the target of the ridicule, I thought they deserved.

"There ain't no Rio Malo river. Never was," Bud replied. This restoked the hysteria and the laughter started all over again. These guys don't get out much.

"Well why do you call it Bud's Rio Malo?" I further inquired.

"Who the hell knows?" said Bud. "It was the original owner's idea." And that was the end of that.

"We get a lot of strangers here," Bud offered.

In a weak attempt at humor, I replied, "Well they call me the friendly stranger. I'm not that friendly but I'm real strange." Bud took my joke as a statement of fact, completely missing the intended humor.

"Yeah, I figured you were," he said. "We get a lot of strange people in this town." He needn't have bothered to tell me because that particular fact was already stored in my memory banks and filed under "bonkers," or was it "bananas?"

To my surprise, there were a few laughs at the back table from the black clad, black hatted cowboys playing cards. I was soon to find out why.

"Come on back here and join us, Sonny," one of them yelled.

10

Ancient Outlaws of the Old West

It had been really hard to break off from my engrossing conversation with Bud, but I forced myself. Besides, Herby and Rock, the new best buds, not to be confused with Bud the bartender or Bud the beer, had so completely bonded that they were oblivious of anyone else in the bar. So I got off the bar stool and walked back to the table of the black clad brotherhood, sitting down in the extra chair one of them had pulled up for me. Once again I had missed all the warning signs. I should have run out the door the second Bud charged me $4.50 for the beer.

I hadn't noticed how old they were. But now that I could see them up close, it was obvious that all of them were at least eighty or ninety years of age. Then I saw the dog, a mangy black Chihuahua that was tied to one of their chairs. In a day that was mimicking the insanity of my prior days during the last week, the five card players introduced themselves.

"My name is Billy the Kid," the ninety plus year old man told me. "Of course, I got that name when I was much younger."

Could he actually be Billy the Kid? I wondered.

"I'm Jesse James," the second man said, extending his hand to shake mine.

"Nice to make your acquaintance, Jesse," I replied. I was now convinced beyond any reasonable doubt, that since I crossed the state line, I missed every available cautionary sign that I was sliding into a churning morass of total lunacy. "I'm Stanley Henry Thompson," I replied, in a weak attempt to also make some sort of statement with my name.

"You know who you look like?" Jesse James asked.

I was hoping that this group of cowboys, manly men, would recognize and acknowledge my own masculine persona. Yes, I was indeed one of them, a bona fide member of the macho brotherhood. I was no doubt a spittin' image (western talk) of one of those Hollywood tough guys.

"Yeah," Billy the Kid chimed in. "Danged if he don't bear a remarkable resemblance to Calvin Coolidge."

"Welcome Calvin," Billy the Kid chortled. "My name is Billy the

Kid." Then he leaned forward and whispered, "Of course, I got that name when I was much younger." Good lord, he forgot he already introduced himself. But no one else remembered either, and I was trying to forget.

"Pleased to meet you, Billy," I said, although I wasn't any happier meeting him the second time than I was the first.

"I'm Black Bart," black outfit number three said, giving me his hardest, meanest look that bespoke of a bullet through the heart for anyone who might do anything as intolerable as spill their beer. I saw his false teeth shift in his mouth.

"This is ridiculous," I thought, trying to keep a straight face. "Who is the next outlaw?" The answer was immediately forthcoming.

"Howdy partner, I'm Cole Younger," said black outfit number four.

I had been waiting for someone to get around to the "howdy partner" thing. That was the mandatory greeting in any gathering of cowboys anywhere, anytime. I was now equally certain it was also the salutation of choice for any gathering of raving nut jobs anywhere, anytime.

Finally, it was black outfit number five's turn. It wasn't hard to guess what was coming next. Couldn't at least one of them surprise me and introduce himself as George Washington or some other out of genre character?

"I'm Butch Cassidy," he said, continuing the schizophrenic admixture of identity crisis and senility.

"My pleasure," I stated, with as much sincerity as I could muster which, at this point, was none.

I suddenly started giggling, initially trying to muffle the snickering with my hand covering my mouth. But then, the god of tee-hee stepped in and I completely lost it. I suddenly burst into laughter, not because I was sitting at a table with five ancient over the hill, black clad cowboys named after the most notorious outlaws of the old west, but because I had somehow found my way to this remote town which proclaimed itself the UFO capital of the world. Also, I had yet to come across any sane person other than myself. Of course, I was always in doubt about my own sanity.

This loss of control on my part did not go over well with Butch Cassidy. As I regained my composure, it came to my attention that Butch had placed a rather large six-shooter on the table in front of him, crossways to his body. Although it was not pointed at me, his body language and that of the others made it very evident that I had managed to piss off the whole group.

"Just what the hell you laughin' at?" asked Butch. "You laughin' at our names or is there somethin' you find funny about us? That kind of nonsense can get a man killed in these parts."

I knew I could never explain to Butch's satisfaction I wasn't laughing at him and his outlaw friends, but rather my own predicament.

"I was laughing because I just realized Bud charges $4.50 for a gallon of gas and the same for a glass of beer," I lied.

"Yeah, that's real funny," Butch replied, with not even the glimmer of a smile on his severe looking face.

He wasn't really buying my excuse for my outburst but he wanted to get to more important things like playing cards so he let it go. The others appeared to let my explanation slide also.

"You play poker, Sonny?" Black Bart asked.

"No, I'm afraid not," I answered. Bud was staring at us and listening to the conversation. The juke box had stopped playing.

"What about black jack? You play blackjack?" Jesse asked.

"Well, I played a little when I was a kid, but I'm not very good at it," I politely offered. "Isn't that where you have to get twenty-one points?"

"Yeah, you've played blackjack," said Billy." I used to play that all the time when I was in jail over in Mesilla."

"Hey, yeah, I remember that," Jesse jumped in. "That was the time you lost all that weight and slipped off the shackles and escaped."

My god they were really nuts. I didn't want to play cards with them, but since they rescued me from Bud, I figured I owed them.

"Play a few hands with us, Sonny," Cole said. "It's only $1.00 a hand."

"I remember the days we used to play for $100 a hand," said Butch.

"Okay, I'll play a couple of hands," I agreed, being careful to watch for the hustle I was sure would come.

Jesse dealt the cards. I came up with 15 but figured I'd hold and lose just so I could get out of there. To my shock, the rest of them threw down their cards and said I won. How could that possibly be? Was this a hustle coming on for $1.00 a game? "You won $6.00,"

60

Bart said.

"Great," I smiled. The mangy Chihuahua stood motionless, looking up and watching closely from his subjacent location on the floor. I was beginning to wonder if he was dead and stuffed or something. I don't think I noticed any movement from him whatsoever. Jesse dealt the second hand.

I had a slightly better hand this time with a seventeen. Again I held, knowing somebody else would have a better hand and win, which is what I wanted to happen so I could gracefully depart. Everybody threw down their cards again. "You're the luckiest guy I've ever seen," said Bart. "You won again."

This was getting a little weird, which was saying a lot using the ludicrous events I recently experienced as the measurement for weird. I just won two rounds of black jack with two very bad hands of cards. They can't be hustling me for the paltry few bucks, are they? I was sure they'd raise the stakes.

Jesse dealt the third hand. I won that hand also. Then I won the next, and the next, and the next until I had won a total of a dozen hands. Nobody else won any. I was sixty dollars to the good and I never had more than one or two draws of cards that I thought could even remotely be winners.

"Man, you're a great card player," Cole said. "You got that right," Billy followed up.

I sat there waiting for one of them to raise the stakes higher to complete the hustle.

"I can't believe I won. I'm really not that good a player," I said apologetically.

"Well, I'm tapped out," Billy came back.

"Me too," said Butch.

The others also said they were out of money. I really felt badly about taking their money and I offered to refund it all saying it was just a friendly game.

"Oh no, you won fair and square," they all replied.

Then Cole spoke. "Look mister, I wouldn't mind playing one more hand if you wouldn't mind, just to try to get a little of my money back."

"No, that's fine," I said.

"Well, you look like a man who doesn't mind some higher stakes" said Bart.

Here comes the hustle. "What do you have in mind?" I asked.

Bart said, "How about this. I'm kind of out of money but, I'll bet my dog Mayor here against your $60. One hand, winner takes all."

"Look Bart," I replied, "I don't want your dog, no offense meant, of course."

He came back fast, "I've lost fifty dollars over the last week. My wife is about to kill me. Please, give me a chance here. What do you say? Bet me your $60 against my dog."

I felt so sorry for him I said, "Okay. One hand, that's it. Winner takes all." I really wanted to help the guy. While I could use the $60 myself, I figured I'd throw the game and let him win just to get him off the hook with his wife. And I sure didn't want his dog, which still had barely moved a muscle. He's got to be dead and stuffed.

"Jesse, you deal the cards," said Bart.

Jesse took the cards and quickly shot two of them to each of us. I had sixteen. That had to be a sure loser. Cole glanced at his cards. "Damn, you won again, mister. You don't play professionally or something, do you? I bet you deal cards over in Vegas, don't you?"

I nearly fell off of the chair. I couldn't lose here no matter how bad my hand. There didn't seem to be a hustle going on. This was ridiculous. These five guys were telling me I was the best card player they'd ever seen and I was thinking they were absolutely the worst card players I'd ever seen.

They all got up to leave. Bart handed me the dog's leash. "Here's your dog, mister. You take good care of him."

"Wait a minute Bart," I replied. "Hey, I really don't want your dog. I don't have any place to keep him. You keep your dog and you can have the $60 too," I said, offering the leash and the money to him.

Bart glared at me now. "I don't need your charity, mister. A deal is a deal. You won the hand and you won the dog and the money fair and square. We keep our word around here and we don't accept handouts," he repeated. He was visibly upset and seemed very hurt.

"Alright, if it upsets you that much, that's fine with me. But, I really can't take your dog. Everyone was standing now and they all had six guns hanging from their waists. Bart moved closer to me, putting his face directly in front of mine. "Mister, I'm a man of honor. I kept my end of the bet. You insult my honor and you're gonna' get shot," he scowled.

His face was boiling red and little beads of sweat were forming on his forehead. I thought he was going to take a swing at me and all

I was trying to do was give him back his dog and some money. This was very weird. Bud's Rio Malo Saloon was very weird.

"Okay, I'll take your dog," I said to Bart.

"That's more like it," he replied, and quickly turned and walked out the door.

I was the only one at the table now. I looked over at Bud but before I could speak, he said, "Don't even think about it. You got yourself a dog. Have a nice life." He turned to walk toward the other end of the bar, then stopped and looked back. "By the way, your dog, Mayor, he's a real special dog." As he was walking away, he laughed. Then he laughed again. "Take it easy, friendly stranger," he said. And, I was alone.

11

The Dog Mayor

Rock and Herby, the two new best buds and soul mates in timidity and mortal fear, were still sitting at the bar chattering happily as I walked past them with the dog, Mayor, following close behind. When I got out the door, I took off the dog's leash, hoping he would run after Bart who was now about a block down Main Street. No such luck. The dog Mayor seemed to know he now belonged to me. He was the mangiest Chihuahua I'd ever seen. Maybe some farmer would take him. I'll drop him off at a farm or ranch someplace. Yeah, that's what I'll do.

The dog Mayor followed me as I strolled toward my truck, still perplexed by the reverse hustle of the five ancient outlaws in black. As strange as things had been lately, they might very well be the exact characters they claimed to be, brought into our modern time by some geeky thirteen year old computer freak who invented a time machine and still slept with his mother.

I actually thought that if I hadn't accepted this little black mongrel following along behind me, the five ancient outlaws would have simultaneously drawn their guns and executed me in some code of the west vigilante style justice. Even worse, there was probably some old territorial law still on the books that would make their shooting me perfectly legal and the honorable thing to do. I thought I'd throw the awful critter into the back of the truck like all the western guys do. I don't think dogs care much for that macho concoction. They're probably thinking, Why don't you ride back here and let me drive you redneck nitwit? See how you like it sliding around the truck bed on this hot, slippery metal floor.

We got to the truck and I opened the driver side door and the black Chihuahua streaked inside the truck before I even realized it happened. "Get out of there you little creep," I yelled.

Apparently he didn't like my tone of voice or demeanor because when I reached to grab him, the hopelessly ugly dog snarled, showed every one of his tiny teeth, and bit my index finger, drawing blood. "Ouch!" I screamed. Then I decided to reason with him.

"Come here, Mayor," I gently called. "Come here, boy."

He wouldn't budge, holding steady as he stood on the far end of the seat by the passenger door and growling at my every move.

"Get over here you little creep," I snapped.

He just snarled, but even more viciously. He apparently was again not pleased with my choice of words or my gracious invitation to get out of my truck. I gave up and climbed into the driver's seat. I thought I noticed a self satisfied smirk on his demonic little face. I was about to start the engine but I stopped and looked over at him. "You disagreeable little creep" I muttered in disgust.

"Why do they call you Mayor?" I absent mindedly asked, knowing the ugly mutt couldn't understand a word I said.

"Because I'm the mayor of this one horse town you dim-witted, tenderfoot son of a bitch?" came his reply. "I'm Mayor Bobby Jeperson."

Understandably, my immediate reaction to a talking dog was not based on any prior experience with such a phenomenon. There was a time I thought my long deceased toy poodle was operating on a much higher spiritual-intellectual plane than I would ever achieve. I truly believed he had a metaphysical conversance with the underworld and was plotting to kill me and ship my body across the River Styx to Hades. But I never actually heard the ghastly little creature talk.

"My god," I shrieked as I jumped out of the truck. "What the hell! What the hell!"

My heart was pounding. "What the hell!" I was frantically pacing back and forth on the sidewalk by the truck. "What kind of dog are you? I must be in some really bad 'B' movie."

The dog stood on his hind legs looking out the passenger side window and calmly watching me trying to recover from the horror. He seemed to be enjoying my fright immensely. I was overwhelmed with shock and disbelief. Is this some supernatural event? Is God sending me a message? How on Earth do I handle this? Those were my immediate thoughts, however running like hell also came to mind.

I regained my composure, but only slightly. I was still very distressed, even fearful. I'm not going to give the little demon the satisfaction, I told myself. I cautiously walked around the back of the truck, mindful of the little mongrel's constant gaze, and jumped back inside.

"Tell me you didn't just talk," I said.

"Alright, I didn't just talk, you deplorable dummy. Does that make you feel better?"

"How many beers did I have?" I asked myself, hoping I was hallucinating because the unfriendly Bud the bartender served me bad beer.

"You can't count either, numbskull. You're pathetic," the dog Mayor, answered.

"I was asking a rhetorical question," I replied, in an attempt to one up him. "And you've got a nasty mouth."

"If you think it's nasty now, think how bad it is after I lick my ass."

"You lick your behind?" I gasped in shock.

"Of course I do. And I smell other dog's asses and sniff where they pee and take a crap. I don't like the idea of doing it, but I can't help myself. That's what dogs do. That's part of the curse I'm living."

"I'd never do that," I said. "You're gross."

"You're still stupid," the tiny dog retorted. "And you look like Franklin Pierce. I learned all about him in eighth grade in 1978."

"You don't know who Franklin Pierce is." I said. "You weren't even alive in 1978. You dogs have a real short life span, remember? And if you keep messing with me, your particular life span is going to get much shorter."

"Ohhhh, you really scare me, you Detroit reject. And Bart said you looked like Calvin Coolidge. That's a laugh. You're definitely a double of Franklin Pierce. Besides, I was so alive in 1978."

"You couldn't have been. You're not human," I replied, wondering how I came to be sitting in downtown Empyrean, Arizona arguing with a foul mouthed, small dog.

"Yes, I am human you stupid dude. I'm just a bit out of sorts at the present time."

The little rodent was not using dude in the "you're cool" sense. He was substituting dude for tenderfoot, or worse. But it didn't matter. I disliked him either way. Besides, I had a very troubled history with small dogs. As with my experience with the toy poodle, I was once again sensing this animal's mental prowess was much more than I cared to confront. I didn't want to admit that I lost the battle with the last small dog to run my life, but I had. And, I wanted to quit with only one loss. Being defeated by a second pint-sized pain in the ass was not a particularly attractive prospect.

"Well if you don't mind my asking, and I'm not a detail man," I reminded myself and informed the dog at the same time, "if you are human, then how did you become a Chihuahua?"

"Look Jack, we've got a lot to talk about. I'm going to tell you a lot of stuff you won't believe, but not right now. All you need to know now is that you and I can help each other."

"My name's not Jack," I said, remembering my earlier unpleasant conversation in Phoenix with a guy who called me Jack. "Why should I listen to you and how could we possibly be of any use to each other?"

"First of all, I heard you don't have a job. Second, judging from this dilapidated truck, you don't have any money either. I can fix both of those things but you have to help me too. Can you understand that?" he asked in a sarcastic voice.

I nodded skeptically, knowing I was desperate to find employment.

"There's a business in town that's for sale. You and I will buy it and I'll work for you."

"You want a job?" I asked in surprise. "Of course, I guess there's not a real big job market out there for unemployed, foul-mouth Chihuahuas. Besides, I thought you said you're the mayor of Empyrean."

"I want more than a job. I need to get turned back into a human form like I was. The job you give me will put me in a position to accomplish that. I'm on leave of absence from my mayor's job because the city council didn't think it would be good publicity for the town to have a small dog as mayor. You know, the picture is on the city web site and all. Personally, I think they're a little too sensitive, don't you?"

I didn't answer because the situation was so insane I found myself aghast.

"But explain to me how you became a Chihuahua," I said, still shocked that I was having a conversation with a talking Chihuahua who claimed to be the mayor of Empyrean, Arizona.

"Like I said, I'll tell you about that later. First we need to go buy that business. Have we got a deal?"

I had to stop and think about that for a moment. Being too hasty had often gotten me in trouble. As I pondered the wisdom of buying a business with a small dog, I considered my options. It didn't take long because I had no options.

"Yeah, I suppose so," I mumbled, completely devoid of enthusiasm.

"What's your problem, numb-nuts?" he asked in his snottiest, most insulting Chihuahua voice. As he talked, his words were sometimes punctuated by unintentional barks. "Ruff-ruffs" were scattered throughout his sentences.

"I never thought I'd be in a business partnership with an ugly Chihuahua, I guess."

"Well I never thought I'd be in a business partnership with a loser like you," the vituperative mutt hissed back. "So we got a deal?"

"Yeah, we got a deal," I replied, wondering how I was letting myself become involved in the weirdest situation I'd ever encountered.

We got out of the truck and started walking. I was following the dog. I hadn't noticed before, but his testicles were extremely large, almost dragging along the concrete sidewalk as we walked.

"How'd you get such big balls?" I asked.

"That was a last second prank, courtesy of the jerk that turned me into a Chihuahua," he fumed. "When I catch up to him, I'm gonna get him for that ball thing too."

"What kind of business is it?" I asked. "I don't have much money, you know."

"I'll help you on the money thing," Dog Mayor said. "Don't worry about that."

"What kind of business is it?" I asked again, getting a feeling Dog Mayor didn't really want to tell me what I was getting into."

"I want to surprise you. We'll be there in a minute or two," Dog Mayor replied, again dodging my question.

We took a right turn and walked up a side street another block and Dog Mayor stopped. We were now standing in front of an unkempt, non-functioning business. As if in support of the non-operating business, a non-functioning neon sign in the front window advertised "Deluxe UFO Tour Company" on blackened fluorescent tubes. A cheap cardboard sign like the one I used for my garage sale read, "Business for Sale"

'Here it is," the town mayor turned Chihuahua said gleefully. "Open the door and we'll go in."

As I reached for the door handle, I looked down at the mangy creature whose head didn't even reach my knee unless he stood on his hind legs. "I'm not buying this train wreck," I said.

"Yeah you are," he countered, walking in ahead of me. "We made a deal and you gotta stick to it."

The inside of the place was an even bigger disaster than the outside. Everything was covered with dust and papers were strewn about the floor. Stacks of unopened mail lined the counter. The most unkempt man I'd ever seen was sitting in a chair propped against the back wall and holding a can of beer, the second last one of the six-pack sitting on his desk in front of him.

"What the hell do you want?" he politely inquired. He evidently had not noticed the officious appearing dog that had walked across the musty office floor and now stood at the foot of his chair looking up at him.

"We want to do some business with you Larry, you worthless pinnacle of human debris," Dog Mayor answered.

"Well, Mayor Bobby," was his snide reply. "I didn't see you down there. To what misfortune do I blame for your honor's darkening my doorway with your repulsive little shadow? You didn't piss on my sidewalk, did you?" He gurgled and then laughed as he lifted his can of cheap beer toward his chapped lips.

"No, I waited until I got inside so I can piss on your leg you pathetic consequence of DNA misfire. How much money do you want for your thriving enterprise here? And don't start high. You got one shot to unload this garbage dump and then we're out of here."

Larry thought for a moment. "Well, there's the assets, you know, the building, the touring coach, the business equipment and of course the good will and the quality name I've built up in our community. Our community with no mayor," he added, and laughed again at what he imagined was his stinging humor.

"The building's falling down around your ears, but you were probably too drunk to notice. Your touring coach, that fifteen year old eight passenger van with no tires and sitting on blocks out front, probably needs an engine or transmission or both. By the way, since you haven't gotten off your dead ass glued to that chair for several years you probably didn't notice that the UFO aliens' heads on the side of your van have vampire teeth and moustaches painted on them. So it needs a paint job too. You need to pay somebody just to take that trash filled jalopy off your hands because the repair bills cost more than it's worth. Should I keep going?"

"Well what about all the business equipment in the office here? And what about the goodwill, my good name?"

"You know the only business equipment in this shit-hole is a couple of dried out ball point pens and a disconnected telephone. As for your good name, your fellow citizens are about to ride your ass out of town on a rail. How much money is it gonna' take to buy this decrepit rubbish heap, Larry?"

"You take over the mortgage on the building and give me $10,000 for the rest of the business. We have a deal?"

"Not even close, Larry. I happen to know what you owe on the building and we'll take over the mortgage. For the rest of the business, we'll give you a thousand dollars and not a dime more."

"You got a deal," Larry said.

"Good. Write down what I tell you on a clean piece of paper and you and Stan sign it. Get a couple of your deadbeat friends in here to witness your signatures. You do know how to write don't you?"

With that, Larry pulled out his cell phone and summoned two of his friends who arrived instantly. I surmised he no doubt promised free beer if they could be here in five minutes. Luckily they were able to instantly clear their calendars of their many important appointments just to witness Larry's signature. Both men were exactly what the mayor had described, deadbeats. He might have meant that as a compliment. These two representatives of the un-washed masses were even grungier looking than Larry. Come to think of it, buying this business was probably just another step down bringing me ever closer to joining their ranks.

"Give him the money," the mayor said, looking at me.

"Wait a minute," I replied, "you said you were going to help me buy this place. Where's your money?"

"Shut up," the mayor said. "Give Larry the thousand dollars and I'll get my part of the money later."

Reluctantly, and without the additional thought I knew I should have given it, I parted with the thousand dollars. That left me a total net worth of $1700 in cash and a pickup truck that probably wasn't in any better condition than Larry's tour coach, except my truck had tires.

"Give my friend here the keys to the building, Larry and get your smelly carcass out of here."

"How about letting me sleep here for a few days, Mayor?" Larry replied.

"That okay with you partner?" Dog Mayor asked me.

Ever the softie for hard luck cases, I said "Okay."

The mayor and I walked out and headed for the bank. He was actually going to give me $500 for his half of the business. I couldn't believe it. This was the first honorable man I think I ever met, and he was a Chihuahua.

Unbelievably, the bank didn't question the Chihuahua as to whether he actually was Mayor Bobby Jeperson. They didn't even ask for an identification card or a driver's license, not that he would have had either with a picture showing him as a Chihuahua. They just put a little ink pad down on the floor and he put his right front paw on it and then they put the withdrawal slip down by his foot and he stepped on it and left an inky paw print as his signature. They gave him, well, actually me, the $500. Everybody in town seemed to have known the mayor was a Chihuahua, except me of course.

"Alright Stan, you go over to the saloon and celebrate our new venture. You can probably use a drink anyway. I've got some other business I've got to attend to."

12

The Embarrassing Yak Incident

Earlier, I had decided to drive back to Desert Chickadee's house and use the phone to call Latisha Wimberly to report my progress in my search for her partner, my ex-wife, Nancy Nussbaum. There wasn't really much to report other than I might have a small lead at Club Feral. As it turned out, Latisha was happy to get my call and excited that there was at least a little progress in the search to find Nancy. I felt guilty because I really hadn't done anything except stop at the club. There really hadn't been any progress, but she seemed to be happy I was at least thinking about finding Nancy.

I often thought about my former co-worker, Jean Monaghan, during my trip west and decided to call her too. She answered on the first ring.

"Stan," she said, "I was hoping you would call. How are things going?"

It took the better part of half an hour, but I described all that had happened after she drove me home that last day of work. I told her I thought about the kiss we shared and, even though we hardly knew each other, I missed her.

"I miss you too, Stan," she said. "I'm glad you bought a business. I know you'll do really well with it."

"I don't know, Jean," I said. "The business takes tourists around to alleged UFO landing sites. That's all it does. It doesn't sound real great to me. It was bankrupt. That's how well it was doing."

We chatted a while longer and said our goodbyes. I liked Jean even more now, a lot more.

On my way to the saloon, I ran a few errands and got the oil changed in my truck. It was nearly five o'clock on what had been a strange but eventful day. I pushed open the door of Bud's Rio Malo Saloon and walked over to claim one of several empty bar stools. Bud served me another $6.50 beer, pointedly reminding me that I wasn't a local. I was going to protest and advise him that I was now a proud business owner in this eccentric berg, but I was too tired to argue.

Besides, for some reason, the usual innocuous din of the saloon had mysteriously ceased to the point of being able to hear the proverbial pin drop. I took a sip of beer, anxiously anticipating some inebriated jokester either dropping the pin or some much heavier version of it, like an empty glass. As I set my soon to be empty beer glass on the bar, I noticed everyone was looking at me, including the ever gracious and effusively inhospitable Bud.

"What!" I exclaimed to Bud, as I tried to find out what the current problem was.

Bud stared for a moment and then nodded his head, his eyes focused on something behind me. I turned to look. "Oh god," I shrieked, attempting in vain to invoke a higher deity to help me through this brand new nuttery, an existing word of which I changed the meaning shortly after arriving in Empyrean. Standing behind me was a Chinese man, staring silently at me like the rest of the wide-eyed customers.

The fact that he was Chinese was not the reason for my current horror. Rather, the fact that he was naked from his waist down was the occasion for my shock. He wasn't wearing pants or underwear of any kind. His elongated tool, proudly hanging just inches from where I sat, joined with the drinking patrons in staring accusatorially at me. Since Mr. Penis' function of emptying beer was in direct opposition to the clients' function of drinking beer, I pondered the rationale of their curious alliance for the mutual castigation of myself.

"What is it?" I again protested to Bud.

"You're on Wang's stool," replied Bud. "That's where he always sits."

"I immediately jumped off the bar stool, not minding the necessary acquiescence to surrender the seat as much as abhorring the fact that my own behind had been sitting on the same spot his naked bottom routinely occupied.

I picked another spot five or six bar stools away and sat down next to some black guy. The mindless banter of the place had returned to its regular level.

"How're you doing?" he asked.

"Well, as soon as I get used to some of the customs in this town, I'll probably be doing a lot better. Why does that guy Wang walk around naked? Who is he anyway? And, please don't tell me his name is Wing Wang or I'll throw myself off this bar stool."

"It's funny you should mention that," he replied, hinting that Wing Wang, as used in some circles to describe the male organ, might indeed be his name. I was getting ready to hurl myself from the bar stool to the floor in a dramatic suicidal gesture, knowing the fall wouldn't kill me, but might possibly get me a few sympathetic free beers.

He continued. "I don't think anybody knows his name. Bud did give him the nickname "Wang," but I'm sure it wasn't in reference to the Wing Wang to which you refer. Bud's not smart enough to connect those dots. Oh yeah, Bud also named a drink after him. He calls it 'Wang's Moon Rocket.' Anyway, Wang doesn't speak a word of English. He comes in every Saturday about this time like he's been doing for the last thirty or so years. He has a few beers and sings a couple of karaoke songs, then leaves. He lives out of town someplace."

I shook my head in disbelief as the man continued talking. "The fact that he's always naked from the waist down doesn't violate any state law or town ordinance so nobody pays any attention to him. But it's a surprise to people who've never seen him before."

"Yeah, you're telling me," I said. "By the way, I'm Stan Thompson."

"It's nice to meet you, Stan. I'm Manfred Starshine."

"Yeah, it's nice to meet you too. Is that your real name?" I asked, fearful of what the answer might be.

"No, I changed it. My name used to be Norman, but I changed it to Manfred because I liked that better. Don't you?"

"Oh yeah, much better," I agreed, thinking that in any place other than Empyrean, it would have been his last name that was unusual.

Another customer sat down on a stool on my right.

"Evening, gents," he said smiling.

"Hello Galen," Manfred greeted him in a bored, knowing voice.

I nodded at the new arrival.

"Stan, this is Doctor Galen Withersby. Galen, this is Stan."

We shook hands and Galen voiced an insincere "Glad to meet you."

"Well Manfred, it looks like you're the only Negro in the bar this afternoon."

"Oh my god, what have I gotten into now?" I asked myself, fully anticipating fists to fly at any moment.

However, no anger was forthcoming from Manfred.

"Stan, Galen is a highly trained Sociologist," Manfred remarked, while simultaneously rolling his eyes toward the ceiling. "It's his business to take note of these profound sociological situations."

"Is he a racist?" I whispered.

"Calling Galen a racist would be a compliment, wouldn't it Galen?" Manfred laughed. "You see, Stan, I think of a racist as someone who hates a particular race. But, that would not describe Galen. Galen hates all races equally. He hates anyone who belongs to any race. That, of course, would include every person on the planet."

Galen, who had obviously sparred with Manfred on many prior occasions, smiled but then began to explain his unsolicited views on such things.

"I concentrate on a specialized branch of Sociology which I created for my Doctoral dissertation. It's called "Raciology.""

"What on earth is that?" I asked, although I was not at all anxious to hear his answer.

But the answer was rapid in coming. "Raciology is the branch of Sociology which explains the general decline of the human race which we are now experiencing."

Manfred, clearly un-rattled by the insanity unfolding to my right, continued to sip his beer and nod, greeting other customers as they walked by. I didn't bother to ask Galen to explain further, somehow knowing that he would do so anyway.

"You've heard of dark matter?" he condescendingly inquired. "That's the stuff that actually makes up most of the universe." His tone presumed he was speaking on a lofty intellectual plane that he alone occupied and was far beyond my comprehension. I'm so fortunate he's a patient man, I reflected wryly, otherwise, I would never know the wisdom he was about to impart.

"Get ready," Manfred whispered, loudly enough for Galen to hear.

"Cute, Manfred," Galen quipped. He looked back at me. "Here's how it works. Races all have stereotypes, do they not?"

"I suppose that's true, although I never thought about it before."

"What about you? What race are you?"

"I'm Irish," I replied, not really knowing if Irish was a race, but I wasn't sure.

"Okay, so what are the Irish known for?"

"Saint Patrick's Day," I guessed.

"Drinking. They're known for drinking. They spend all their waking hours in pubs."

"Well, yeah, but don't a lot of races drink?"

"Of course, and that's precisely my point. The other races wouldn't drink if it wasn't for the Irish. The Irish infected all the other races with their endemic alcoholism."

"You're blaming the Irish for all the drinking that goes on in the world?" I asked in amazement. My eyes were wandering in the direction of the exit as I contemplated my escape.

"It gets better," said Manfred.

"The Irish alcoholic plague was spread by negative germ-like organisms called Zuyglyphens. They travel through dark matter and their sole function is to spread the negative characteristics of each race to all other races. So, not only do you see the alcohol plague spread across the races of the earth, but also the negative traits of each race have thoroughly contaminated every other race. Hence the decline of the human species. Do you understand now?"

Manfred, continuing to drink his beer and ignore Galen, had himself reached a level to which I could only aspire. He had learned to appreciate lunacy as an art form. Before I could answer, Galen cautioned that I should ignore Manfred as he could not understand the powerful science, which supported his sociological assertions. I glanced over at Manfred who was rolling his eyes again and trying not to burst out laughing and spill his beer.

"Jees, look out!" exclaimed Galen, ducking his head low.

I ducked too, in reaction to Galen's shout. Manfred, not at all fazed and not bothering to duck, continued drinking his beer.

"Why are you scaring the hell out of me?" I asked in an irritated tone.

"One just flew through the room, that's why. It just missed your head. You gotta' be careful. They travel....whoa! Look out again! Man that was close!" Galen shouted, ducking again. "I was starting to say they always travel in pairs when that other one flew by. They're bad today."

"Who, what?" I asked, although no one else in the room seemed to be paying any attention.

"It's the flying humanoids, man. Don't you ever watch the television show, 'Spooky Things and Scary Stuff?' Usually they only come around if you're talking about them. They always seem to know. But lately, they've just been out of control. Every time I look up one's flying by. They're all worked up about something." I looked around the ceiling area again, but saw nothing.

"So Galen," I interjected, "did you say your dissertation was on the new branch of Sociology you created called "Raciology?"

"Yeah, exactly. I'm on the cutting edge, way ahead of the pack."

"And you got your Ph.D. in Sociology?"

"I don't have my Ph.D. yet. I'm what they call an A.B.D, All But Dissertation. My Ph.D. committee asked me to take a hiatus after I presented my dissertation on Zuyglyphens and dark matter and the decline of the human race. They wanted me to do more work on this subject and fully develop it into the specialized branch of science it deserves. As soon as I've completed this project, I'll go back and present my dissertation and pick up my Ph.D."

"How long have you been on hiatus?" I replied.

"It's been thirty-one years," he said. "I call my committee back each year in August and tell them what I've got but they always want more and insist I keep working for another year. They are so hungry for this new science I invented. It really gets me emotional."

I looked at Manfred, but he was ignoring Galen.

"Oh, I have to go," Galen suddenly said. "I'd like to talk to you more, but I've got some important things going on right now. Take it easy."

I wasn't sorry to see him leave.

"How did you like that little sociology lesson?" Manfred asked.

"It was great, Manfred," I replied. "Can I buy you a beer? I'll tell Bud to spray them for Zuyglyphens before he brings them to us."

Manfred agreed to my offer of a beer and I signaled for Bud to come over.

"By the way, Manfred, what do you do around here?"

"I'm the Keeper of the Gate to Non-visible Worlds."

Bud arrived to take our order. I had originally planned to have another beer however I now needed something much stronger to counteract my sorrow when I found out that Manfred, whom I thought was the only non-crazy person in town, now appeared to be as loony as the rest of the population.

Before I could order, however, Bud informed me that the pants averse Mr. Wang wanted to buy me a drink because I had so politely relinquished my, rather his, bar stool to him. "He wants to buy you a Wang's Moon Rocket."

"Sounds good to me," I said. I need something stronger than a beer and if a Wang's Moon Rocket was free, that would be just fine.

"I wouldn't do that if I were you," cautioned Manfred.

I looked at Bud. "What are the ingredients in a Wang's Moon Rocket?"

An irritated Bud rattled off the list of contents of the exotic concoction. "It has three shots of Chinese vodka, three shots of Chinese white wine, a shot of lotus juice and two shots of caffeinated yak piss. The yak piss is not from concentrate and not the powdered kind. It's fresh, made right here at the Rio Malo Saloon."

"Yeah, that's exactly what I wanted," I replied laughing.

Bud didn't crack a smile and walked away with the usual scowl on his face to fix the drink and get Manfred's beer. In a short time he returned, handing Manfred his beer and pushing my Wang's Moon Rocket across the bar to me.

"Cheers," said Manfred.

"Cheers," I replied, hoisting the golden mixture to my lips.

Wang's Moon Rocket had a superb flavor, yet left a slightly sour aftertaste which seemed oddly familiar, but more like something I might have smelled rather than consumed at some time in the past. I finished it quickly and signaled Bud to bring me another. It seemed like he was back in no time, delivering another saffron tinged Wang's Moon Rocket. Once again, I made quick work of it.

Manfred had continued talking, describing his spiritual healing vocation and inquiring if I might be interested in having my third eye opened to the secrets of the vortex or attending an intuitive reading. As I was pondering becoming involved with Manfred, either the first or second Wang's Moon Rocket kicked in. Suddenly I was drunk as a skunk, high as a Georgia pine, plastered, well, you get the picture. And just as suddenly, I realized I needed to rid myself of some of the beer of which I had earlier partaken.

I had never been to the men's room at Bud's Rio Malo and I was sure that it would be a special treat. In order to get to the men's room, one had to go through a doorway in the very back of the room and proceed about twenty feet down a hallway. I pushed open the door cleverly labeled "Cowboys" to find that the restroom was in better condition than I could ever imagine and was actually clean.

The odd thing about the place, however, was that the two urinals were located directly below two windows sitting at eye level and providing a view of the animal pen just outside. As I dutifully stood at the urinal "doing my business," as the saying goes, I saw a half dozen strange looking animals in the enclosure. I had no idea what they were until I read the small sign beneath the windows. "The animals you see outside are yaks. In many parts of the world their urine is revered for its spiritual healing power."

Even in my highly inebriated condition I immediately grasped the significance of the yaks gazing inquisitively toward me. Bud wasn't kidding. He really did put yak piss in my cocktail. However, in my intoxicated state, I focused my rage on the yaks instead of the man who mixed the yak piss into my drink. I began screaming the most dreadful curses out the window at them. "You frigging yaks! Your frapping minion Bud put your piss in my frapping Mang's Yoon Rockets! I mean my Yang's Roon Mockets." I was having some trouble enunciating.

As my alcohol sodden fury peaked, I concluded that some sort of retribution was in order here. I would kill the yaks first and then kill Bud the bartender. My eyes scoured the men's room for a weapon. There was nothing but a waste basket and a toilet plunger. The latter would have to do. I grabbed the toilet plunger, still screeching profanities as loudly and quickly as they came to mind, and ran out the back door. With one hand on top rail of the enclosure, and the other hand holding the toilet plunger, I attempted to bolt over the fence and into the yak pen. I would quickly end the lives of those six evil pissers.

I almost made it over the fence, and would have too if it were not for my left foot hanging up and interrupting my ballerina like leap. That miscalculation caused me to fall unceremoniously into several mushy piles of yak manure. I was screaming curses even more loudly, if that were possible. I got up and stood facing them with my toilet plunger held high, poised to kill the first of the yak piss dispensing S.O.B.'s.

But now, in a reversal of aggressiveness modes, the largest of the six offending beasts, and apparently the frigging supreme yak leader, turned and advanced to within ten feet of where I stood. He was stamping his front feet, grunting and braying and making some kind of bleeping, insensible animal sound. I thought I detected a smile on the devil's face. Yes, I was sure he was laughing at me in a secret yak laugh that only other yaks know. And now, as I looked behind him at the other five yaks, they too were laughing at me. They were laughing at me because I was the idiot who drank their spiritually healing piss.

And to pour salt in the wound, their snide, private yak laugh shrieked un-remittent joy at the deception that I had suffered at their hands, actually hooves. But, as I stared toward them in my inebriated stupor, I was horrified that instead of six yak faces, I saw my own dear father's face on every one of their yak heads. "Hi, S.H.I.T, his six yak reincarnations said, laughing in unison. "Got you again! Are you really stupid enough to believe yak piss heals your soul?"

Once again my evil progenitor was capitalizing on the profane initials of the name he had cursed me with the day I was born. With laser like focus on my mission to kill all daddy-faced yaks, I screamed triumphantly as if the victory was already won. Propelled by the liquid afterburners of two Wang's Moon Rockets I charged forward, my lethal toilet plunger pointed directly at frigging supreme yak leader. But then, seemingly as furious at me as I was at his yak pack and bartender agent Bud, he galloped forward at full speed to meet me in mortal combat.

In a maneuver violating the laws of knightly combat and chivalry, the no-class yak ducked his head, causing me to miss the fatal blow I attempted with the toilet plunger. Then, with his head still lowered, he charged forward and I felt the painful thud of the yak leader's snout against my crotch and his teeth clamped down on my penis, which was shielded only by my khaki pants. My screams immediately escalated to the highest soprano level ever reached on Planet Earth. "You've un-manned me you cowardly beast!"

"I told you not to drink those Wang's Moon Rockets," a voice behind me commented.

I was lying on the ground holding what I was sure was either a badly mangled or decapitated penis and I looked over to see Manfred. He easily climbed over the fence I found so formidable earlier and helped me to my feet.

"You're a mess," he concluded.

"Yes, I am," I agreed, as I leaned on him and hobbled back toward the fence.

13

Where Should I hide the Handyman's Body?

"I've never seen anything like this before. Nope, this is the worst I've seen in my entire life. Wow! It's really bad."

My business partner, Dog Mayor, and I were listening to handyman Virgil Tarsenberg, aka "Tarzan," report on the sorry mechanical state of the touring coach we recently acquired along with the other worthless assets of the bankrupt Deluxe UFO Tour Company. It was Monday morning and Dog Mayor and I were taking stock of our less than astute investment.

Rhonda, who decided she would work at Deluxe UFO Tour Company, came out of the office to listen to Virgil. Dog Mayor heard enough and went inside to set up his desk. I wasn't sure how he would do that with only a small nose and four paws lacking opposable thumbs. And, I wasn't sure Rhonda's career choice was an especially wise one in view of the fact that we had no customers and no money to pay her salary. Apparently, she was no more of a detail person than me.

At first, I wasn't sure I wanted to get involved in running a business, especially one that had already proven its lack of viability by becoming bankrupt. But after thinking about it over the weekend, I was now positive I made the wrong decision. However, getting out of the deal would no doubt be impossible, short of just walking away and writing off my $500 investment. And besides that, if I walked away, I would forego the opportunity of being able to throw additional good money after bad.

Like most entrepreneurs who own a failing business, I wanted to make sure I lost every last dime I had. I would no doubt ride this horse until it died. The only comforting thing was that its day of demise would come soon as my total operating capital was less than $2,000. That meant that I couldn't afford to pay employees, the mortgage, or any operating expenses for that matter. In fact, I suddenly realized I had now gotten myself into the exact situation in which I found myself when I fled, I mean migrated, from Detroit.

"Boy, this is something else," Virgil continued, as he lay on the ground underneath the decrepit vehicle sitting on four concrete blocks. "It's definitely in the worst shape of any car I've ever seen in my life."

Virgil Tarsenberg, who was rabidly convinced that he was a direct descendant of some long dead French king, was Rhonda's cousin. I had already decided to kill him as soon as I figured out where I would hide his body. On the other hand, I didn't really want to handle dead bodies so I would have to find an accomplice for that part of the operation. I was thinking this through very carefully. Was Tarsenberg a French name? Why did I care?

Virgil was one of those technically superior trades people with special expertise in absolutely nothing, but convinced they know everything about everything. I had encountered more than my share of these pompous plumbers, auto mechanics, electricians, etc whose life's mission is to rave about how excruciatingly horrible my particular problem happens to be.

No matter if it was a stopped up toilet, dead battery, or blown fuse the resident expert on the particular matter would launch into a prepared tirade as if on cue. The pronouncement that my particular problem was the worst he'd ever encountered and had never seen anything like it before in all his days was certainly reason enough to kill him. No jury would ever convict me.

I was convinced all these glass half empty purveyors of gloom used the same script, which concluded with a dark forecast of imminent doom because the guy who originally installed the garbage disposal did not use the little plastic widget thing. This oversight triggered an electromagnetic wave that caused the earth's tectonic plates to shift resulting in a re-alignment of the continents. If only he had been there he would have done the job right because, you see, he always carried little plastic widget things with him. In fact, on one occasion, he had saved humanity from extinction because he had a little plastic widget thing in his pocket at the exact moment the seven continents were going to collide and the earth would shatter. How stupid I was not to call him in the first place. None of this ever would have happened.

But luckily, by golly, he could fix the problem. And he would too, but not right now. He had to leave to go on another job at some other victim's home. If I could only find out whose house he was going to, I could call the home owner and we could kill the Virgil clone together. If he wouldn't mind handling the body, I would be more than happy to commit the murder.

And the other thing that validated my strong suspicions that all these specialized trade experts worked out of the same office and used the same script was that they all dressed alike. They all wore those dark blue work pants cut extra low in back so when they bent over, the panoramic crack in their ass would rise up over their belt like some sinister, dark moon ascending into the night sky on some alien planet.

On the other hand, maybe the "puttin' on the crack," as it was called by the professionals, was meant to be a friendly anal smile of reassurance before the bill was presented. One quick note, the professionals may be distinguished from the apprentices because the former carry a defibrillator with them as standard equipment in the event it is needed when the bill is presented to the unsuspecting customer.

The present iteration of the Virgil clone, oddly enough actually named Virgil, was a lanky, not particularly bright looking guy whose conversation provided instant confirmation of that physiognomic observation. That he was covered with grease goes without saying, even though it was only eight o'clock in the morning and he couldn't have possibly done any work yet. I knew that for a fact because he said he had just come from "Dinky's Diner" where he began each of his days with Dinky's breakfast special and a meeting with a half dozen of his peers to analyze the latest news and political developments. Their daily assessment of world affairs was then typed up and sent by special courier to the White House for the president to read. Only then was Virgil available to address the more mundane problems of the day.

The old van had no tires and three foot high weeds had grown up all around it. That the van was worthless was hardly a surprise. When automobiles are put up on blocks and the tires are removed, that means the desperate owner sold the only part of the vehicle that had any value, the tires. In keeping with the long established tradition of not hurting the feelings of cars which no longer run, these aesthetically minded individuals put their deceased automobiles up on concrete bricks. They remove the tires and enhance the beauty of the neighborhood by displaying the rotting vehicular hulks in full view of every house on the street.

And that was the precise situation with Deluxe UFO Tour Company's touring coach, which in reality was an eight-passenger van with two hundred thousand miles on it. It was proudly exhibited on the vacant lot next door to the Deluxe UFO Tour Company business office. It was a bold and impactful advertisement that the so called business was actually out of business.

I was becoming increasingly frustrated with Virgil's repetitious assurances that the touring coach was not salvageable and nobody but an idiot, that being me, would ever have bought such a blatantly obvious piece of junk. He didn't use the word blatantly in his assessment however.

After half an hour of Virgil's insinuative and doomful discourses on my mechanical incompetence, I finally reached the breaking point. I threw a convenient shovel at him and said "Then bury the frappin' thing you idiot. I don't want to hear any more."

"I'm going to fix it for three hundred dollars," he quickly said. "I have to charge you extra for the tires, you understand."

I walked back inside the office. Even though I had sobered up from my Saturday tirade, I remembered the list I put together of those people whom I would kill in order to create the perfect world. The six yaks were number one through six on my list. Bud the bartender was number seven. I added Virgil as number eight.

Dog Mayor, hopefully only temporarily consigned to the body of a black Chihuahua, was standing on his desk intermittently talking and barking. He still had trouble enunciating words because uncontrollable "barks" would unexpectedly blurt from his little mouth and disrupt his conversation.

Dog Mayor had assumed the role of business manager of our fledgling firm. That was not an overly demanding job since the firm had no business. I informed his honor that Virgil was going to put the touring coach, or broken down van, depending if you are an optimist or pessimist, in working order.

"Virgil's an idiot," he half barked and half spoke. That's what I called him. At least Dog Mayor and I agreed on something.

Rhonda, who had just entered the office after hugging cousin Virgil "goodbye," heard Dog Mayor's "insensitive remark," which is how she intended to phrase it. However, in a misfire of civility, she shouted, "don't talk about my family that way you black haired little shit."

It was at this point I realized there was going to be a bit of tension in the working relationship between Dog Mayor and Rhonda.

14

Fifteenth Century Chinese Warriors

We had gotten down to the business of the day. Larry, whose real name was Lawrence Thigpen, the former C.E.O. of Deluxe UFO Tour Company, was going to take us on an inspection of UFO landing sites, which were the income producers of the business. At least they had been at some time in the past. According to Larry Thigpen, in the last five years UFO's had allegedly landed at ten different sites. Originally, all ten sites had been highly radioactive, Thigpen swore, but mysteriously, the radioactivity had disappeared.

I briefly pondered that claim. Is he not familiar with the radioactivity half-life concept, being in the business and all? Doesn't it take ten thousand years or some ridiculous stretch of time for radioactivity to deteriorate itself out of existence? I couldn't remember exactly how that went because I probably never knew in the first place.

But, it seemed that Larry, henceforth to be referred to as Thigpen, had not even considered that radioactivity doesn't just disappear. I wondered if our future customers, if there would actually be any, would know the difference. On the other hand, why should I worry? With the meager amount of working capital in the company bank account, we wouldn't be in business long enough to worry about customers anyway.

Since I didn't believe in the existence of UFO's, the missing radioactivity was not a concern. I considered Deluxe UFO Tour Company a sort of tongue in cheek venture that nobody, including the customers, took seriously. I was even considering hiring some cheap labor to dress up in alien outfits and jump out from behind the rocks and scare the tourists. That would be the higher priced tour, of course.

As further indication of how financially strapped we were, we had to drive my old truck to the ten UFO landing sites. Thigpen said his jeep was in the shop but I suspected it was really just out of gas. The mayor obviously couldn't drive and Rhonda didn't have a car. That left me and my twenty year old truck into which we were now trying to squeeze.

Thigpen opened the passenger door and the Dog Mayor scurried past him, his little black body hopping up on the seat to sit between us. However, because of Rhonda's size, Thigpen had to sit in the middle so he slid across the seat and picked up the Chihuahua to hold on his lap. This seating arrangement didn't agree with the Dog Mayor and he promptly bit Thigpen on his right thumb.

This small scratch drew a tiny spot of blood and a profanity laced response from Thigpen. He passed Dog Mayor to Rhonda who, because of her size, had no lap in which to hold the dog. That forced her to hold Dog Mayor in her arms. This was a much more satisfactory situation for him because half his little body rested on her arms and the other half on her substantial breasts. There was a smile on the Dog Mayor's homely face as his head sat on her left boob. Rhonda noticed it too but chose to suffer in silence.

Thigpen directed me to drive west out of town for a few miles until I arrived at a county road leading back into the hills. As we drove out of Empyrean's city limits there were fewer houses and soon only the vast desert. It was a wide, brushy blanket of sage green with intermittent saguaros and lots of cholla with their round, needle covered branches. The desert stretched far to the west, eventually meeting the sky on the distant horizon.

"The UFO landing sites are in there," he said. "I got 'em all numbered and there's a little story on each one back in the office somewhere. I forgot to bring it." That was not a good start, but considering the general dysfunction in Empyrean, it was exactly what I should have expected. Besides, since I don't believe in UFO's, I wasn't taking any of this nonsense seriously.

One reason I convinced myself to buy Deluxe UFO Tour Company was because of my experience with Hector's tourist trap. Hector appeared to be making a good living selling junk to tourists. Being a marketing guy, I thought I could also do well with something like that, except I didn't have the money to buy any inventory. But Deluxe UFO Tour Company didn't require inventory. All it needed was an office to work in and a van to haul willing tourists around the countryside to look at spots where UFO's had supposedly landed. It seemed like a good racket and the customers would have fun on the UFO site tour. I hoped. I figured Thigpen just stuck signs in the ground at imaginary landing places anyway so who cares about their little stories. I could make up some new ones.

"You didn't bring any beer with you, did you Stan?" Thigpen asked.

"No he didn't," Dog Mayor replied for me. "Listen Thigpen, we're here on business. Let's get on with it. We've got a lot of work to do."

We had been driving on the county road heading back into the hills for about ten minutes. The asphalt ended about two miles back from our present location and the road had turned into tan colored dirt. About fifty yards ahead on the left side of the road was a large, pink rock towering seventy-five feet above us.

"Pull off the road and go around to the back of that rock," said Thigpen. As I drove around the flat ground to the back of the rock, I saw a red sign with white letters, "UFO Landing Site # 1."

"The space ship landed right over there just a year and a half ago," Thigpen said. I looked "over there" and saw nothing but a flat spot on the reddish-tan ground with a few bushes and a dozen or so empty beer cans lying around.

"Looks like the aliens had a party when they landed," I cleverly pointed out. "They were probably underage and flew down to earth to drink beer and party then shifted into warp drive and got home to their planet before midnight." Nobody laughed

"That's it?" I asked, astounded that someone would pay to see this bare, featureless spot and nine others like it when there was an entire desert out there with thousands of these exact kinds of spots, hopefully without as many beer cans.

"There's a scary story behind this one," Thigpen whispered. He shivered as he spoke, but I assumed it was just for effect. He must be a marketing guy too.

We were now on our way to the second landing site. The first site had been a total non-event for me and I was thinking that Rhonda and the Dog Mayor were having exactly the same thoughts. However, the latter of the two now had an even bigger smile on his face as he enthusiastically rubbed his hairy carcass around the former's breasts, ostensibly attempting to find a comfortable spot to position his body. But he was testing a whole lot of spots, and his smile bespoke of a male kind of acknowledgement that he knew that I knew exactly what his honor the Mayor was really doing. His honor, or I should say his horniness, was maximizing his feels. What a phony little rodent, I thought.

"Stop that you little peckerhead," Rhonda abruptly squealed. "Stan, you need to fire this lecherous little vermin. Don't you think I know what you're doing dog boy?"

"Take it easy, Rhonda," the mayor objected, inadvertently barking twice. "I was just trying to find a comfortable spot."

"Yeah, right, Teeny Paws. How's that suit your so-called masculinity?"

"Please, you two," I said. "You have to learn to get along. I can't fire him, Rhonda, because he's half owner."

Since we were about ten minutes from the second so-called landing site, partly to diffuse the tension between Dog Mayor and Rhonda and partly because I failed to score any laughs on my initial attempt at humor, I thought I would make a second attempt. I had a UFO joke.

"Did you know that we had a UFO land in Detroit a few years ago?" I asked the group of two persons and a dog.

"Really," Rhonda said in amazement. "What happened?"

"Well, this space ship came down and landed at a gas station that was closed. It was Sunday morning. Two aliens got out of the ship and looked around but all they saw were these gas pumps. So, the two aliens walked up to one of the gas pumps and said, 'Take us to your leader.' The gas pump didn't say anything. So the alien again said, 'Take us to your leader.' The gas pump still didn't say anything. The two aliens looked at each other, turned around, and walked to their space ship and flew back to their own planet. They gave their report to their alien leaders. 'We can easily conquer the planet earth,' they said. 'They can't even talk and all they do is stand around with their pricks in their ears."

No one laughed. "Don't you think that's funny?" I asked.

Rhonda looked over and smiled slightly. "That's a good one, Stan," she said, without a hint of sincerity. It's odd how seriously these people take their UFO's.

We arrived at the second UFO landing site. This site was much different than the first. We had to walk a hundred yards to get to the spot that was located at the top of a large cliff. The valley was about thousand feet below and the cliff's walls were sheer drop-offs going straight down. A misstep here would be fatal.

A flimsy orange plastic mesh fence, making no pretense of being even a tiny bit safe, was constructed at the edge of the cliff. If someone inadvertently leaned against this feeble, mesh barrier, there was an excellent chance that person would plunge into the valley far below. I knew from experience the public is inadvert as hell. It was a deathtrap lying in wait. Bringing people to this dangerous spot would be very bad judgment. And why bother? Other than sure death, there was nothing here out of the ordinary. Like UFO landing site #1, there was reddish-tan mud, a few bushes and half a dozen beer cans. The aliens seem to like their beer.

The only difference between the two sites was the second site had only half as many beer cans as the first. I attributed this phenomenon to the assumption that when the aliens drank their beers at site # 2, they walked over to the cliff to relieve themselves, and in their inebriated state, plunged to their deaths. At the first site, there was no cliff to fall off when they took a leak, as they probably referred to it. They simply "did their business" and walked back to the party site and had more beer.

"Where's the "UFO landing site # 2" sign?" I asked.

"The kids come here and throw the signs over the cliff. There are probably fifty signs at the bottom," Thigpen replied.

We were still standing at the top of the cliff and, for some reason, which eludes me to this day, I walked over to inspect the rickety fence more closely. With no warning, the ground beneath my feet suddenly gave way and I began falling downward. The edge of the cliff directly beneath the fence had eroded back toward the precipice's sheer rock wall, leaving only a protruding earthen shelf less than a foot thick which supported two fence posts and the plastic mesh fencing. I was standing on this earthen shelf when it collapsed from the strain of my extra weight.

As my body fell, I grabbed a piece of the fence with my left hand. It stopped my plunge momentarily, but when I clutched the mesh with my right hand to get a better grip, the fence began to tear. I slowly started to slip away as the fence shredded, gradually at first, but increasingly faster. I could hear the rotten material ripping as Rhonda screamed and Dog Mayor intermittently barked and yelled incoherently. "Damn! Oh, damn!" Thigpen shrieked.

Though I was grateful for their tidings, the squealing was doing little to save me. They need to get a grip, I thought. On the other hand, I had a grip, and it wasn't doing me any good. I wished I could further ponder this philosophical conundrum, but time was running out, both for intellectual inquiry and my remaining life on earth.

What a way to die, I thought, as the tearing sound ended and my plunge began. Though I was rapidly picking up speed, it seemed like everything was happening in slow motion. It was just like in the movies. I just picked the wrong one to star in. From my physics class, I knew I was traveling at one hundred and twenty-two miles per hour. Why did I remember that? I never remembered anything else, except my grade of course. I wished I could forget that too.

Downward I soared, numb to the terror I should feel. It would be over in seconds. The reddish-tan cliff wall rushed past, speeding upward as if I were standing in one spot watching it shoot by me into the blue sky. The wind roared in my ears and flattened my face as my hair whipped wildly in the brisk air stream.

The sense of slow motion continued, but I now seemed to be floating in the air as a sense of profound peace overwhelmed me. I was no longer afraid. It was a very strange feeling. I should be terrified and couldn't understand why I wasn't. But plunging toward the earth at one hundred and twenty-two miles per hour allowed little time to ponder this particular issue. The fall couldn't possibly last more than six or eight seconds, barring a strong updraft or my suddenly sprouting wings. Then I thought about how I'd look with wings. That was important because I was certain I was going to heaven and would become an angel. And they have wings. That's what Sister Scaresus Terriblyus (our nickname for her) told us in the sixth grade.

But as I gazed at the massive cliff wall, I suddenly realized that instead of plunging downward, I was drifting upward. I must be dead, I concluded, as my body ascended to a point six feet from the edge of the cliff. I was now floating in midair just off the cliff's rim, staring at Rhonda, Dog Mayor and Thigpen who were gaping back with expressions of astonishment.

I looked down at the vast panorama of nothingness between me and the desert valley far below as I slowly floated over to the group and my feet once again stood on solid ground. Rhonda threw her arms around me, and the Dog Mayor jumped at my leg. "Sorry about that," he said, realizing that in his excitement, he had urinated on my shoe. Even Thigpen, whom I really wasn't crazy about, put his arms around me and cried.

"What just happened?" I gasped. "Am I dead?"

My questions were soon answered. As Rhonda sobbed uncontrollably with her arms around my neck, I blankly stared into the brush at the north boundary of the alleged landing site. Partially concealed behind a tall bush was a ghost-like creature with an oval head and large, teardrop-shaped black eyes. "Good Lord! Who, what, is that?"

Everyone turned to watch as the figure emerged from behind the bush and slowly advanced toward us. He was creamy-white, about six feet tall and very skinny. His arms and legs were pencil-thin with no sign of muscle. The five fingers on each of his hands were slightly longer than those of humans and each of his small feet had five toes. He didn't have a nose and his mouth was a narrow, expressionless slit. He moved quietly and effortlessly.

Not believing in UFO's, aliens and the like, I never studied the features of aliens shown on television and in movies. But the creature's appearance was precisely the stereotypical depiction of how an alien supposedly looked. I recalled that aliens are usually represented with non-descript faces with two eyes and a mouth. That's exactly how this being looked. If ever there was such a thing as an alien, he must be one.

There was something comforting about him, however. While he looked like all the pictures I'd ever seen, his face had a peaceful, friendly expression on it. His demeanor was kind and reassuring. If he was an alien, he was different than anything I could have imagined. That the creature's abrupt arrival coincided with my plummeting to what would have been certain death gave me pause. He must have done something to stop my fall.

He walked up to our group and raised his right hand. "Peace," he said. He was dignified and genuine. For some reason I couldn't explain I wanted to be his friend and it was obvious the others did too. He smiled. "My name is Nhoame." His dark eyes peered directly into ours and he seemed to speak to each of us individually. We told him our names. That the dog, Mayor, could talk didn't seem to surprise him.

I was certain he had intervened when I fell off the cliff. I thanked him for saving my life.

He looked at me then spoke in a gentle voice. "One cannot prevent all the unhappiness in the universe, but one can do what one can do."

"I'm glad you were here," I said.

He looked behind him, sensing something we did not. He turned back with a look of concern on his face.

"What is it?" I asked. "What's wrong?"

"They are almost here. They will capture me and take me back."

"Who? Who will capture you?"

"There is no time. I must go."

"No, wait. Let us help you."

"They are very dangerous. I don't want to involve you."

"Nhoame, you saved my life. I'll protect you."

Rhonda valiantly stepped forward. "Don't you worry, Nhoame. We'll all protect you."

We heard brush rustling and voices in the direction of the road.

I pointed at a clump of rocks in the nearby trees. "Hide over there!"

Nhoame moved quickly and got out of sight just as four strange looking men walked into the clearing and stopped twenty feet from where we stood. They were big and muscular, and three of them were of Chinese descent. The Chinese men were wearing red silk robes and odd looking hats with circular brims protruding from the sides. Each of them had a long, black pig tail and a large sword hanging from a black leather belt. These men were exactly as described by Latisha Wimberly. Could they be the ones who kidnapped my ex-wife? If so, buying them a beer was my first thought. Not really. Well, maybe.

The side decorations on the men's hats looked like little black ears, giving them an Oriental, Mickey Mouse-like appearance. Their weird attire suggested they might have come from some other time in the distant past. That was my guess, but I was the world's absolute worst when it came to fashion. Their red robes and gigantic swords could be the current rage for all I knew. I would think their swords would be a nuisance on packed New York subways, but one must sacrifice comfort in the spirit of fashion.

The three Chinese men stood behind the fourth man who was the apparent leader. This man, who was also large and muscular, moved forward several steps. He was about six feet tall and I couldn't tell if he was carrying a weapon. He looked gruff and quarrelsome. Evil oozed from his every pore. There was no question he was a tough customer. He wore western clothes, but even with my nonexistent appreciation for style, I knew this "just wasn't him." But I didn't want to find out who "was him." That could be an unhappy experience. He was obviously a person who could get very mean very fast. I sensed we weren't going to be close.

"Did you see our friend pass this way?" he asked.

"Nobody's come by here," I replied. "Tell us what he looks like, and if we see him, we'll tell him you're looking for him."

"That's all right. We'll find him." He turned to walk away, but the three sword-carrying Chinese men in red silk robes took exception to this decision. The one to our far left screamed something in Chinese, shattering the quiet of the morning and startling us. What was especially shocking was the high-pitched tone of his voice. The intimidating warrior screamed in a shrill warble like an excited little girl. A second warrior, apparently stirred up by the first man's yelling, also began to squeal. The third Chinese man, as if to demonstrate that he could shriek with the best of them, began an ear-splitting tirade in an even higher voice.

I was astounded by the soprano wailing, but suddenly concerned things were morphing into a dangerous situation. As it often does in times of stress, my mind wandered in untimely philosophical speculation and I closed my eyes. Still wailing, the Chinese warriors sounded like three little girls arguing with each other. But they were now jumping up and down and alternately pointing toward our group and their evil leader.

Evil leader growled something in Chinese to the three distressed red-robed men. Suddenly, they all turned and walked away.

That was easy. Too easy.

15

The Surprise Under Rhonda's Skirt

We were still standing at the top of the high cliff that nearly killed me. Evil leader and his three soprano Chinese warriors had disappeared behind the trees as they walked toward the dirt road on which we had driven to this momentous spot. Remembering my military training, I sent Thigpen on a reconnaissance mission to make sure the nasty quartet was indeed gone.

He came back to report in a couple of minutes. "It's clear to the road, Captain." He rendered a crisp, though cock-eyed salute, nearly poking himself in his right eye as he slammed his hand against his forehead. He apparently forgot that one is supposed to stop their saluting hand before it actually hits them. Besides, I had only reached the rank of sergeant. He had given me an undeserved promotion, not that I paid much attention to anything the guy said.

"It's all clear, Nhoame. You can come out now." I said.

Nhoame emerged from his hiding place and walked over to where we were standing, a look of relief on his face. Rhonda, Thigpen, Nhoame, Dog Mayor and I walked down the path to the road. I was puzzled Dog Mayor remained uncharacteristically quiet during our unsettling encounter. It wasn't like him.

The truck was in sight now. We would cancel the rest of the UFO site tour and take Nhoame back to town and figure out where he could hide. As we walked out of the brush toward the truck, two Chinese warriors with drawn swords ran out from behind a large rock on the far side of the dirt road. They stopped fifteen feet from where we stood, raised their swords, and screeched in high-pitched girly voices. Thigpen's reconnaissance mission had been about as successful as his bankrupt business.

"They want us to surrender," explained Thigpen, as if he was interpreting their Chinese wailing.

"No shit," Dog Mayor chimed in, with his usual sarcastic snarl. The two Chinese warriors were visibly disturbed to see a small black dog talking, but they looked like they were going to kill him just the same. In fact, I figured they would kill the little beast first because they seemed to consider him some kind of evil omen. And, of course, he was.

But events began moving very rapidly. Rhonda quickly stepped forward and assumed a protective stance in front of the group. The perceptive Chinese warriors took note of this defensive maneuver, although it would be impossible not to notice a large, intimidating woman poised to strike. They began to vigorously shake their swords, their voices trilling at their falsetto limits, and forewarning that bad things were going to happen.

Rhonda, to everyone's horror, had begun pulling up her tight fitting, ankle length black skirt. Briefly reflecting on my military training, I could not recall any combat maneuver even roughly similar to this one.

"Good lord, Rhonda," I yelled, "Are you going to screw them to death?" She didn't answer, but continued to struggle with her skirt, which was now stretched tightly around her body just above her knees. Puzzled by this strange turn of events, the two warriors stopped screaming and watched Rhonda grappling with her skirt as it rose ever higher above her thighs. Equally curious, the rest of us forgot about our immediate peril and stood in awe, gazing upon the physics-defying disrobing transpiring before our eyes.

Though the warriors had their swords lifted high, they were momentarily frozen in wonderment as they gazed at the valiant battle Rhonda was waging. The defiant skirt was now wrapped around Rhonda's waist like a sumo belt and the gaping male observers were dreading what would come next. But the Chinese warriors suddenly regained their composure and were moving closer, menacingly pointing their big swords at us.

It was then that Rhonda reached down between her thighs, causing those of us standing behind her to gasp in dismay. The intimidating warriors in front of her immediately stepped back, looks of terror on their faces. What sight had these poor devils witnessed?

We soon realized the source their dread was not what they witnessed, rather what Rhonda was holding. From my vantage point, it appeared as if she had the two warriors in the sights of her somehow weaponized vagina. It was a misperception on my part because what I didn't know was that Rhonda had pulled out an odd looking gun stowed somewhere between her mountainous thighs. She was now pointing this strange weapon at the Chinese warriors who were again squealing, but now in pleas for mercy.

Rhonda, however, was having none of it, the word mercy apparently absent from her already scarce vocabulary. It was apparent that there was some sort of personal score about to be settled. The warriors shared that understanding and they slowly backed away, edging toward the safety of the rock behind which they had originally hidden.

They were clamoring for mercy when a brilliant light streaked between them and where Rhonda stood. One of the red-robed warriors instantly exploded in a blinding flash and shreds of his red robe shot skyward then fluttered down like flakes of crimson snow. This unhappy reversal was more than sufficient motivation for the second warrior to throw down his sword and run screaming for the safety of the rock.

He had just vanished behind the tan boulder when a second streak of light from Rhonda's weapon pulverized the big rock sending dust and thousands of tiny pieces into the sky. The badly shaken Chinese warrior went screaming into the trees, wailing like a little child who had just been punished, which of course he had.

"What is that thing, Rhonda?" I asked.

"It's a neutron gun, Stan. I stole it when I was abducted by the UFO guys."

I didn't have time to discuss the pros and cons of neutron guns as I had no idea how they worked, nor did I care. We were scrambling to get into the truck. Nhoame sat in the middle and Rhonda rode shotgun, or should I say neutron gun, with Dog Mayor once again royally enthroned on her left breast. Thigpen jumped into the back of the truck, sitting down with his back to the cab. I hurriedly swung the truck around in a U-turn and we began our bouncing safari down the dirt road toward the safety of town.

We arrived much faster than I expected, but I remembered that it always seems further going to someplace than from someplace. At least that's how it seemed to me. Rhonda said Nhoame could stay at her house tonight and she and Desert Chickadee would work up some kind of disguise for him. I dropped them both off and Thigpen, the Dog Mayor and I headed for Bud's Rio Malo Saloon. I definitely needed a drink, even though it was not yet noon.

I parked the truck in front of Bud's and Thigpen, who had moved from the back of the truck into the cab, jumped out followed by Dog Mayor. We went inside and Bud, who was having a very good day, conceded that I might actually have become a local. It finally registered with him that I bought Thigpen's business.

The three of us ordered beers. Thigpen sat to my right and the

Dog Mayor to his right. Luckily, the Dog Mayor had to nurse the singular beer he could have because of his greatly reduced Chihuahua size. That would save a little money on the bar bill.

Thigpen asked me how I knew the term "reconnaissance," as if it were some secret word that only military people know. I told him I was in the military ten years ago. Then he told me he was also a veteran, one who had seen real combat.

"What war were you in?" I asked.

"Well, you see, it's like this," he said. "I got this metal plate in my head. A bullet went through my skull right here." He pointed to a small, circular mark above his right ear. "It blew my damn brains right out the other side of my head. You talk about a bummer, I mean, what the hell? It took the top of my skull off. Every time I go through airport security, every alarm in the place goes off. They think I have a gun hidden in my ass or something. You'd think they'd have a little more respect for a fighting man."

"Man, I'm really sorry. What war did you say you were in?"

"Well, you see, that's the problem. The part of my brain that went out the other side of my head had the memory cells. So I got major memory problems. I can never remember exactly which war I was in."

"Man, I'm really sorry to hear that."

"Oh, that's not all. Besides the memory cells, my contentment cells got blown away too. Blam! Right out the same frappin' hole my memory cells went through."

"What are contentment cells?"

"Well, I do remember about that. The psychiatrist's clinical definition is contentment cells are what make me a happy boy. You lose your contentment cells and you end up with extreme aggression tendencies. That's what I got. I can get pissed off at the drop of a hat over the slightest little thing. So I gotta' take these happy pills."

I shook my head. "Wow."

"But, thinking about it," he continued, "I'm pretty sure I was in Viet Nam, or maybe it was World War Two."

Man, the poor devil was really screwed up. "You weren't in World War Two," I said, which I soon found out was the wrong helpful hint. His aggression tendencies abruptly kicked in.

"How the hell do you know?" he said loudly. "You weren't there. You weren't there when we took Rome. You weren't there when we took Okinawa. If there's anything I can't stand it's you civilian types who talk about the military when you were never even in the Boy Scouts."

"No, I was in the military, Lawrence," I replied, realizing he had already forgotten and thinking that using his formal full name would provide me with some sort of moral high ground. One always searches for that pedestal of righteousness when one engages in profound philosophical discussion while sitting in a saloon. Some ancient philosopher said that I think.

"If you weren't there, how the hell can you be so sure I wasn't in World War Two?"

Although he we was thoroughly pissed off and completely convinced that he was indeed a veteran of World War Two, I persisted. "World War Two ended in 1945. You're only thirty nine years old."

I was certain the obviousness of this disclosure would end the discussion.

"So what the hell does that prove?" he yelled.

"The damn war ended before you were born!" I said. "Are you not connecting the dots here?" I thought that would end the debate, but it only threw gasoline on the fire.

"You're a damn communist," he said.

He was silent for a moment then said, "Your argument is full of holes, Stan, but as I think about it, it had to be the Viet Nam War. Yeah, that's the war I was in."

Thigpen and I were on our third beers now. Dog Mayor was really pissed. He had to stand on his hind legs with his tiny front paws on the bar and drink his beer by putting his head into the glass and slurping the beer with his little red tongue. He had finished about an eighth of his first beer.

"No, I'm afraid you weren't in Nam either," I said.

Thigpen was becoming increasingly agitated. "Now how in the hell do you know that, you son of a bitch? You weren't there in that war either."

I tried to reason with him, but only got in deeper. "I didn't have to be there because you're still only thirty-eight years old. I can't remember what year the Viet Nam War ended, but you would have been in diapers, at best.

Bud walked over to where we sat. "He was in the Gulf War, the first one." He turned and walked away.

"See, I told you," Thigpen shouted.

"So that's where you got shot in the head," I said respectfully.

"Well you see Stan, that's your name, right Stan?"

"Yeah, Larry, my name is Stan."

"Well you see Stan, I did get wounded in the military, but I got shot in my ass."

"I thought you said you got shot in your head," I said now thoroughly confused.

"I did get shot in my head, but not while I was in the military. Although my disability papers say I got shot in my head while I was in the military, it was only so I would get a higher disability benefit. And that's legal because my military psychiatrist said that getting shot in my ass in the military set off some kind of sympathetic reaction in my brain which caused me to be even more forgetful and more aggressive."

It was an incredible story and I listened closely as I sipped my beer.

"I told him I was that way because of my previous injury where I got shot in my head. I said my memory and contentment cells were somewhere in the Ohio woods. But then he said, and I remember his exact words, 'If anyone asks, just tell them you got shot in the head. Just don't tell them when you got shot in the head. Next Patient!' That's exactly what he said, Stan. Your name is Stan, ain't it Stan?"

"Yeah, that's right Larry. It's Stan. But how did you happen to get shot in the head in the Ohio woods?"

"Oh that's a funny story," he said.

I was sure I wouldn't find the story funny, but just as certain I would find it bizarre. I predicted that one right.

"I was raised out in the country on a farm," Larry said. "We had this crazy old coot living next door to us and he shot me. Ain't that funny?"

"No, it's tragic. He must have been a severely disturbed man."

"He was. He thought he had been reincarnated as Buffalo Bill, you know the buffalo hunter and Wild West show guy. And you know what? I really believe he was."

"So how did he come to shoot you?" I asked.

"Well, he was out walking around the woods one day and so was I. As I said, we lived in Ohio and there weren't any buffalo there, but he saw me and thought that I was a buffalo, just the same. Wishful thinking on his part I guess. Anyway, he shot me in the head."

"My god! I can't believe what you're telling me."

"Oh that's okay. I don't have no hard feelings about it. They locked the old guy up and he never harmed anyone else. He's happy as can be as long as he gets a buffalo steak for dinner every day."

"I guess I'll stay out of the Ohio woods," I said, dismayed by his story.

"What war were you in, Stan?"

I took a sip of beer. "I can't say I was ever in a war."

"You can't remember either, huh?"

"No, I remember. I just wasn't in combat like you."

"Oh," he said solemnly, as our eyes met. That was the moment we reached that moral high ground, that pedestal of righteousness to which all beer drinkers aspire. We were now friends.

"I like you, Stan. You think you can find a job for me in your new business?"

I realized I shouldn't promise him a job. He had operated the bankrupt Deluxe UFO Tour Company and that hadn't turned out well. How good an employee would he be? Dog Mayor and I had no working capital and no way to pay salaries or other expenses. There really was no business. No one had taken a UFO landing site tour for at least two years.

In addition to having no money for other expenses, we also had no money for advertising to drum up business. On the other hand, Rhonda had given herself a job at UFO Tours as had Dog Mayor. I would also be working there. I figured Nhoame would also need a job to hide from the evil guy and his squeaky voiced Chinese warriors. Hey, I might as well hire everybody in town.

"Yeah, of course I have a job for you, man. I was hoping you'd ask. Of course, the pay ain't all that great."

"I don't care about the pay. I just want to have someplace to go. You know what I mean?"

I thought about that for a moment then looked and him and smiled. "Yeah, Larry. Everybody needs someplace to go."

16

The Un-man and Nurse Fluckenberger

In a strange sort of way, I was starting to turn my life around. I came to Arizona to find a job and I did. Of course, it didn't pay a salary, but not being a detail man, I was nonetheless proud that I was now employed. Besides that, I found the general location where the kidnappers might be holding my ex-wife, Nancy. If I could just get my new business to generate some income I could claim I had a real job. And if I could just locate and rescue Nancy, my dual quests would be successful. I felt strangely optimistic.

Thigpen loaned me his cell phone and I made a quick call to Latisha Wimberly and told her about the events of the morning. The Chinese warriors looked exactly as she described Nancy's kidnappers. "I was on the right track," I confidently told her.

I also called Jean Monaghan. It was another pleasant discussion with the promising signals of the beginnings of a romance. I was tempted to ask her to come out to Empyrean for a visit. I was, after all, a prominent business owner in town. But my particular business wasn't actually doing any business and I was sleeping on the living room couch belonging to Desert Chickadee a.k.a. "Thunder Squaw. I decided inviting Jean for a visit was a bad idea.

It was only three o'clock in the afternoon, but I was already tired. It had been a long day. I signaled to Bud to bring me another beer.

Thigpen decided he would head back to the UFO Tour office and clean things up now that he was an official employee. He was even less of a detail man than I was. He didn't care what job he got or that he wouldn't be getting a salary.

I sat alone at the bar staring into my beer. One always finds inspiration when sitting alone staring into their beer. I was silently probing the deepest recesses of my comprehension. Can one actually see the bottom of the glass or does one need to drink more to reach that higher ethereal plane located there? That too is a mystery. How can a higher plane be located at the bottom of something, such as a beer mug? Why are there so many questions and so few answers?

For some reason I felt the need to verbalize my thoughts. "Why am I seeking the universality of truth, the one word that would answer every question, the reality of good and evil? Could I find that ultimate actuality at Bud's Rio Malo?"

"You must know where to search," a voice beside me answered. "I can help you find truth."

At first, I thought it was an angel. I had been staring so intently into my beer that I didn't see the woman sit down next to me. It was disappointing when I realized no supernatural force had intervened here. I was so close to solving it this time. And this mere mortal presumes to know the answer to my most profound inquiry. This woman cannot answer my interrogatory. How dare her! I turned to confront her, to banish her to her own assigned spot in the universe, to castigate her for intruding into my profundity, to thrash her for her impudence.

But I never follow through on my threats. "Hello, can I buy you a beer?" I cheerfully asked.

"I thought I would buy you a beer, Bub," she replied.

I always disliked the generic salutation, Bub. Bub seemed so guttural, so coarse, so impersonal and base. But the way she said it turned me on.

"Great! That would be great!"

The woman sitting beside me was unique in several ways, but I really can't say how. Once again, however, I should have recognized the warning signs. It's always bad to get involved with something one doesn't understand. For me, the lack of understanding covered a great deal of territory. The woman's face was attractive, but with pronounced, almost exaggerated features. Her voice was pleasant, although it carried a bit more bass than I would expect. I found that exciting. She had dark hair, deep red lipstick, and was not stingy with the makeup covering her face. She wore a black, billowy dress that hung like tapestry on her crossed legs, which she intermittently brushed against mine. Her hand was now on my leg, gently rubbing just above my knee but carelessly moving higher every few strokes.

"Why don't we go to my place?" she suggested.

She only had to ask once and I was following her out the door. I noticed Bud shaking his head "no" as I rushed past him. Screw Bud. He's the guy that put yak piss in my drink, hardly qualifying him as my moral compass.

I followed her silver Mercedes in my old truck and we reached her home soon. It was a big, expensive house. She pulled her car into the garage and I parked my truck in the driveway. The inside of the house was right out of a magazine. It was too rich for my blood, but I could adapt. I noticed she liked horses. There were pictures and statues of horses all over the place.

"Let's go into the bedroom," she said, getting right to the point of why we were here.

I followed her down the hallway into a large master bedroom. Good lord, she really did like horses. To say the room was decorated in an equestrian motif would be a gross understatement. Like the living room, the walls were covered with pictures of horses and race tracks.

"Take off your clothes and get into bed," she said forcefully.

This was the precise dream of every guy who ever sat in a bar wondering if life would improve, if there was really a one word answer for the mystery of the universe. Yes, this was the answer every half sloshed guy sought. She was that beautiful take charge woman who found him irresistible in his drunken, bleary eyed stupor and was ordering him to prepare for sex. Yes, this was it! This was the answer!

"Alright," I said, and began to unbutton my shirt.

She smiled at me. "I'll be right back. I'm going into the closet to get into my silks."

In seconds I'd stripped completely and was underneath the covers. I was anxiously anticipating the ecstasy that every philosophical inebriate is certain awaits him. Superb, unapologetic sex is the sacred birthright I may now claim. I had paid my dues straining to peer through a thousand beers seeking the answers that lay at the bottom of the glasses. I had found the answer, solved the riddle, and had stepped forward to accept my reward. Momentarily, the woman would re-appear in a black, silk nightgown staring hungrily at my god-like golden body. Yes, it had all been worth it, all those hours of searching from the bar stools. The moment of recompense had arrived.

Suddenly, the closet door flew open and she appeared.

"God almighty," I screamed, with the horror of a man who accidentally stuck his testicles into a bear trap. "What the hell are you doing?"

Instead of a beauteous woman in a black silk nightgown, that same person now stood at the foot of the bed dressed in a jockey's outfit with a red silk shirt and bright yellow silk pants. The bizarre bedroom attire was accessorized with a black riding hat, goggles, and knee high black boots. She also had a riding crop that she menacingly slapped on her left hand, clearly intending to put into use on my bare bottom.

She stared at me with an expression of anticipatory ravishment, preparing to pounce as she lustfully appraised my compromised circumstances. Even more frightening, while she was in the closet she had not only changed clothes, but also genders. She was actually a he, not that I'm a detail man.

The un-woman's flowing dress had cleverly concealed the large bulge in her crotch area, which had now taken on a life of its own. It had greatly enlarged and extended like a boa constrictor in the attack mode. It was wildly writhing under his tight yellow jockey pants, searching for just the right moment to lunge at its terror-stricken victim, that being me. He was desperately struggling to pull down his skin-tight jockey drawers, but they somehow became entangled with his massive wazoo.

She, rather he, ripped the covers off my nude body and jumped up on the end of the bed, and continued wrestling furiously with his squirming appendage still tangled in his jockey pants. He lost his balance and fell off the bed onto the floor. I heard a loud crack when his twisting body crashed on the carpet.

"I broke my shoulder," he screamed. "Oh god, it hurts."

I had jumped out of the bed just as he leapt onto it, and was frantically gathering my clothes.

He laid there moaning, pleading for my help.

I had already decided to add him to my growing list of future homicides. Why should I help him? He tried to seduce me. He made an idiot out of me. Bud knew what was going on. I ignored the signals. I was pissed off. Screw you. You deserved what you got. I'm not helping you. There was no way that was going to happen, man.

In a few minutes I had gotten him dressed and wiped the makeup off his face. I was now driving him to the hospital in his Mercedes. We pulled up to the emergency room and I dropped him off and then drove into the parking lot where I left the car. By the time I got inside the hospital they had taken already taken him into the patient area for treatment. I sat down to wait for him.

In a few moments a woman in a nurse's uniform appeared. She seemed very efficient. Her great efficiency was only exceeded by the monumentality of her breasts. They cast a large shadow and nothing further need be said.

"Hello. I'm Nurse Fluckenberger. I just wanted to let you know your friend is going to be fine. He dislocated his shoulder. It's painful but not serious. You'll hear him scream in a few minutes. Doctor has to push it back in. That's my favorite part."

I was a bit taken aback by her remark. It sounded like she would enjoy the suffering the un-woman jockey would have to endure. She saw the anxiety on my face and quickly explained her remarks.

"Oh," she said laughing, "what I meant was I enjoy putting shoulders back into the socket. They can sometimes be a challenge, but I always get it right. It provides a sense of professional satisfaction."

She surprised me with her next comment. "I haven't seen you before. Have you been in town long?"

I explained my brief timeline since my arrival in Empyrean. I didn't discuss any of the weird experiences that befell me as recounting them would only cause anxiety for me.

"Look," she said. "I don't know if you're married or have a girlfriend or a boyfriend and I don't care. My friend Bonnie Bistenwaller and I will be at the Rio Malo tomorrow night. Why don't you meet us there?" CC is very interesting, although she's very, very quiet. If you can keep your eyes off my breasts long enough, you might enjoy talking to her. Can you be there?"

"I wasn't looking at your breasts," I protested pointedly (no pun intended). I thought you said her name was Bonnie Bistenwaller. Why do you call her CC?"

"That's because B.B. is too hard to remember."

"Oh," I said. I wasn't interested in meeting anyone. I was already thinking of Jean Monaghan and me as a couple. Besides, the object of my last amorous adventure was in the Emergency Room with a dislocated shoulder.

"I wasn't looking at your breasts," I repeated, though I don't know why.

"Yeah, right," she said. "Are there icebergs in Wichita?" She turned and walked away.

Did she say icebergs in Wichita?" What on Earth is she talking about?

In about an hour and a half Nurse Fluckenberger brought the patient out in a wheel chair. His right arm was in a sling. He was okay to go home, but I would have to drive because he was on heavy duty pain pills. I fetched the car and was back in a few minutes.

"Thanks very much," Nurse Fluckenberger," I said. "By the way, what did you mean when you said, "icebergs in Wichita?""

"You never heard that one?" she said, in a genuine expression of shock. "You were looking at my breasts, right? Okay, are there icebergs in Wichita? Are you not connecting the dots, Stanley?"

In truth, not only was I unable to connect the dots, I really hadn't been looking at her breasts. I mean, I had looked at her breasts, but not in the lustful manner of which she accused me. I was observing her breasts as more of a "believe it or not" moment. My attention to her breasts was from an engineering point of view. They appeared to be a serious safety hazard. The issue was, if this dualistic mammalian shrine should somehow tumble down upon unsuspecting pedestrians, how large would be the casualty count?

We were soon on our way back to his house. "I have to apologize," he said. "I misled you and you have taken very good care of me."

I didn't tell him I had already added his name to my homicide list.

He continued. "Is there anything I can do to make it up to you?"

"No, forget it," I replied.

"I insist," he went on. "There must be some way I can make this all up to you."

"You don't owe me anything," I insisted. We arrived at his house and he punched the little button on the garage door opener and I pulled the Mercedes inside.

Because of the pain pills he was taking, the hospital wanted me to spend at least an hour with him before leaving him alone. Actually, they wanted me to stay longer but that was all I would commit to.

We walked inside the house and he offered me a beer. I didn't need one but accepted his offer just the same.

"I understand you bought "Deluxe UFO Tour Company" he said.

"Yeah, I guess I did. It wasn't my smartest move, but I haven't made many smart moves lately."

"Well, don't let it get you down. Obviously I didn't make that smart a move today myself. So, what are your plans for the business?"

"That's a good question. Your mayor, the Chihuahua, and I bought the place together. Neither one of us has the money to operate a business so I'm not really sure why we bought it. As far as plans go, we'll get it into as good a shape as we can."

His reply provided some answers that I actually wasn't seeking. "The mayor bought the business because he's trying to get his life back. Since he got turned into a Chihuahua by some outlaw alien, things have been pretty rough for him. The city council put him on special leave, you know. They didn't think it would be good for the town's image to have a dog for mayor. Dog Mayor figures that owning the UFO Tour business will keep him on top of UFO activity and he'll be able to find the alien who turned him into a dog and convince him to return him to his human form. I think he's screwed, to tell you the truth."

"You talk about aliens and people turning into dogs as if it's all just a routine occurrence around here. Why isn't this stuff on any of the news channels? It would be big news anywhere else."

"We keep things pretty much to ourselves in Empyrean. Now the mayor thing, some reporter from one of the networks did get hold of that story. But, it was the same old thing. They decided it was a hoax and killed the story. Besides that, the mayor wouldn't cooperate. He wouldn't talk when the reporter came to interview him. Unbelievably, the mayor is the only proof we have that aliens really do show up here on a regular basis. As far as UFO's and aliens go, most people think that it's all a hoax. It's amazing what can be going on right under people's noses, but they refuse to accept it."

"Listen," he continued, "I feel pretty bad about what happened today, and you've been real decent about it. I'm going to make you an offer and you can take it or leave it. I'll loan you and the mayor twenty thousand dollars at no interest. If the business makes money, you give me an amount of interest you think is fair at the end of the year. No papers to sign or anything. If you lose all the money, that's okay, you don't owe me anything. If you do well and expand, I get a piece of the action. Is that fair enough?"

"Yeah," I replied, shocked by his generosity. "It's more than fair. Why would you do that for us? You don't know me at all. I might take your money and leave town the next day."

"No you won't. You're an honest man. The mayor, pain in the neck that he is, is also an honest man. He'll make a good partner and he's good with the books. We got a deal?"

"Yeah, we got a deal. What's your name, anyway?"

"I'm Howard Winklethorpe."

Howard wrote a check to me for twenty thousand dollars. I would take it to the bank first thing in the morning.

17

The Pancake Mountain Alliance

As I was still sleeping at Rhonda's parents' house, Tuesday morning, as all mornings, began with Desert Chickadee's regularly scheduled dance at dawn. This ritual, which the neighbors had no doubt calculated into their house values with a deduction of thirty thousand dollars, had now begun. The house faced east and Desert Chickadee performed her sweeping north to south and back again cascade across the front yard. She danced with amazing nimbleness in view of her size.

The couch on which I slept faced the large picture window in the living room. Desert Chickadee's substantial shadow floating across the front blinds enhanced the ambiance of this quotidian event. What this meant for me was that as I slept, the morning's gradual sunrise was intermittently blocked by Desert Chickadees shadow as she swept back and forth in front of the large easterly facing picture window. The every eight seconds regularity of Chickadee's shadow blocking the sunlight had the effect of a continuously flashing light, as if one were being tortured in an interrogation deep in the jungles of Burma. It was driving me to near madness.

Rhonda was at the breakfast table having a cup of yogurt, mindful of its healthful implications. To maximize the health benefits, Rhonda was pouring the cup of yogurt along with five additional cups of yogurt over a stack of a dozen pancakes. Sitting next to this carbohydrate mountain was a large bowl of oatmeal, also a healthful victual, except this particular serving was submerged in pure cream and a third of a cup of brown sugar.

I sat down to join her. "Rhonda, I have something to tell you."

She looked across the table as she chomped her pancake and gulped her coffee. "Yes, what is it, Stan?"

"When we first met," I continued, "I must confess I didn't believe you when you said you were abducted by a UFO. I never believed in UFO's and space aliens and I thought you were crazy. I just wanted to say that I was wrong and I apologize."

She laughed, unconcerned by my early skepticism. "Oh, that's okay. I knew you didn't believe me but I figured you would come around sooner or later."

"Well, there's something else."

"What's that?" she asked, wolfing a giant section of the pancake mountain on her plate.

"One of the reasons I came to Arizona was to find my ex-wife, a woman named Nancy Nussbaum. She has a partner by the name of Latisha Wimberly. A few weeks ago Nancy was kidnapped by what Latisha described as large Chinese men wearing red robes, long pigtails and carrying swords. These men talked with very high pitched voices."

Rhonda was unfazed. "It's probably the same group we ran into yesterday."

"That's what I was thinking! They have to be the same guys who took Nancy. I traced these men to Phoenix and a nightclub called Club Feral. When we got tangled up with those characters yesterday I realized they had to be the same guys. I thought I should tell you about that."

"Is that why you came to Arizona?"

"That's one reason, but I also had to find a job."

"You got a job. You're the boss of the Deluxe UFO Tour Company. You're like the C.E.O."

"Yeah, I can't wait to get my year-end bonus. That's if the company survives for more than two weeks. Maybe we could all draw a paycheck sometime too."

Rhonda laughed. "You said you weren't a detail man. I'm not a detail person either."

I abruptly changed the subject because I was curious about something. "Rhonda, what exactly was that weapon you used yesterday?"

"Like I told you, it's a neutron gun."

"It seemed to do a lot of damage. I thought neutrons were harmless."

"They are harmless subatomic particles until you combine them in the correct mixture with dark matter and focus that energy on a target. It will blow your ass to smithereens."

"I'd hate for that to happen."

Rhonda laughed. "Yeah, it would ruin your day for sure." She paused for a moment. "There's something I should tell you, since we're into true confessions. I knew those Chinese guys. They work for the aliens who abducted me. That's why I blew the one guy away. He was real bad to me."

I was beginning to understand Rhonda. She wasn't as crazy as I thought. Or maybe I was losing it. But things seemed to start making sense. Then I thought about our new friend we met at UFO Landing Site Number 2. "Where's Nhoame?"

"He's getting ready for the day. Nhoame!" she yelled. There was no answer, but someone I didn't recognize walked into the kitchen followed by Desert Chickadee.

"How do you like him?" Desert Chickadee asked. "My friend Cole Younger gave me some clothes for him. They're almost the same size."

Nhoame was dressed in black western style clothes, looking exactly like the five outlaws who sat playing cards every day at the Rio Malo. This was the perfect disguise. And if anybody tried to mess with him, the most famous outlaws in the west were there to protect him. I wondered again if they were really who they said they were. Chronologically speaking, it was impossible. But in Empyrean, chronology didn't matter.

I shook my head in amazement. "Nhoame looks fabulous."

Then Nhoame spoke. "I want to thank you for all you have done for me. You must have many questions and I will try to answer them now. I am from a planet many light years from your galaxy. The men were hunting me yesterday because I escaped from their so called Chinese monastery to the south of town. It's really a compound used for training potential victims to be hunted for sport."

"See Stan," said Rhonda, "none of us really knew what that place was. We thought it was a monastery run by Chinese monks for religious purposes. I guess we should have wondered about that a long time ago, but, it was always there. They never bothered nobody."

"What exactly is it?" I asked. "You say they train potential victims to be hunted?"

Nhoame shook his head. "It is a training facility for intergalactic slaves. It's actually run by the Salabians, a war-like people from the planet Salab. The Chinese warriors are employees. You see, the Salabians raid peaceful planets throughout the universe and take slaves. They train these slaves in compounds like the Chinese monastery outside of town. They've set up a small planet called Rhostugasht. In your language, that means death world.

Those of us who are sent there are to be prey for the Salabian warriors who go to Rhostugasht for sport. It's like the gladiators of ancient Rome but there is one difference. They make sure that the slaves cannot win. It is a great confidence builder for their warriors. They always kill their prey so that is why I escaped. If I return to the Chinese monastery compound I shall die."

"But, who are the Chinese in the compound. Why do they talk with those high voices?" I asked.

"The Salabians went back in time and rented Chinese eunuchs who served the emperor in the Royal Court in the fifteenth century. The Salabians brought them into this century to train slaves like me in combat skills before we are sent to Rhostugasht to die."

"But, why do they want eunuchs?" I asked.

"Because eunuchs have no testicles and are very loyal to their masters. That's also why they talk in high voices. And they have no interest in women and focus completely on their jobs.

"So, what are we supposed to do?" I asked. "Do we just lay low forever?"

"I have many friends at the compound. The class graduates in just a few days. I want to rescue them before they are shipped off to Rhostugasht be killed."

"That sounds like a tall order. How many need to be rescued?"

"There are exactly ninety-nine of them. I was the hundredth."

"How many Chinese eunuchs are there?"

"There are forty of them," Nhoame replied. "Actually, including Gan, there are only thirty-nine because Rhonda killed one of them in the group you met yesterday. The man leading that group is named Gan. He's also the leader of the Chinese compound. He is a Salabian and the most dangerous one. I'm surprised Mayor Bobby didn't recognize him. Gan is the one that turned him into a Chihuahua."

"I did recognize him," said the Dog Mayor, just arriving after his morning stroll to mark his territory. "You know," he digressed," I always said I owned the whole town when I was the mayor. Now that I'm a Chihuahua, I feel like I have to pee on every bush and lawn in a one mile radius to make sure other dogs know I still own the town. Now I call it my territory instead of my town. The trouble is I can't pee on everything because my bladder isn't big enough. I'm on empty once I reach the end of the block. I mean, that's it. That's my only territory now, one lousy block. It's very depressing."

"Getting back to the original subject," I interjected, "why didn't you say you recognized Gan?"

"I hate to admit it, but I was afraid. Like Nhoame said, Gan is very dangerous. At some point I need to confront him and force him to turn me back into a human."

"Gan is the one who molested me when I was abducted," said Rhonda.

"Gan is the one who has been kidnapping people from all over the Universe," Nhoame added.

"There's one more thing," I said. "I bet Gan is the one responsible for kidnapping my ex-wife, Nancy."

"So all four of us have a reason to find Gan and defeat him," said Rhonda. "We need to free Nhoame's friends, make Gan change the Mayor back into a real person, rescue Stan's ex-wife, and I need to take revenge on him for molesting me. We can do this together. We can defeat Gan."

Another thought suddenly entered my mind. "Nhoame, could they could be holding my ex-wife at the monastery. You didn't happen to see an attractive blond woman there, did you?"

"I'm sorry, Stan. I didn't see any woman there, only men."

"She's got to be someplace near Empyrean," I said.

I looked out the kitchen window into the Wilkenshaver's backyard. Just a few weeks ago I arrived from Detroit. Now, I was suddenly involved in a freedom fight for alien gladiatorial slaves, the de-Chihuahuaizing of Mayor Bob, a search for my ex-wife, and intergalactic sexual harassment revenge. And I purchased a bankrupt business. But I was finding myself in Empyrean, Arizona, just like the town's motto promised.

Of course, it could be argued that Empyrean is the town where all nutcases go to find themselves. I supposed I was crazy, but what crazy really means is that a person keeps thinking it will get better. This was as good as it gets and it wasn't that bad. I had some real friends whom I could count on to help me and I would help them. They were all doing things off the menu but so was I. That everyone in town was the same way was comforting. I could finally answer the question I had asked myself for years. Am I crazy or just not very smart? I was crazy, but I had taken a stand for the first time in my life.

"We're all in this together, Rhonda" I said. "Thigpen will help too." Nhoame, Dog Mayor and Rhonda were smiling.

I was smiling too. "By the way, I've got some money to get the business going."

18

A Matter of National Security

We were sitting at the kitchen table in Rhonda's parents' house watching her polish off the last of her breakfast. I wanted to ask some questions so we could make a plan to right the wrongs of the evil alien Gan the Salabian.

I started with Rhonda. "Why didn't Gan recognize you when we ran into him yesterday?"

"Because it's been two years and I gained so much weight. But I remember him, very clearly. He hasn't changed at all."

Then Nhoame spoke. "By the way, there's one other little detail I forgot to mention."

Mindful that I was not a detail man, I was always watchful regarding that facet of my personality. Along the way (my life) I missed some major cues for disaster, but I was getting more careful. At least I thought I was. Somehow, I was sure that Nhoame's little detail would not be so little and cause me to regret my newly acquired sense of chivalry. I was right.

Nhoame continued. "Besides being eunuchs, the Chinese warriors are also vampires."

"What?" I gasped, thinking that even a Wang's Moon Rocket would not provide the necessary comfort to handle this new revelation.

"I don't believe in vampires."

"Well you should," Nhoame said, "because there are thirty-nine of them at the Chinese compound."

I looked out the window and mumbled. "How did I find the one town in the country that has a talking Chihuahua for a mayor, space aliens and Chinese eunuch warriors who are also vampires? How did I do that?"

No one answered. "You mean these guys with the swords and falsetto voices fly around and suck peoples' blood? Is that what you mean, Nhoame?" I didn't understand why I was so upset with this newly revealed aberration. It shouldn't have been a surprise in view of all the other surprises that had come so quickly. Ripley's Believe It or Not could open a museum in Empyrean. I might just as well walk around with a permanent look of astonishment on my face so I wouldn't have to change expressions when the next amazement happened along. But Chinese eunuch vampire warriors were a bit much.

Nhoame was calm and reassuring. "Don't worry, Stan. The vampire iteration of the Chinese warrior eunuchs won't bother us. They never go after blood here in Empyrean. The pickings are too slim. What they do is turn into bats and fly into Phoenix once a month on a Friday night and victimize those poor devils who are into the bar scene.

They wait until their chosen victim is intoxicated and they follow him or her to a dark place and bite them. It's a nice outing for the Chinese eunuch vampire warriors, but it's also a good time for us to attack the compound. They only leave one or two guards to watch the place. The problem is, Gan is also there when the Chinese eunuch vampire warriors are gone. He never takes any chances."

"Why don't they bite the aliens in the compound?"

"They never bother us aliens because we have green blood. The vampires prefer red blood. Besides, when the vampires suck the blood from the people on the bar scene, they get a two for one deal. They not only get the blood but also get a 'high,' depending on the blood alcohol level of their victims."

"When these Chinese eunuch vampire warriors fly into Phoenix and bite people's necks and suck their blood, do the victims also turn into vampires?"

"No, not at all," Nhoame replied. "That just happens in the movies. You see, since the Chinese eunuchs by definition don't have testicles, their bite is not infectious from the standpoint it turns the bitee (the one who is bitten) into a vampire. If you want to create other vampires, you must have your sex organs. These guys are in it for the blood."

"Oh," I said. "So what's the plan?"

"How about taking an exploratory trip to the Chinese compound this Friday night when the Chinese eunuch vampire warriors have flown to Phoenix?" Nhoame replied.

That idea sounded good to everyone, but only Nhoame, Rhonda and I would go. The Dog Mayor was too small to be of any help because he was a Chihuahua. If we encountered any problems at the compound, the Dog Mayor would be frozen into in-action and simply stand there and shiver and urinate uncontrollably. Militarily speaking, he was not the ideal soldier to assign to front line duty.

With our plan made, I decided to go down to the office. I invited the Dog Mayor, Nhoame, and Rhonda to ride along. Once again, we all rode in the front seat of my truck that had continued to amaze me with its reliability. Nhoame sat in the middle and Rhonda, holding a smiling Dog Mayor on her left breast, rode shotgun. When we arrived, Thigpen was already there. Oddly, there was another vehicle parked in front of the office. It had a U.S. Government seal on its door.

"This is not good," I mumbled. I was thinking that Rhonda's neutron gun annihilation of the Chinese eunuch had probably not gone over well in some quarters, particularly law enforcement. On the other hand, if these guys were from the fifteenth century, technically they were already dead. "Besides, they were stealing people's blood," I was preparing myself to defend our actions to the government official inside our office. Rhonda had a right and a duty as an American to kill the blood-sucking, no-balled, sword wielding soprano."

I parked the truck and we all went inside. Thigpen bid me good morning and introduced the government man.

"Stan, uh, that's your name, right Stan? Yeah, it is. Stan, this is Agent, what's your name again, sir? Thigpen asked.

"I'm Special Agent René Orbostrowski. Don't ask. It's French."

"Orbostrowski is French?" I asked.

"No. Why do people have so much trouble with that name? René is French."

"That's a girl's name, ain't it Stan?" Thigpen said.

"No, Larry. It's only a girl's name if you're not French."

"Well if Orbostrowski is a girl's name if you're not French, what about René?" Thigpen said.

"No, I meant René is a girl's name only if you're not French."

"Well what about Orbostrowski if you are French?" Thigpen continued, in what had become a grueling examination of the completely inconsequential. "Is Orbostrowski a girl's name then?"

"God almighty, no, Larry," I said. "Have you ever met a girl named Orbostrowski?"

"Well, yeah Stan. That's why I asked. I met a girl named Orbostrowski up in Winslow last year. But let's see now, she wasn't French. Did she have a boy's name then?"

"Shut up!" René the government agent abruptly screamed. "What the hell is wrong with you people?"

Of course, we all knew. We just didn't tell him. We were all frapping lunatics.

"All right," Agent Orbostrowski continued, "who is the owner of this ludicrous disaster?"

"I am."

"Well I need to talk to you in private. Everyone else has to leave."

"Can the dog stay? He gets nervous if he's not with me."

"I don't care if the little shit stays," Orbostrowski replied. "He's sure one ugly mutt."

"As the group filed out of the office with Orbostrowski watching, an abrupt "Fuck you, Orbostrowski!" suddenly sounded.

"Who said that?" he asked.

"Who said what?" I said.

"I thought I heard a profanity aimed in my direction."

"I didn't hear anything," I said.

It was the Dog Mayor taking his revenge for Orbostrowski's insensitive comment that he was an ugly mutt. But I had to agree with Orbostrowski. Dog Mayor was ugly. But there was no use getting Orbostrowski involved in the Chihuahua conundrum.

Orbostrowski looked around the office suspiciously. Other than him and me, only the Dog Mayor was in the office. Orbostrowski shook his head, apparently concluding he was hearing things. He then laid out his proposition.

"Here's the deal," he said. "You're taking people on UFO landing site tours. We both know your business is ninety-nine percent bullshit. There really aren't any UFO landing sites since UFO's and aliens don't exist."

Incredibly, this crack government agent did not notice Nhoame, an alien dressed in a black cowboy outfit and a six gun in his holster standing just three feet from him before he dismissed him and the others from the office.

"However," he continued, "in the remote possibility a UFO should happen to land in this god-forsaken area, it would undoubtedly land in Quadrant 3." He spread out a map that divided the area surrounding Empyrean into four quadrants. That there were four quadrants was not a surprise. "Therefore," he went on, "as a matter of national security, the U.S. Government needs you to confine your UFO tours to Quadrant 4 because that is the spot in which UFO's are least likely to land."

In fact, Quadrant 4 was precisely the spot where all the UFO and alien activity was occurring. The Chinese compound with the one hundred alien slaves, Gan the Salabian, the ten UFO landing sites already on the Deluxe UFO Tour route, and the site of the encounter with the Chinese eunuch vampire warriors all lay in Quadrant 4.

"Okay," I agreed. "So you want us to confine all of our tours and other activities to Quadrant 4. Is that right?"

"You got it, Bub." The name Bub didn't turn me on this time, nor would it ever again.

"Okay, that will be fine," I replied.

"Well I appreciate your patriotic cooperation. Of course, Uncle Sam will make it worth your while to cooperate."

Dog Mayor's ears perked up now.

"Oh?" I questioned. "We certainly could use the help. We just opened the business. It was bankrupt, you know?"

"Yeah, I know," replied Agent René Orbostrowski. "For your cooperation, the government is prepared to give you ten thousand dollars per month."

To say I was shocked would be an understatement. I didn't think this rat trap would generate ten thousand dollars in revenue in ten years. I'm sure now that I must have had a look of supreme astonishment on my face. The Dog Mayor was strangely silent. I couldn't speak either. I was thinking, where do I sign, where do I sign?

Government Agent René Orbostrowski, noticing the look of shock on my face, mistakenly thought he insulted me with a low offer. He abruptly spouted a second proposition before I could enthusiastically accept the first extremely generous offer.

"Okay, hold on," he followed up. "Look, I'm really sorry I insulted you, but it's a part of my job to low ball people like you in these situations. You're not pissed off at me, I hope."

My god, this guy is just like us. He's just as crazy as we are. I was going to jump over the counter and kiss him for the ten thousand dollars a month offer. That was an incredible amount of money for us to do nothing, which is how I always figured the government operated anyway. I could sit in Bud's Rio Malo all day long on that. But, apparently, he wanted to give us even more.

Before I could speak and screw things up, René Orbostrowski threw out another offer. "Look," he said, "on a deal like this you should be getting a minimum of twenty thousand dollars a month. But since I pissed you off, how about we go twenty-five thousand dollars per month for you to keep your operations in Quadrant 4?"

But now, I recovered the composure that I never had at any time in my prior life. I established a degree of professionalism. "That offer is a little better René, but I have to tell you, I'm really disappointed."

The Dog Mayor began to shiver. His trembling was so conspicuous, René Orbostrowski noticed. "What's wrong with that homely little shit? Is he cold?"

"No, he's just screwed up."

"Look Stanley, I can only go to thirty-five thousand per month on this deal. I need to get authorization for any more."

"We need fifty thousand a month," I replied, otherwise we'll keep our tours in Quadrant 3 where all the action is."

"Dog Mayor threw up and was shivering so badly he shook himself right off the desk. I heard him yelp when his little black carcass hit the floor.

"Sign right here," René ordered. "You drive a tough bargain Stanley. It's fifty thousand a month for ten years. You keep your UFO landing site tours in Quadrant 4. Quadrant 3 is mine. We got a deal?"

"We got a deal," I said, hoping Orbostrowki didn't notice my reeling head and that, like the Dog Mayor, I was also shaking.

That was all there was to that. I signed the copy of the contract and Dog Mayor, intent on doing his part, promptly peed all over the floor the very second Government Agent René Orbostrowski walked out the door.

This is good. It's only ten o'clock in the morning and I've already had the best possible day I could ever imagine. I definitely intended to quit while I was ahead. The rest of the group, Rhonda, Thigpen and Nhoame walked in.

"Great news," I told them. "We got a government contract to keep all our UFO tours in Quadrant 4. We actually have a business going here."

The rest of the day was spent getting the office straightened out and trying to organize. But since we didn't have any business, we didn't have much to organize. So, I called Jean in Detroit to tell her I was having some good luck with the business.

19

Personnel Problems

Gan the Salabian, the sinister alien charged with getting the one hundred alien gladiatorial slaves trained for their ultimate sacrifice, was in conference with Yao Wie. Yao Wie was the warlord leader of the Chinese eunuch vampire warriors. They were meeting in Yao Wie's office at the Chinese Compound and the tone was not amicable. Yao Wie was upset because one of his warriors had been disintegrated by Rhonda's neutron gun.

"Where sumo wrestler woman get neutron gun?" he asked, in his shrill voice. "You Salabians not careful like Chinese people. You need be more detailed."

"That's not my fault," Gan replied. "She stole it from the space ship when we abducted her."

"Why you take sumo girl?" Yao Wie persisted.

"We needed to do experiments on the earthling. She wasn't a sumo wrestler then. She was hot."

"What you mean, hot? You mean she burn you?"

"No, I mean she was a fox, man."

"What you mean fox-man? You mean like boy fox?"

"No," replied a frustrated Gan. "I mean she looked good, like beautiful."

"You Salabians not do experiment. You molest her. You Salabians perverts. I no work with you no more. I take my people and go back to fifteenth century and work for emperor. You bad guy. I pro-feminist women's rights guy."

"Hey, look Jack, we got a contract with your emperor. You have to work for us."

"Name not Jack. That not true if you do bad things. Emperor want beauty in world."

"You should talk about beauty and perverts yellow fellow. You forty yellow guys carry your chopped-off, shriveled up balls in little tin boxes in your right pockets and fly around sucking blood out of people. Look who's calling the kettle black, here."

"Where kettle? You call me yellow fellow again I put you in little tin box. On top that, only 39 us guys out there because you get one killed by neutron gun."

"I told you that's not my fault. The crew on the space ship is responsible for that. They let her steal the neutron gun when they had her on board."

"You got big sumo girl pissed off. She come to get us now. What you do 'bout that?"

"Hey Jack, you provide the muscle. I'm the brains of this operation."

"You got no brains. You dumb idiot," Yao Wie replied, in oxymoronic overkill. Yao Wie's tenor voice rose increasingly higher as he became more upset.

Gan, the perceptive alien overseer, sensed the conversation was not going well. He decided to put his foot down with the rebellious warlord. "You gotta' beef up security." He was concerned because it was the Friday and the Chinese eunuch vampire warriors would fly to Phoenix to suck the blood of Club Feral patrons. "We can't have your entire crew flying away to Phoenix every month to suck blood. They need to lay off that stuff."

"You nuts? They vampires. Must have blood. Lucky you Salabians got green blood. Otherwise, you have thousand holes in your neck."

"I'm telling you, Yao Wie, we are vulnerable when your blood sucking platoon flies out of the compound. You need more men to guard the place when they're gone."

"We got manpower shortage problem so Emperor only allow forty eunuch warriors to leave Forbidden City. Emperor's Personnel Manager say hard to recruit warriors cause first line of job description say must cut balls off and become eunuch. Applicants not like that. It too much like American companies."

"Tell your personnel manager to eliminate the first line in the job description. American companies call that cutting off the balls thing "performs all other duties as assigned." That's always the last line in job descriptions. The employee never reads it until it's too late. Whenever you want to make an employee do something he doesn't want to do, like cutting off his balls, you simply refer to that last line. You just say, 'Oh, by the way, we need to cut off your balls. It's in your job description.' That's how the American companies do it."

"That good idea. In meantime, why you Salabians not put more soldiers here?"

"Hey, we have manpower problems too. We got wars going on with two different galaxies. You talk about manpower shortages. No way can we put more troops down here."

"Your problem, pervert guy. We do our job, but men need R & R in Phoenix. One Friday night each month is okay. That bar night for twenty-somethings. They local tribe who make Friday night a religious ritual. Easy to get blood cause those people drunk, not feel bite. And Chinese men get drunk from twenty-something blood. Alcohol already in blood they drink. That save time and money. My men no need buy drink to get drunk. Ha, Ha. Now, what you do 'bout sumo girl?"

"I didn't know the sumo girl was pissed. I didn't recognize her the other day. It's been two years since I last saw her."

"You dumb son bitch, pervert guy. Emperor not like you. You take advantage sumo girl."

"That was a one time thing, man. We have an inquiry going. We'll punish whoever is responsible."

"You stop, pervert guy. You sound like Wall Street financial guy, all bullshit. Next thing you say is I so sorry but I keep my bonus anyway. You need shut up and do job better."

Gan noticed Yao Wie's English had improved considerably when it came to cursing Wall Street financial types. They were not only despised on Earth, but the entire universe scorned the scumbags. And Gan had been called one by Yao Wie. That was the absolute worst, most despicable insult.

"We're at an impasse, Yao Wie. We must work together to get the job done here."

"We do our job. You not do your job. Where guy who escape. What his name?"

"His name Nhoame. Damn it, now you have me talking like you. I mean his name is Nhoame. I'm on his trail and I'll find him."

"You Wall Street guy. You full shit."

"Can you at least keep a few extra men at the compound this Friday? I think something is going to happen. I feel it more than I see it."

"No. Men need R&R, Wall Street guy."

20

Night Raid

As planned, Nhoame, Rhonda and I met at the office for our reconnaissance trip to the Chinese compound. When the Chinese eunuch vampire warriors assumed their bat form and flew into Phoenix, as was their monthly Friday night custom, the Chinese compound would have no guards. In a last minute decision I decided to bring Larry Thigpen. He would provide a little extra muscle in case something unanticipated should occur. The way life had been going lately, it should be anticipated that something unanticipated would happen.

Nhoame, Rhonda and I got into the truck cab, and with Thigpen sitting in the back of the truck, we left for the Chinese compound. When we had gotten within one mile of it, I turned the lights off so we could approach without their seeing us. When we were one hundred yards from the compound I pulled the truck onto the shoulder of the road and shut off the engine.

The compound was surrounded by eight feet high adobe style walls giving it the appearance of a fort. It was illuminated by numerous lights, but strangely, none were exceptionally bright, contrary to what one might expect in a prison-like facility. We approached the compound from the north with Nhoame leading the way to his escape tunnel located underneath the east wall.

The desert was dark, but a three quarter moon provided just enough light to see the ground and avoid the spine covered cholla cactus surrounding us. Three hundred yards to the east, a pile of bulbous rocks stacked on a small mountain glimmered softly in the gloaming's last moments. A few minutes later, we arrived at the tunnel through which Nhoame had escaped. I looked up at the moonlit sky, which was so clear the Milky Way itself seemed to be lighting our way. That celestial harmony silently assured us we had the spiritual high ground and provided heavenly validation of our mission. For sure, we were the good guys.

With Nhoame leading the way and Thigpen and I following, we crawled through the mud passageway under the wall. While we easily managed to pull ourselves through the six foot long tunnel, we had to scrounge some wooden sticks to dig out more mud to enlarge the passage for Rhonda. There was no way her sumo wrestler's body could fit through the snug space. I felt badly for her. I mean, we were all friends here. She didn't need to be so self-conscious about her size. After all, she was a sumo wrestler.

The four of us were now creeping through the dimly lighted complex toward the prisoners' quarters. The four walls enclosing it defined its simple layout. The complex was relatively small and efficient. It consisted of a main yard surrounded by living quarters for the guards and cells for the prisoners. The one story living quarters were built against the compound's wall.

Staying close to the walls and in the shadows, we soon arrived at our destination. There were twenty five cells in all, each holding four prisoners and enclosed by vertical bars. Cell doors were fastened by some kind of exotic lock, a bizarre looking device that Nhoame explained was brain wave resistant. Some of the aliens, particularly those from Nhoame's planet, had telepathic powers such as he used to rescue me from my fall from the cliff. Therefore, special locks had to be installed to prevent escapes. Nhoame however, had figured out a way to open the telepathic resistant locks, which were not so telepathic resistant after all.

Although it was early in the evening, all of the prisoners were apparently asleep. Nhoame explained that Chinese guards drug the prisoners on the Friday night each month they go to Phoenix. He then demonstrated how he opened the lock on his cell door when he escaped. It seemed like he just stared at the lock on the cell door nearest to him and it popped open. He had it figured out. We could easily release the prisoners from their cells right now. The big challenges would be getting them out of the complex and figuring out where we would take them and how we would transport them.

No one was around so we decided to explore further. We crept through the semi-darkness, being extra quiet as we passed in front of the guards' quarters in case one or two of them had stayed behind and have soft drinks instead of the blood-alcohol refreshments from the necks of Phoenix party goers. We had almost reached the end of the living quarters when we heard voices.

Nhoame quickly identified Yao Wie, the no-nonsense chief of the Chinese eunuch vampire warriors and the evil Gan the Salabian. Rhonda too, recognized Gan's voice and was anxious to confront him. She also wanted to break out the prisoners tonight. However, being the take-charge leader that I am, I told Rhonda we were not going to do either of those things.

"No, Rhonda," I said firmly."

"Why not? Isn't that why we came here?"

"Yes it is, Rhonda. And even though I'm not a detail man, I don't believe I can fit ninety-nine aliens in the back of my truck." That would make a nice drinking song, however.

"Besides," I continued, "even if we did let them out of their cells tonight and got them through the tunnel under the wall, what do we do then? We'd have ninety-nine aliens standing in the desert." Yeah, for sure that was a great drinking song.

As we stood near the window where Yao Wie and Gan were talking, I was congratulating myself on my leadership and controlling the impulsive Rhonda. Yes, I was the brilliant leader and my little army, confident in my wisdom, obeyed my commands.

That there was a major disconnect became immediately obvious. Without warning, Rhonda bolted from the group, and with three lunging steps, landed at the door behind which Yao Wie and Gan were having their conversation.

With a mighty scream of "Geronimo!" followed up by a thunderous "You perverts," Rhonda, with neutron gun in hand, smashed through the door. We had no choice but to rush into the room behind her, arriving in time to see a shocked Yao Wie and terrified Gan the Salabian jump to their feet and raise their hands high. Hellfire and damnation had arrived in the form of a three hundred pound out of sorts female sumo wrestler with a deadly neutron gun pointed directly at them.

"I tell you so!" Yao Wie screamed at the trembling Gan.

"No I tell you so! I mean, I told you so," Gan screamed back. "Stop making me talk like you. I not Chinese. I mean I'm not Chinese, you no-balled soprano shithead."

"Who you call shithead, you, you, you ugly guy?" Yao Wie responded, stumbling for the English translation of the Chinese profanity pouring through his brain, but unable to find the synapses to make the connection with his mouth.

"Shut up, you two," an obviously in charge Rhonda screamed.

"Rhonda, please stop," Nhoame asked. "This won't help us. Remember, there are thirty-eight eunuch vampire warriors coming back later."

Rhonda acquiesced to the logic of Nhoame's request.

"Alright," she said, "but there's one thing I need to do. Gan, come over here."

Gan was shaking so badly I thought his body would fly apart into a thousand pieces and crash on the floor. He cautiously walked over to where Rhonda stood.

"Come closer, you S.O.B."

This would not be good.

He moved closer to her and suddenly, her massive right leg shot up to his crotch, squarely connecting with that most sensitive section. "As the real estate people say, location, location, location," Rhonda quipped.

Gan fell to the floor, shaking and holding his testicles. Yao Wie, having witnessed Gan's unhappy fate, was also trembling.

"No, I innocent," he squealed.

"Get over here now, yowee, or whatever your name is," Rhonda ordered.

Yao Wie reluctantly stepped forward, bracing for the impact of Rhonda's vengeful right leg. Once again her pile driver limb sped upward and landed squarely in Yao Wie's crotch. He reached to grab his testicles, but remembered at the same moment as Rhonda that eunuchs don't have testicles. Either he didn't remember this minor detail before he reacted or else he fondly remembered this absent remnant of his manhood. In either case, he fell to the floor writhing, either feigning or actually experiencing some kind of sympathetic pain.

But Rhonda was not content with Yao Wie's pretend pain so she made him stand up. She then administered her encore punishment, which was to hit him over the head with the butt of her neutron gun. He fell back to the floor holding his slightly bleeding head with both his hands. He laid there screaming what we assumed were Chinese epithets. On the other hand, they could just as easily have been Confucian proverbs. But it's all about the tone of one's voice, isn't it? I guessed his screams were the former rather than the latter.

Thigpen, who had been uncharacteristically silent, felt the need to provide his profound observation.

"Bitchin!" he said.

We tied Gan and Yao Wie face to face and left them lying on the floor. As we walked out the door, we heard Yao Wie giggling in his little girl voice.

"Oh Gan," he moaned romantically.

"Oh God, let's get out of here," Thigpen said.

We made a quick exit across the open yard to the east wall and our secret tunnel, which, would undoubtedly lose its secret designation when the guards uncovered the breach.

As we walked through the desert toward my parked truck I wanted to chastise Rhonda for blowing our cover but I didn't have the heart. It was supposed to be a reconnaissance mission but Rhonda wanted revenge. Maybe she would be happier now, but it made our mission to free the ninety-nine alien prisoners much more complicated. She had blown our cover. Even Thigpen realized we made a major error in exposing ourselves. They would be waiting for us now, maybe even make a preemptive strike against us. He also seemed to sense that Rhonda felt bad about losing her temper so he decided to console her.

"Don't worry about it, Rhonda. Why one time I remember in the war………."

The poor devil couldn't remember the anecdote he was going to relate to comfort Rhonda.

"Well anyway," he continued, "That's another story, but I don't know what it is."

Rhonda patted him on the back.

"That's okay, Larry. I'll be smarter in the future."

Besides, Nhoame didn't seem concerned and that seemed to calm the group. At least, it calmed me. We would have to figure out our next move, but I had no clue what that would be. "Nhoame would find a way."

21

Rock and Herby Disappear

When Rhonda had her meltdown at the Chinese compound she created several unfavorable situations for herself and the rest of us. The first bad thing was that she alerted Yao Wie and Gan the Salabian, now a couple, that the compound's security had been compromised. The result would inevitably be a tightening of procedures making it more difficult to rescue the ninety-nine aliens. The second bad thing was that she exposed Nhoame's whereabouts to the evil couple. They now knew where to find him.

It was not only Nhoame and I who recognized these troubling developments, but also Thigpen. On the ride back to Empyrean, even Rhonda seemed to realize the trouble her temper tantrum would unleash. But none of us had any idea how soon trouble would begin.

Thigpen and I dropped Rhonda and Nhoame off at her parents' house and headed for Bud's Rio Malo. Our adrenalin was still running high and the time honored cure to calm ourselves down was to have a beer. I wasn't certain about the scientific basis for that prescription and Thigpen didn't care. It was approximately eleven-thirty when walked in the door of Bud's Rio Malo. It was Friday night and the regulars were there and things were "rockin," at least according to Larry Thigpen.

The hot news at Bud's Rio Malo was a breaking news report on television. There had been a big fight at Club Feral in Phoenix an hour earlier. When the police searched Club Feral's premises, they discovered thirty-eight red silk robes hidden in a box on the roof. According to several hundred inebriated witnesses, the red silk robes belonged to a group of very amorous Chinese men.

What the police didn't know was the Chinese eunuch vampire warriors had been hiding their robes on the roof for months. Without the robes there, when they landed and changed from their bat forms to humans, they would have no clothes. Of course, they couldn't walk into the crowded club naked. That would make them even more conspicuous than they already were. Or would it?

These two hundred customers, although reeling from the "huge number of drinks" provided by the Chinese men, verified this assertion of excessive amour by displaying multiple hickey marks on their necks. On closer inspection of the hickey marks, the police found two small puncture wounds associated with each hickey. Many of the patrons with the hickey marks were also feeling very weak in addition to very drunk.

Police Detective Bradley Costigan who had been working undercover at Club Feral, reported that he became suspicious by the many dazed customers walking out of the bar accompanied by Chinese men. He further reported that he had seen at least several of these Chinese men injecting something into the victims' necks. This slight embellishment was added by Detective Costigan to impress his superior, Captain Marmsley, with his observation skills. After considerable thought, ten seconds later Captain Marmsley reached a startling conclusion and called in his report to the Mayor.

"Mayor, what we have here is a biological attack by cross-dressing Chinese government agents. Their intent is to incite a war with China and a rebellion of the world-wide transvestite community. It's a nasty plot Mayor, no doubt the most sinister I've ever experienced. We need to lock down the city immediately and call out the National Guard. The perpetrators are still at large. I would also recommend you notify Homeland Security to raise the terror alert level. This is as bad as it gets Mayor."

The mayor, always on the lookout for opportunities for publicity, called a news conference and read Captain Marmsley's report word for word. He wanted to "get ahead of Homeland Security to protect our precious citizens," he was quoted as saying. Panic immediately spread across the city and anyone wearing a red dress, especially males, were suspect.

The terrorists, thirty-eight intoxicated Chinese eunuch vampire warriors, had metamorphosed into thirty-eight intoxicated vampire bats. They ditched their red silk robes and flew off in every direction, each bat assuming that the particular direction in which he happened to be flying was the correct route home.

At approximately eleven thirty, only half a dozen of the intoxicated mammalian aviators had found their way back to the compound. Upon landing, they transmogrified into their human form and retrieved their red robes lying in the compound's courtyard from which they had taken them off for their trip to Phoenix. It's always good to use big words when describing the vampire human changing to vampire bat process and, of course, the converse. It's also always wise to own two or more red silk robes.

"Aieeeee!" a man named Gee screamed. The others looked at him and laughed as he danced around holding his wing-wang (translation: male organ.).

It is also always wise to shake out your clothes when you leave them on the ground in the desert. Little friends of the desert looking for a place to stay overnight may crawl into them. In this case, a scorpion had taken refuge in Gee's red robe and when the unlucky man put the garment back on, he got stung on his wing-wang. The next morning would bring a hangover and pain in forbidden places. It would not be a fun day.

Gee, the second in command after Yao Wie, decided he better check in with his boss. Limping from the scorpion sting and dizzy from the alcohol overdose caused by the blood/alcohol level of the victims he had bitten, it took all his strength to walk across the central courtyard to Yao Wie's residence. But he managed to do it and was knocking on the front door when he heard high pitched giggles and moans from inside Yao Wie's quarters. He heard movement and shuffling and then Yao Wie screamed for him to open the door.

An astonished Gee found Yao Wie and Gan the Salabian tied together on the floor.

"Untie us," Yao Wie screamed.

Gee, his vision blurred by alcohol, struggled to untie the two men but he couldn't see the knots in the ropes.

"What wrong you?" Yao Wie screeched, in his most furious soprano voice.

"Not have glasses sir," a terrified Gee replied. "No see knots."

"You no wear glasses. You drunk" Yao Wie replied.

At that moment Gee, kneeling over the two men, passed out and fell forward across their tied up bodies.

"What hell go on?" Yao Wie screamed.

Hearing the commotion, the other five eunuch vampire warriors ran to Yao Wie's quarters, all of them falling down several times before reaching his door. Finally, one of the boozed up group was able to pull Gee's unconscious body off of the two men and loosen the ropes to free them.

"Some locals breached our security," Gan the Salabian announced.

Somehow, breached our security sounded more official than crawled through a hole under a wall, but Gan, of course, didn't know about that detail. Besides, he was upset that a few ragtag locals got the best of him. Gan wanted to even the score. He also wanted to recapture Nhoame, however, that was a secondary objective because, in addition to the security being breached, his dignity had also been compromised. That was the real bummer. Nobody messes with Gan. Of course, somebody already had.

"All right Yao Wie," Gan said, here's our plan. I have a hunch that our escapee Nhoame is staying at the sumo wrestler girl's house. You send your men to Empyrean to the Wilkenshaver home tonight. By striking back fast, we'll surprise them. Beat up the sumo girl and bring our prisoner Nhoame back here. Actually, bring sumo girl back here also.

"You pervert," Yao Wie replied. "No want sumo girl back here. She cause too much trouble already."

"Well I want her here and I'm the boss," Gan yelled at him.

For some reason, Gan was infatuated with Rhonda, although he had also developed feelings for Yao Wie as they spent the last two hours tied together. But, he found Rhonda more attractive.

"You Wall Street pervert guy." Yao Wie yelled. "You men drink coffee and go sober. Then you go get Nhoame guy and sumo girl. Go quickly!"

In a few moments, the six Chinese eunuch vampire warriors had changed back into their bat form and were flying toward Empyrean. They had to initially land on the roof of the Hotel Empyrean where they had a third set of red robes stored for just such occasions as their visit to town tonight. They had completed the brief flight and their wardrobe adjustment in just a few minutes and were now standing on the front porch of the Wilkenshaver home.

They had stopped at several other homes that they had mistaken for the Wilkenshaver residence, but finally got directions from the third irritated neighbor they awakened with their midnight knock on the front door. The reason for this irritation was probably due to the fact that no one wants to open their front door at midnight and discover six drunken Chinese men in red robes standing on the porch and asking directions? Of course, there's always the one person who would be delighted with that prospect.

The Wilkenshaver house was completely dark and the six interlopers decided to break in rather than knock, thereby surprising the people inside. The living room window to their right was the only one they needed to try. It wasn't locked and they raised it. Gee stuck his head inside the house and then crawled through the window and onto the couch beneath it.

With his head extended over the glass coffee table and his hands placed on the seat of the sofa to support his body, he pulled his legs through the window and placed his knees on the top of the couch's back. His body was now in a steeply inverted position with his legs at a level well above his head. Still suffering from alcohol over-indulgence, his nearly upside down position caused the blood to rush to his head and he blacked out and fell forward across the glass coffee table and an ear-shattering crash landing.

Gee's unconscious body shattered the table's glass top and several pieces of china displayed on it. Fortunately, the sound of breaking glass momentarily brought him back to consciousness. Unfortunately, though a vampire, the sight of his own blood oozing from half a dozen minor cuts terrified him and he screamed three times and passed out again. The other five intruders, realizing surprise had been lost, began crawling through the window just as lights began coming on inside the house.

Desert Chickadee, holding a baseball bat, was the first to appear. She soundly connected with the first of the group, catching a dumbfounded eunuch vampire warrior in his forehead and knocking him cold. He fell next to the unconscious Gee. The next intruder suffered the same fate and fell on top of the two men lying on the floor.

Rock Wilkenshaver, shotgun in hand, was the next to enter the room. He yanked the pump on the twelve-gage shotgun and pushed a shell into the chamber. Before he could bring the gun to a level position and aim, he accidentally pulled the trigger and the it fired with an earsplitting blast, shooting out the living room lights and blowing a two foot hole in the ceiling. One of the Chinese intruders began a hasty retreat through the front window, in the process, violating the number one rule when someone has a shotgun filled with bird shot. Don't expose your heinie. Rock Wilkenshaver's next blast smashed into the surprised eunuch vampire warrior's posterior, blowing him the rest of the way through the window and onto the front porch. He was now running down the street squealing and holding his bleeding backside stinging from two dozen tiny holes.

Rhonda, following close behind Rock, had charged another intruder and was sitting on top of him pummeling his face as the perplexed warrior stared at the I Love Art caption stitched across her nightgown. Seeing the fight was hopeless, the last intruder had already dived through the front window and was running down the street holding his backside with both hands just as a precaution. Nhoame stood and watched the spectacle from the dining room ready to move in if he was needed. However, it was obvious the Wilkenshaver clan needed no help when it came to self-defense.

The sheriff was as unhappy to be called to the Wilkenshaver home as the Wilkenshavers were when he arrived. Friday night was karaoke night at Bud's and Sheriff Elliott Landers was getting ready for the final round of competition when he got the call. A dedicated cross dresser, he was wearing his very best 1970's female rock star outfit of black mini-dress, glitter, feathers, and fishnet stockings when he arrived at the Wilkenshaver's house. He was furious about having to be there as he was on track to win the night's song fest. He called himself Lady Go Go, vaguely reminiscent of long gone decades.

Of course, by virtue of a special deal he had with Bud, he always won the Friday karaoke contest. However, without being present to sing his final selection, "I enjoy being a Girl," it would be difficult for Bud to fix the voting so Sheriff Landers would win. He was still secretly hoping that the other contestants would somehow self-destruct so he could win anyway.

"Nice outfit, Elliott," Desert Chickadee enviously remarked, as Sheriff Lander's entered the demolished living room. "But you need to shave your legs."

"I hate that," Sheriff Landers replied. "My skin is so sensitive I always get razor burn."

"Deal with it, Elliott," an annoyed Rhonda interrupted. "You know, Elliott, most towns wouldn't tolerate their top lawman running around in women's clothes."

"You're always very hurtful, Rhonda," he replied, but then got down to business. "What in the world's going on here?" he asked, as he pointed at the three unconscious Chinese men. Rhonda was still sitting on a fourth Chinese man punching him in the face. The living room was destroyed.

The still excited Desert Chickadee described what happened in great detail while a deputy handcuffed the four Chinese men. With the excitement over, Rhonda suddenly realized she had not seen Herby.

"Where's Herby?" she said. "Herby! Herby, where are you?"

There was no answer. Desert Chickadee left the living room to find Herby, beginning her brief search by looking underneath her bed. She thought she might find Herby there because he was just that kind of guy. That was where her husband Rock usually hid when there was any kind of trouble. For some reason, Rock stepped up to the home invasion tonight and performed well. But he was also missing. There was no Herby Titsmore and no Rock Wilkenshaver. After quickly checking every room in the small house, she stormed back into the living room.

"Herby's been kidnapped Sheriff. And Rock's gone too."

Sheriff Landers had seen Herby before but completely forgotten what he looked like because Herby was completely forgettable. He knew Rock however, because he was a long time local.

"I need a description of Herby ladies," he said. "Oh, I need one for Rock too."

Desert Chickadee and Rhonda quickly penciled the descriptions for the sheriff and he would put out an "all points bulletin." There were not, however, many points in Empyrean. Other than the town itself, the local drive-in ice cream joint on the south edge of town was the only other point. Neither Rhonda nor Desert Chickadee figured much would come of the "all points bulletin."

Earlier at the Chinese compound, when the eunuch vampire vampires staggered back to the courtyard to take off their robes to change into bats, Gan realized they were in no condition to accomplish their mission to kidnap Nhoame and Rhonda. He decided he would undertake the job himself. Using his state of the art Salabian teleporter, he arrived at the Wilkenshaver residence at the exact moment as the eunuch vampire warriors. He could see them stumbling across the front yard and bumping into each other on the small front porch. He knew they would blow it. Then Gee fell forward and crashed onto the coffee table, waking up the entire household. Gan would handle this job himself.

When the brawl began, Gan made his move. Timid Herby was the last to head for the living room. Gan, who had entered the kitchen through the back door, realized he couldn't kidnap Rhonda, so he opted for Herby. Rock, who had just blasted the eunuch vampire warrior's rear end, turned to see the evil Gan holding a laser gun of some type to Herby's head. With his finger pressed against his lip, Gan signaled Rock to be quiet and motioned for him to come into the kitchen where he and Herby were standing. The three of them left through the back door and were immediately whisked to the compound by Gan's Salabian teleporter.

Sheriff Landers, with his descriptions of the kidnapped Herby and Rock distributed on an all points bulletin, got ready to leave with his four prisoners.

"Sheriff, we know where Herby and Rock are," Rhonda said.

"Where would that be Rhonda?" Sheriff Landers absentmindedly said, as he looked into a mirror and touched up his make-up.

"They took them to the Chinese compound outside of town."

"Now what makes you think that?" the Sheriff replied, as he admired the red silk robes of the Chinese prisoners standing next to him.

Even Desert Chickadee who had known the sheriff for over forty years couldn't believe he wasn't connecting those dots.

"Elliott, for God's sake. All the Chinese men at the compound wear those same red robes, just like those guys standing next to you. Anybody home up there, Elliott?" she said, pointing toward his head.

"Don't get sassy with me, Barbara Jean," the sheriff replied. He always hated it when Barbara Jean, aka Desert Chickadee, called him by his first name because that meant she was insulting him.

They had gone out together in high school and everyone expected them to get married. Along the way however, something happened and they were suddenly not together anymore. They had baggage, but no one knew what it was. And they still talked to each other like they always did, she addressing him by his formal name of Elliott instead of by his nickname Ellie. He still called her Barbara Jean and not Desert Chickadee, her self-proclaimed Indian name. He was the only one in town she allowed to not call her Desert Chickadee.

"Elliott, six Chinese men invaded my house. They are obviously from the Chinese compound south of town. Rhonda's and my husbands disappear at the exact moment they broke in to my house. Come on Elliott. Even you oughta' see a connection here."

"Yeah, I see your point, Barbara Jean. Look, I'll need to get a search warrant before I can check out the place and the court house is closed on Saturday. I'll have to contact Judge Simmons at home but it will have to be in the morning, okay?"

"Okay Elliott. Let me know what you find out."

Elliott nodded and left the house with his prisoners. In less than two minutes, they reached the building holding the sheriff's office and jail. The prisoners were brought into the process room and instructed to remove their red robes and wait for the deputy while he went to the supply room to get some prisoners' uniforms. On his return, however, the room was completely empty with the exception of four red robes lying on the floor by the barred but open window. The four men had transformed themselves into bats and flew out the jail window and back to the Chinese compound.

22

Manfred Starshine

Rhonda and Desert Chickadee walked into Sheriff Elliott Landers' office promptly at eight a.m. Knowing Desert Chickadee, aka Barbara Jean, he expected her to arrive at precisely that time and she did. "What did you find out Elliott? Are you going to go search the Chinese compound and rescue poor Rock and Herby this morning?"

From the moment he met her forty years earlier, Elliott feared giving Barbara Jean bad news. That she didn't take bad news well was a blatant understatement with a predictable outcome. "Well, you see, Barbara Jean, there's a little problem with that."

"What do you mean by little problem, Elliott? You and I both know Rock and Herby are at the Chinese compound waiting for somebody to go out there and rescue them. It's so simple even you ought to be able to understand."

It was plain to see that Desert Chickadee was working herself up, but Elliott had no choice other than continue. "It's like this. Technically, the Chinese compound is like an embassy, a special space for foreign countries. That compound was here before Arizona became a state. A long time ago our government signed an agreement with the Chinese government to provide the compound "embassy status." That means we can't just barge in and search the place."

"What do you mean Elliott, you wimp?"

Desert Chickadee's temper was rising, and with unsurprising genetic congruity, so was Rhonda's. "We can't just leave Rock and Herby out there until they decide to turn them loose. They'll never let them go."

"I can't help that. Unless we know for sure they're being held prisoner, we can't request a search warrant for the place. Even then, it would have to go through the State Department. And, I doubt they would approve it anyway."

"I'm not happy about this," Desert Chickadee growled.

"I knew you wouldn't be Barbara Jean, but there's nothing I can do about it."

"Well, you haven't heard the last of this." Elliott was sure he hadn't heard the last of it. Desert Chickadee and Rhonda turned and walked out the door, but he knew they would be back.

The two women drove over to the office of Deluxe UFO Tour Company. Dog Mayor, Thigpen and I spent the night at the office and Desert Chickadee wanted to get the mayor's opinion on the situation. Maybe he could suggest a course of action. As the two women walked into the office, Dog Mayor was standing on his desk at the back of the room. "Hey Rhonda, are we going for a ride today? I want to sit on your lap, such as it isn't."

"Shut up you little sex fiend," Rhonda snapped. "They kidnapped Herby and Rock and we need your help getting them back."

"Who kidnapped Herby and Rock?" Dog Mayor asked.

Actually, the sheriff had already informed the Dog Mayor about last night's events. Even though he was on indefinite leave because of his temporary status as a canine, he was still the mayor and everyone in the town government kept him informed about things. He'd seen the sheriff earlier in the morning, but didn't want to wake Thigpen and me to give us the bad news.

"The Chinese guys took them last night," Rhonda said. "The sheriff arrested four of them but they escaped."

Desert Chickadee walked over to Dog Mayor's Desk. She was about to speak, but noticed a small puddle under a vase of purple flowers. She looked at Dog Mayor. "Your vase is leaking."

"No it ain't," Thigpen said. "His Honor pissed on the flowers."

"For God's sake, Mayor. What the hell's wrong with you?" Desert Chickadee said.

"I'm a dog, in case you didn't notice. I had to mark my territory. So what do you want?"

Desert Chickadee shook her head in disgust. "Our numb nuts sheriff refuses to search the Chinese compound because it's got "embassy status" or something. But, you know all about that don't you, mayor?"

"Yeah I do. I'm trying to figure out a plan as we speak. Don't worry we'll get them back."

Barely awake, I was sitting on my cot in the corner of the office. "We'll go get them Desert Chickadee," I assured her.

Desert Chickadee looked relieved. "I know you will, Mayor, and you too Stan. That's why we came to see you. We knew you would do something about this awful situation."

I smiled sympathetically, brimming with false bravado. "We'll make a plan to get our friends out of there. Right, Mayor?"

I made these heroic remarks without having any idea just how I would accomplish what I was promising. Because of our disastrous reconnaissance mission the night before, the Chinese compound would now be super vigilant and extra nasty about defending their turf.

Thigpen decided he would also reassure Rhonda.

"Yeah, don't worry Rhonda. We'll get our friends back, won't we ....?" Thigpen, again forgetting my name, looked in my direction. "Stan, Larry. My name is Stan."

"Yeah I know," Thigpen replied. He cupped his right hand over his mouth and whispered, "Her name is Rhonda, right Stan?" I nodded my head. Thigpen didn't even want to think about trying to remember Desert Chickadee's-Barbara Jean's names. His metal encased brain might short circuit.

"I hear you knocked out a couple of guys last night, Desert Chickadee," said Dog Mayor.

"Yeah, I did your honor. I guess the sheriff told you that too."

"As the mayor, I need to know these things."

"I'm glad you're on my side," Desert Chickadee said. Normally, a tiny black dog standing on a desk panting and wagging his tail wouldn't inspire a great deal of confidence, but Dog Mayor was a man (under normal circumstances) who could get things done. Desert Chickadee had known him for a long time and had absolute faith in the annoying little creature. He cared about people and that's what always got him elected. But it felt odd to address a small dog as "your honor."

At times he was difficult to deal with, but Desert Chickadee knew how to handle him. The Dog Mayor liked to engage in a little pre-business ritual of insults and sarcasm. Once the verbal sparring was over, the business at hand could be discussed. And that's the point at which we had arrived. The moment was at hand for the mayor to hatch the brilliant scheme to solve the problem, the masterful action plan to vanquish the oppressors from the planet.

"Manfred Starshine is the man to handle this situation!" he blurted excitedly.

"What?" I asked, shocked by his absurd suggestion. "How can he possibly help us get those guys out the compound?"

"Manfred and his brother-in-law, Galen Withersby, are the ones for this job. Trust me on this."

"Galen is married to Manfred's sister?" I replied, stunned. "Galen is a racist. How can he be married to Manfred's sister?"

Dog Mayor's scratching behind his ear with his right rear foot didn't enhance his stature as a decision maker. "Galen is not a racist. He's just crazy, and like lots of crazy people, he has a streak of genius in him. We'll tap into that genius and go rescue our friends, simple as that. Manfred will keep Galen under control. He understands him better than anyone else."

The Mayor made it sound easy, but I knew it was going to be a lot tougher than he envisioned. But I bought into the plan because I didn't have a better one myself. I told Desert Chickadee and Rhonda to go back to the house and Thigpen, Dog Mayor and I started toward Manfred Starshine's store in the center of town.

It was still early, but tourists were on the move, looking for ways to spend their money. As we walked south on Main Street, I felt better about my situation. While I was the co-owner of a business that hadn't seen a customer in two years, the $50,000 monthly government subsidy negated the relevance of that annoying detail.

It didn't take long to reach Manfred's building and I was looking at the signs hanging in the glass windows. In the left window was a sign offering "Healing." A second sign proclaimed "Vortex Site Tours Since 1989." In the right window, there was a schedule for "Intuitive Readings." This hardly looked like the base from which to launch the rescue of our two friends from the formidable Chinese complex.

Even though Nhoame said he hadn't seen any women at the compound, I had a feeling my ex-wife was being held captive somewhere in the area. I was hoping we could rescue her as well as Rock and Herby.

As Dog Mayor, Thigpen and I walked through the front door into the merchandise display area, we saw Manfred talking to a customer in the small room at the back of the building. A door with a curtain of beaded strands separated the two rooms. In a few minutes, the customer finished talking with Manfred and pushed the beads aside as he exited.

The main room was stocked with hundreds of books as well as decorative symbols hanging from walls and ceilings. There were mystical items as well, crystals, special healing rocks and rocks from secret vortex locations. There was an endless supply of rocks with special powers and life changing properties. If I had known about these wondrous stones when I had my problems in Detroit, I would have purchased the entire bleeping store.

Manfred saw us and walked from the back room to where we stood. He was dressed in his finest celestial costume, a long yellow robe arrayed with red, gold and silver half-moons, meteors and stars, a white shirt with a straight, snug fitting collar and black round cap with no visor. The outfit set off his dignified white beard. He appeared every bit the authentic mystic or whatever it was he intended to look like. His white sneakers were sort of an atmospheric distraction, but it all seemed to work so who cares?

"Good morning guys," he said with a smile.

"Good morning, Manfred," I said.

"Hi Manfred," Thigpen said, recalling Manfred's name because I just said it.

Dog Mayor started to say "Hello," but inadvertently barked twice. He shrugged his little shoulders and said, "Oh shit!"

It wasn't much of a greeting but Manfred smiled. "I knew you guys were coming. You wish to incorporate my brother-in-law's insanity into your plan to rescue Rock and Herby."

I was amazed. "How did you know?"

He smiled. "A deep rooted, cognitive perspective on the axiom of corporeity provides an intuitive window on the future. You know what I mean."

"I haven't a clue what you're talking about." I was sorry I asked the question, but was thinking two or three Wang's Moon Rockets would provide the necessary insight into his thinking. Unfortunately, I had developed a strong aversion to drinking yak urine.

I was becoming more concerned about Rock and Herby. When Rhonda first told me about their kidnapping I was worried we might not be able to rescue them. This thought continued to distress me to the point that I was almost certain our chivalrous intentions were no match for our Chinese adversaries.

23

Galen WIthersby, Ph. D. N. (N signifying "Not")

Manfred called Galen Withersby to make sure he was available before we dropped in to visit him at his home office. Luckily, Galen would see us right away because he had a busy afternoon schedule. I was sure no one including Galen had any idea what he might be doing that afternoon. On the other hand, no one really cared because Galen was in his own world, wherever that was.

We rode with Manfred and arrived at Galen's home in a just a few minutes. The great thing about a small town is you never have to drive very far. Manfred's sister, whom incredibly was Galen's wife, was at work and it was Galen who answered the door.

"Good morning, gentlemen. It's a great day, is it not?" he declared.

Under the circumstances, it really was not a great day however, we didn't respond as such because we collectively understood the futility of disagreeing with Galen on any subject. Differing with Galen even on something as inconsequential as the pleasantness of the day would lead to a loony labyrinth of tilt-a-whirl non-reason and infinite pondering.

We concurred it was a wonderful day. That someone finally agreed with him pleased Galen immensely. He gestured for us to follow him into his home. It wasn't exactly clear whether Galen meant for his attire to project a professorial appearance or demonstrate that he was truly deranged. He was dressed in a white shirt, tie, dark brown corduroy pants and a tan wool jacket with brown elbow patches. This collegial winter garb was appropriate as winter apparel in the northern climes, but today's temperature was a 102 degrees.

The rest of us, including Manfred who had changed from his mystical outfit, were wearing shorts and tee shirts. If Galen was trying to convince us he was crazy, I was a believer. Final affirmation of that point was his long, gray hair blowing in every imaginable direction without the assistance of even a slight breeze in the hallway through which we were walking. I didn't care to ponder than phenomenon.

At the end of the corridor was the converted bedroom that served as his office. It was a large room with enough space for a desk, four file cabinets, and two chairs. Papers were piled on every available surface. Manfred and Thigpen sat down while Galen, excusing himself, returned momentarily with a third chair for me. He assumed the Dog Mayor would be happy sitting on the floor.

Dog Mayor, however, was not pleased with that arrangement and didn't hesitate to inform Galen as to his seating preferences. "Did you forget someone, Mr. No Ph.D. Withersby? I'm the mayor of this town, you know." By the irritated look on Galen's face, it appeared he had considered the propriety of canine seating options. He should have gotten Dog Mayor a chair and been done with it, but this simple solution was an unsatisfactory alternative for Galen, mainly because it was simple and practical. He belabored the point. "You are a dog, Mayor. Are you not aware of the species dissimilitude inherent in the seating customs of our society?"

Oh, oh. This would be trouble. Then Thigpen abruptly yelled, "Give him a damn chair, Galen." That handled Dog Mayor's complaint. Galen left the room to fetch (no pun intended) Dog Mayor a chair.

"Disputatious little mutt, isn't he?" Galen remarked, when he returned with the chair.

Dog Mayor let it go, mainly because he didn't know what disputatious meant. Neither did the rest of us.

"So how can I help you gentlemen?" Galen asked, in his most academically haughty tone.

"Cut the arrogance Galen," Manfred replied. "We've got a serious problem here and we need you focused on the solution, not on showing off your non-existent bona fides."

"Manfred, Manfred, you delude yourself. You are so jealous because I operate within the realm of real science and you conduct your business in a hodgepodge of fantasy. Poor Manfred. Poor, poor Manfred."

Of the two, I would vote for Manfred as the one more likely operating within at least some semblance of reality. While I wasn't sure his magic rocks could change lives, and I doubted the existence of vortexes other than tornadoes, Manfred was at least rational. Galen had his mind focused on some mysterious off-planet goings on, completely unaware of events occurring immediately around him. Needless to say, neither man would get my vote for director of the country's nuclear weapons arsenal.

Manfred had briefly outlined the situation on his earlier phone call to Galen. The question was how to get Rock and Herby back without someone getting hurt or possibly killed. And Nhoame wanted us to rescue his ninety-nine fellow prisoners, which were slated to be shipped to the death planet Rhostugasht in the next few days. And my ex-wife Nancy also needed to be rescued. And Dog Mayor wanted Gan to return him to his human form. This was a rather lengthy shopping list.

Galen, however, immediately had the answer. "Excuse me for a moment. I must go to my supply cabinets in the external storage facility."

"By external storage facility he means his garage," Manfred said, as Galen scurried out of the room.

He returned shortly and placed a four inch tall bottle on his desk. "It's simple. I have the solution right here." The clear glass bottle was labeled Mediterranean Oregano Leaves and it was completely empty.

The first to speak was the military minded Thigpen who had expected nothing less than a case of dynamite or a box of machine guns. "You're going to kill them all with an empty spice bottle?"

The frustrated Galen looked at Thigpen. "Of course not, you idiot. Look more closely at the bottle." Thigpen, Manfred, Dog Mayor and I simultaneously leaned forward, straining our eyes to see something in the empty bottle. There was nothing but the bottle's label glued on its outside surface.

"Notice anything else?" Galen asked.

"Well yeah, I do now that you mention it," Thigpen said. "It also says "Gourmet Collection and Net Wt. 0.5 ounces.""

"No, no, no!" an exasperated Galen shot back. "Look at what's inside the bottle. It's completely full for Pete's sake."

That Galen insisted something was inside the empty bottle could have been interpreted in one of two ways. The first was that we could consider it affirmation of the long held opinion of everyone in town that Galen was deranged. Since he had already proven that point, however, that affirmation was unnecessary. The second way to interpret Galen's insistence that the bottle was full was to assume he was an ultra-positive guy along the glass half-empty, glass half-full continuum. Neither option seemed to fit.

We sat back in our chairs and stared blankly at Galen who was beaming a toothy, self-satisfied smile that looked like it was about lurch out of control and encircle his head.

"You see them, don't you?" he happily chirped.

Manfred had learned from long experience with Galen to maintain his patience. Even Dog Mayor was holding his tongue. (He wasn't literally holding his tongue because he had teeny paws and lacked an opposable thumb.) But either way, the thing was dripping all over his chair as he sat panting. He didn't appear to be frustrated with Galen's opinion that a completely empty glass was completely full.

Even Thigpen, who had been boisterous earlier, realized that maybe there was more to the empty bottle than we could see.

Finally, I couldn't take anymore. "Alright Galen, what am I missing here?"

"I'm glad you asked. You remember what I told you about the Zuyglyphens in the bar that night? Well there's a spice jar full of them sitting in front of you."

"What are Zuyglyphens?" interrupted Thigpen.

"Yeah, I'd also like to know what you're talking about, Galen," said Dog Mayor. "And how are Zuyglyphs or whatever they're called going to help us rescue Herby, Rock, and the rest of the prisoners?"

"Let me explain, Mayor," Galen said. He paused. You know, it's awfully hard to call a ten pound dog slobbering all over my carpet, Mayor. Get yourself straightened out and back into your human form."

"How would you like a ten pound dog to come over there and bite you in your dumb ass?" Dog Mayor responded. He thought for a moment. I can't reach high enough to bite you in the ass because I'm not tall enough. And your heinie doesn't look all that appetizing. If I could get back into my human form I would kick you in your ass instead of biting it."

Manfred was exasperated. "Will you please get on with it, Galen? Tell them about the Zuyglyphens before I bite you in the ass myself."

"I agree with the Mayor," Thigpen said. "Galen's ass doesn't really look that appealing to me either."

"Stop!" I said. "Get on with it, Galen, or we'll be here all day. Say what you have to say so we can either come up with a plan to rescue our friends or lock you up in an institution for the terminally absurd."

"Stan, Stan. I had such high hopes for you. Then you went into a partnership with a talking dog and purchased a bankrupt business. Who are you calling absurd, Stan?"

Galen had me there. I was just beginning to feel good about myself and he tells me that. He's not a glass half full guy.

"Alright, listen up!" Galen said assertively. Galen's authoritative tone caused Thigpen to jump to his feet and snap to attention and salute. "Yes Sir!" he said, in his best military voice. He realized he was the only one standing at attention and sat down. "Flashback," he said.

"Zuyglyphens," Galen continued, "are germ-like organisms that travel through dark matter. They are invisible, as you can see by the seemingly empty spice glass. Strike that. I meant to say as you cannot see by the seemingly empty spice glass. Their function is to spread the negative characteristics of all races and cultures to all other races and cultures. As an example, that night in the bar I used the Irish propensity for alcohol consumption as the negative racial characteristic of the Irish which has been spread to all other cultures through Zuyglyphens."

I glanced at Manfred out of the corner of my eye. Oddly, he seemed to be listening to Galen.

"Anyway, the Zuyglyphens in that spice jar sitting in front of you have been weaponized," he continued.

"What do you mean weaponized?" asked Dog Mayor. "Weaponized with what?"

"I have over a dozen types of weaponized Zuyglyphens, Mayor," Galen said proudly, but this particular type is one of my favorites. This is called the "genus siestacillus." It will do the job very nicely, I guarantee."

"What is genus siestacillus?" Manfred asked. "And what will it do?"

"Manfred, Manfred. Must I explain everything to you? It's very obvious everyone else understands exactly what genus siestacillus is. Why must I always explain for you?"

"Excuse me Galen," I said, "but I don't know what genus siestacillus is either." Galen looked distressed that there were two ignorant people in the room, but judging from the blank looks on Thigpen's and Dog Mayor's faces, they didn't have a clue either. "Alright, I'll explain," Galen said, in a bored voice.

"Genus siestacillus" is the Zuyglyphen carried trait of 'sleepness.'

In other words, people in Mexico take afternoon siestas. By isolating Mexican Zuyglyphens that carry the sleepness trait, I can collect them into a small container like this spice glass. This makes for a concentrated mixture of sleep-infused Zuyglyphens." There was silence for half a minute as Galen sat beaming, waiting for applause we guessed. But there was only silence.

"So what," Thigpen said. "What does all this mean and how will it help us rescue our friends?" Galen was bewildered now. "Don't you people see? You go to the Chinese compound and uncork this bottle and the eunuch vampire warriors fall asleep. Ha, ha. It's wonderful isn't it? There's enough genus siestacillus in this little bottle to put the whole town to sleep for the next twelve hours."

Galen had everyone's attention now. We were skeptical, but Galen was just balmy enough to have something, if there really was something inside the bottle. "Galen," I said, "our lives will be on the line when we confront the Chinese. I wonder if we could see a demonstration of your genus siestacillus?"

"I knew you'd ask," he said. "Choy. Here Choy. Come on Choy." Choy was Galen's shih tzu. "Might as well test the genus siestacillus we're going to use on the Chinese warriors on a Chinese dog," he said laughing. "Actually, the shih tzu is from Tibet, but China thinks it owns Tibet as well as the rest of the world, so I call it a Chinese dog. For that matter, if China owns the world, every dog must be a Chinese dog." He paused to think about that.

Choy bounded into the room and jumped on everyone and was a nuisance. No one likes other people's dogs. "Okay," Galen said, "everyone hold your noses when I say now. What I will do is stick this tiny syringe into the rubber cap on the spice bottle and draw out a miniscule amount of genus siestacillus. Then I'll press the pump on the syringe and release it into the air in front of Choy's nose. As dog's have a heightened sense of smell, Choy will immediately pass out. Is everyone ready?"

Galen put on his rubber gloves and stuck the syringe into the rubber top of the jar. He pulled the pump back very slightly and then withdrew the needle. "Now!" he said. He held the syringe directly in front of Choy's nose and pressed the pump. Choy, instantly asleep, dropped onto the floor with a little thump. But Choy's little thump was followed by a louder thump as Dog Mayor, unable to hold his nose with his thumb less paws, passed out and fell from his chair onto the floor. Then Galen, who was kneeling by the sleeping Choy, suddenly fell to the floor causing a third and even louder thump.

"The dumb shit zapped himself," Thigpen said laughing. Approximately one and a half seconds later, he too passed out and fell off his chair. This caused an even louder fourth thump in what had become a concert of drum beat thumps in successively increasing volume. Manfred and I looked at each other and I think I had begun to smile when I fell to the floor and everything went black.

"Wake up. Wake up, mister."

I was struggling to open my eyes.

"Hey Buddy. Come on. Wake up."

I wanted to keep my eyes closed. The world out there looked much too bright. I don't live on that shining planet. I'll stay here where it's dark and comfy.

"Hey! Come on, mister. Wake up, will you."

I forced my eyelids to open a crack. I could see the fuzzy outline of a creature from this illuminated world. They must all wear protective goggles in this shining place I thought. "What planet is this?" I asked, slowly opening my eyes to the glaring ceiling lights.

"It's planet earth, mister," someone said. I blinked several times and finally got my eyes open. "You and your friends had a sleepover and Galen Withersby's wife got home from work and found you, a swishy male nurse said. When she couldn't wake you boys she called 911. The ambulances brought you and your three sleepy friends to the emergency room. Your dogs are at the veterinary hospital. You people must have smoked some weird stuff."

"We didn't smoke anything. Where are my friends?"

"Yeah, that's what they all say," swishy voice replied. "Your spaced out buddies are in the next three rooms. They're all awake, and now, you are too. Isn't this just a happy day? Oh they will be so delighted to see you. Isn't the best day ever?"

"You're very irritating," I said.

"Oh don't you have a cute little squint?" he warbled.

I thought about strangling him, but sensing my hostility, he kept his thin body with its pursed smile and short hair safely out of my reach. He was dressed in a white uniform cut snugly to emphasize.......well, whatever it was he was trying to emphasize.

"How long have I been here?" I asked.

"They brought you in late yesterday afternoon. It's almost noon and you need to get out of here."

I learned from my earlier emergency room visit with Hector the rattlesnake man that emergency room people become very irritated when pseudo patients such as myself darken their doors with any kind of wound less serious than a severed foot or impalement by a telephone pole. Thankfully, I was not suffering either of these afflictions, but I wasn't injured enough to warrant emergency room care, in swishy voice's opinion. I was therefore fair game for reproach and he wasn't holding back.

Thankfully, Thigpen walked into the room and rescued me.

"Come on........., a. it's time to go, a............"

"Stan, Larry. My name is Stan."

"Oh yeah, come on Stan, let's get out of here."

I was awake, but still wobbly and Thigpen helped me out of bed. He steered me through the doorway and we walked over to the nurse's station to sign out. "Come back soon, boys," the male nurse quipped. "We hope to see you again real soon, hopefully under more serious circumstances." The rest of the nurses laughed at his little joke that he probably used a thousand times before. I'll add him to my list of potential homicides I plan to commit. He'll be number one on the list, I decided, displacing yaks one through six presently occupying that spot.

Manfred and Galen were in the hospital lobby waiting for us. Since we were all a little shaky from our mal-administered dose of genus siestacillus, we promptly concluded that a visit to Bud's Rio Malo to partake of a medicinal beer was in order. As our bleary eyed group walked toward the revolving door, Rhonda came in and stopped in front of us. "Stan, Gan the Salabian wants to meet with us right away to release Herby and Rock!"

24

Go Fly a Kite

"If I wanted to know it, I'd already know it," Special Agent René Orbostrowski stated firmly. He was responding to Rhonda and me who had gone to his Empyrean office to tell him we wanted to rescue Herby Titsmore and Rock Wilkenshaver from Gan and his band of Chinese eunuch vampire warriors. Although Gan said he would release Herby and Rock to Rhonda and me, it was on the condition that we come alone and meet him in a remote spot in the desert. We sensed it was a trap. We also felt that things had gotten out of hand.

"I don't want to know there are aliens around here or anywhere else on earth. I've never seen an alien, and if they're out there, I don't want to know. Period. Look Stan, we both know your business is a hoax. No flying saucers or UFO's ever landed in Quadrant Four where you agreed to confine your UFO tours. Quadrant Three is another matter. A UFO may have landed there one time, but I like not knowing for sure. The truth is out there so stay home. That's what I do."

"Then why is the government subsidizing my Deluxe UFO Tour Company business?" I replied. "And why do you want me to stay out of Quadrant Three?"

"Simple," replied Orbostrowski, "certain highly placed people in the government are convinced that UFO's and little green men do exist. So we go through the motions and pretend that my office is monitoring any aliens that supposedly land in Quadrant Three. Since no UFO's have landed in Quadrant Three, my annual UFO Control Report always states 'No UFO Landings to Report This Year.' When it's phrased like that it sets up the expectation that there could possibly be aliens landing next year and we will continue to be vigilant, which is how I always end my report. That proves that we are doing one heck of a job keeping them out of here and I get a raise every year."

"Well there aren't any dinosaurs running around Quadrant Three either. You're doing a great job keeping the dinosaur population under control also," I said sarcastically.

Ignoring my intended sarcasm, Orbostrowski thought about that for a moment then said he would forward an intra-departmental memo suggesting a monitoring area for dinosaurs as well. "I mean, what we could have here is some ancient, unknown dinosaur type that survived the great extinction. Now you did state that you saw what appeared to be dinosaurs in the Empyrean area, did you not Stan?"

"No René, I did not state that I saw dinosaurs in the Empyrean area or any other area. We are here to get help in rescuing our friends from the alien Gan the Salabian."

"Well, it's like I said Stan. If I wanted to know it, I'd already know it. And I don't want to know about this imaginary alien guy, Gan the Salabian. Besides, your two friends are probably off somewhere on a three day drunk which sounds like a pretty good idea to me right now."

"Well what about the Chinese compound?" I countered.

"Sheriff Landers already told Rhonda that the Chinese compound has 'embassy status.' The only way we could get into that place is to go through the State Department and request a special exception for a search warrant. That would take months and they'd never approve it anyway. Even then, unless someone observed a United States citizen being kidnapped and put inside that compound, we'd never get approval to search it."

No help would be forthcoming from Special Agent Orbostrowski. Rhonda and I walked out of his office into the bright sunlight. The meeting with Gan was supposed to happen in less than two hours and we were on our own. Rhonda and I had no choice but to go alone, otherwise Gan wouldn't meet with us.

"Okay, here's what we'll do," Rhonda said. "We'll go meet Gan and when he shows his ugly face, I'll pull out my neutron gun from under my skirt. We'll force him to turn over Herby and Rock."

"Well don't wear that tight skirt again. It took you so long to get that skirt up the last time we could have watched a full length science fiction movie. I have a feeling Gan will move a lot faster than the Chinese warriors."

"Good point Stan, but I already thought about that. I left a loose skirt at the office to wear for just such an occasion like this. The neutron gun is such a nice accessory, don't you think?"

Rhonda revealed a sense of humor I hadn't noticed before. We were walking the three blocks back to the office to get my truck and would leave shortly for our rendezvous with Gan. We soon arrived and the Dog Mayor was there to meet us. He'd already heard that we were going to meet Gan and get our friends released. Like us, he was very suspicious of Gan's motives in arranging the meeting.

"You better be careful," he cautioned. "I don't trust that guy."

"Well it's not like we trust him either, but what else can we do?" I asked.

Rhonda had gone into the back room to get her neutron gun and put on her full skirt. She would be able to get to the gun fast if she needed it. As Rhonda and I walked out the door, I wondered if we were doing the right thing. This could turn out badly, but there didn't seem to be any other option. We drove out of town on Main Street heading south and I was wondering if I might be able to rescue my ex-wife when we saw Gan. There hadn't been any mention of her and I had begun to wonder if I somehow got off on the wrong track thinking she was in Empyrean. Wouldn't Gan have said something about her if he was holding her captive?

Main Street also served as the state highway and we continued on it for just over five miles when it intersected with Forest Road 1091. We took a left turn and headed east toward Devil's Point. In the west, there are lots of places named Devil's Point, or Devil's Peak or Devil's something or other. I attributed this oddity to two possibilities. The first was that the Devil visited all of the places named after him, in which case he would have been a very busy tourist. The second possibility was that the Devil simply must have been one very popular fellow out here in the west. I couldn't decide which reason made the most sense. There I was doing it again, letting my mind wander off in some irrelevant philosophical inquiry that no one on earth cared about other than me. As I thought about it, I realized I didn't care that much myself.

Gan instructed us to meet him at two o'clock, less than five minutes from now. The sun was slowly moving westward. Shadows of cactuses and trees were beginning to form and would soon stretch across the desert floor. As I drove, Rhonda looked out the window. "The desert is beautiful, isn't it?"

I nodded. "Yeah, it is."

Devil's Point lay just ahead. It was named Devil's Point because the cluster of rocks sitting on the edge of a deep canyon was capped with a long vertical rock pointing at the sky. Hence, some clever poet in the distant past christened it Devil's Point. There was no end to the wonders to be found in and around Empyrean.

"What in the world is that thing?" yelled Rhonda, pointing at the sky to our right.

I looked out the right window. "It's a kite, a Chinese kite."

As I pulled my truck to a stop, we recognized the man holding the string attached to the kite. It was Gan. The large red kite was rectangular and had squares at each end, giving it the appearance of two boxes floating in tandem. Why Gan chose to be flying a kite at this particular moment was puzzling and bizarre. However, as puzzling and bizarre were perfect descriptors of my life as of late, I gave no further thought to this seemingly insignificant activity. I would soon realize that was a big mistake.

Rhonda and I got out of the truck and walked the fifty or so yards to where Gan stood.

"You like to fly kites?" he asked.

"Actually, I do like to fly kites, but not under these particular circumstances. Where are our friends, Gan?" I asked, feigning a threatening tone.

"You'll see your friends soon. First, I want to fly my kite."

Things were getting crazy again. On the other hand, things had been crazy since the day I got laid off in Detroit. Gan's flying his kite was really no change. I was standing somewhere in the Arizona desert watching an alien from outer space fly a kite. Could things get any crazier? It was a dumb question and I was about find out the answer. Yes, things could.

"Here, you fly the kite," Gan said, handing me the string. Once I had a grip on the string, Gan flashed an evil smile. "Make sure you keep the string tight and the kite stays exactly where it is in the sky. That's very important if you ever want to see your friends again."

As I held the string, I figured I could let it loose at the opportune moment.

"You, sumo wrestler girl, come with me," he ordered. His mood had abruptly changed and was now foul and intimidating.

"You go to hell you ugly jerk!" Rhonda said.

That was not the reply Gan was seeking and his face turned even darker. But, he unexpectedly smiled. "You will do what I say, sexy lady. You will also return the neutron gun you stole from the idiots on the space ship. Give it to me now."

"And what if I don't?" Rhonda snapped.

"Then skinny Herby will die immediately."

Rhonda looked concerned about this prospect however she was

still trying to out-bluff Gan. It wasn't working. "Why is that?" she asked.

"You see that the kite is attached to two strings. Your precious little friend Herby is balanced on the edge of the cliff behind the rocks over there, with one of the strings attached to his waist. The wind from the west is blowing the kite east, oddly enough. The string attached to Herby's belt is trying to pull him east also, and thus over the cliff. The only thing stopping the kite from pulling Herby over the cliff is your friend Stan. Stan must use his string to pull the kite to the west and keep it in its exact position. If Stan lets loose of his string, or if his string should get broken, like if my men over in the bushes shot it in two, then, goodbye Herby."

"And now, we will bid you farewell Stan. My girlfriend and I are leaving. Give me the neutron gun, darling, and remember there will be no tricks. Do something wrong and my men shoot Stan's string and Herby goes over the cliff."

Rhonda reached under her dress for the neutron gun. Gan stretched his neck and strained his eyes to see whatever might be seen. He had a contented smile on his face. He won and he knew it. Rhonda handed him the neutron gun.

"I'm sorry Stan," she said. "Will you let Herby go now, Gan?"

Gan began laughing "No darling, I'm afraid not. But Stan will let him go, sooner or later."

"But you promised," Rhonda screamed. "You promised you'd let Herby go if I gave you the neutron gun and came with you. You promised!"

"No I didn't," replied Gan. "I never said I'd let him go. I just said he would die if you didn't do what I said. "And even if I did promise, I'm a pathological liar and I'd break my promise anyway. Ha, ha, ha," he laughed.

"Well he's going to die if we leave Stan here like this," Rhonda cried.

"Yes, I guess he is," Gan said laughing. "Oh well. Happy landings, Herby. It's all on you, Stan. How long can you hold onto him? It's supposed to get much windier by the way. In fact, the wind is picking up now." He laughed again, enjoying his cleverness.

Having no choice, Rhonda walked with Gan over to the bushes where his men were hiding. He yelled something and then he and Rhonda walked around behind a small hill. I heard a truck start and pull away and dust began blowing behind the bushes as the truck drove southwest on a ranch road off to the right.

That left me holding the kite, fighting to keep it in place so it wouldn't drag poor Herby over the cliff. My arms were beginning to ache. It was a big kite and Gan was right; the wind was growing stronger. There was no one in sight and it was unlikely anyone would be driving out to visit Devil's Point. The wind began to gust. I struggled to control the kite. It dove downward wildly, scaring me that it carried Herby over the cliff. But the kite suddenly climbed straight up and back to its safe position.

My arms throbbed and the string cut into my hands. The gusts were growing stronger, at one point nearly pulling me to the ground. The heavy kite was shooting back and forth across the sky and I was gradually losing control of the red monster.

"Hang on Herby," I shouted, knowing he couldn't hear me above the intermittent moans of the wind.

The kite string cut deeper into my hands and blood seeped from my palms. I kept telling myself the string must remain taut with the kite. If I allowed any slack, the string tied to Herby's waist would immediately tighten and he would be pulled off the cliff. It was becoming much more difficult to handle the kite in the wind's erratic blasts. I had managed to wrap the string around the back of my right elbow to relieve the cutting pressure on my hands and pain in my arms.

Suddenly a powerful draft pushed me forward and whipped the kite into a steep, but brief climb. I held on with all the strength I could muster, leaning backward into the strong breeze. The wind tore at the kite, pushed it wildly to the right and then whipped it back to the left. Without warning, the string snapped and the kite shot eastward and the string attached to Herby drew tight. The kite dove into the canyon and disappeared behind the pine trees.

I started running toward Herby and the canyon, hoping beyond hope that the little guy could hang on for just a few moments. As I ran, I saw the ominous red kite once again shoot skyward above the pine trees on the canyon's edge. Then it plunged into the canyon once more. "Herby's dead!"

As I rounded the corner of the little group of pine trees I could see the kite shoot upward out of the canyon and the string once again become taut. "Thank God. Herby's still alive. He managed to hang on." But as I got closer to the string, I was shocked to see it was not attached to Herby at all. There was no Herby. He'd never even been there. The kite string was attached to a pine tree. Gan had cleverly tricked us and made a fool of me. I was left flying a kite in the desert and he walked off with Rhonda, the neutron gun, and still had Herby and Rock in captivity. I was feeling very stupid.

As I walked over to the pine tree to which the kite string was attached, I noticed a sign leaning against its trunk. I knelt down to read it. It said: "I am a tree. My name is Gary" I was bewildered by this latest absurdity. My first thought was that the sign was left by Gan in an off the wall attempt at humor. On the other hand, I was confident Gan had no sense of humor so I ruled him out. That meant some stand-up comic wannabe with a lot of time on his hands must have left the sign. But why would such a person leave a sign way out here where it would never be read? This made less sense than pondering if Gan had a sense of humor. The only other conclusion was the chilling realization that the tree itself, rather himself as his name was Gary, was responsible for the note.

As I turned to leave, I was startled by another daftness. There was a second sign, this one leaning against a rock. This sign said: "I am a rock. My name is Edgar. P.S. The pine tree is not named Gary. He's lying. His real name is Martin."

Wishing to get out of there as quickly as possible, I started walking again. Then I saw a third sign, this one leaning against a cholla cactus. This one said: "I am a cholla cactus. My name is Elaine. I wouldn't trust the rock if I were you."

My god, was there no end to it? I was walking away even more quickly now, and as I looked over my shoulder, I could see the red boxy kite wildly climbing and diving like a fighter plane in its own imaginary dog fight.

Then I began thinking about poor Rhonda and how I let her down. I always blame myself when things go wrong, no doubt because of my guilt laden Catholic upbringing. Tornadoes, hurricanes, yeah it's me. I caused them. But I reasoned it wasn't my fault that Gan had gotten the best of us. He was shrewd. Besides, I can learn from this experience. Nuts! I screwed up.

25

We All Knew; We Just Didn't Tell You

It was nearly dark when I got back to town. There were no lights on inside the office so I parked my truck and went down to the Rio Malo to have a beer. As I walked through the door of the saloon, Bud, as usual, acknowledged me with his most ungracious nod. Why do I come here? The place was crowded, but I spotted Manfred, Galen and Thigpen sitting at a table in the back of the room. As I got closer to their table, I noticed a fourth beer on the table. Then I saw Dog Mayor's little black head peeping over the table top. He'd been hidden by the glass of beer. I pulled up a chair and sat down next to Thigpen.

It was then I saw a tall, clear glass filled with a light bluish concoction. The blue liquid, which represented the ocean, was topped off with a tropical display of a section of upside down dark green lime representing an island into which were stuck a red umbrella and a green plastic palm tree appearing blown over by the wind. Small pieces of peanut shells symbolizing capsized boats were floating upside down in the bluish micro-ocean. Red maraschino cherry juice was poured over everything.

That someone would order a tropical drink in the middle of the desert would be judged rather odd in any town other than Empyrean. I later learned the boutique cocktail was called a "THAV," an acronym for Tsunami, Hurricane and Volcano, and not coincidentally, also the name of a Norwegian goddess with a serious grudge against males. I shuddered as it dawned on me whom that triple catastrophe, man-hating beverage and empty chair awaited.

Latisha Wimberly walked up to the table. "Hello, Stan," she said.

I turned around as Latisha bent over to hug me. Although I was initially surprised she would be here in Empyrean, I realized I was actually glad to see her. I gave her a sincere hug in return.

"I think you're actually glad to see me, Stan."

"Yes, I'm happy you're here."

"After our last phone conversation I decided I had to come. Things looked like they were getting interesting."

"Latisha walked into our office earlier," said Thigpen. "By the way, how did it go out there, a...........?"

"Stan, Larry. My name is Stan."

There was a perplexed look on Thigpen's face. "Yeah, I knew that. You didn't change your name recently did you, Stan?"

"No, my name has always been Stan."

"So how did it go, Stan?" Thigpen asked again. The suspicious look on his face signaled he thought I was lying to him about changing my name.

Larry was having one of his "short of memory cell" days. He would straighten things out in an hour or two, but I answered his question.

"As you know, I'm not a detail man. So if you don't count Rhonda's getting kidnapped and me flying a kite while it happened, I would call it a successful day." Everyone at the table, even Dog Mayor, suddenly had shocked expressions on their faces. I did see that detail. "What?" I asked.

"Oh Stan," the Dog Mayor replied rolling his eyes, "tell me you didn't fall for that old trick of handing off the kite string with the guy on the edge of the cliff thing."

Apparently, everyone at the table knew about that trick but me. Where had I been all my life? This was unbelievable.

"Stanley," Latisha said. "You didn't."

I was embarrassed "Yeah, I'm afraid I did fall for Gan's trick."

I thought about it, momentarily envisioning my reacting to my tablemates with an explosion of exasperation and guilt, reminiscent of an argument with my father. But instead of repeatedly screaming damn, my customary reply to him, I opted for a more civil response. "Why haven't I ever heard of the kite string trick?" I screamed in my loudest voice.

There was immediate silence in the entire saloon and everyone in the place was now looking at me. Random chuckles started and were followed by giggles, then outright laughter. "He never heard of the kite string trick," someone hollered. Not having a beer in front of me, I grabbed the Dog Mayor's nearly full brew and chugged it. Other than the dog food taste on the rim of the glass, the beer afforded some comfort. My chugging the beer provided even more unintended amusement for the crowd, but after what seemed like five or six hours, the laughter subsided.

In an effort to change the subject, I decided to relay the other happenings of the day. That also turned out to be a mistake. "On the bright side, I did meet a pine tree named Gary."

"You met Gary?" said Thigpen. "Hey, how's he doin' anyway?" My God, how does he know Gary? I mean, who has a pine tree in their circle of friends? Even though I knew it would compound the lunacy, my curiosity as to how Thigpen made the acquaintance of a pine tree was so overwhelming I had to ask.

"How did you happen to meet Gary?" I inquired.

"Oh, I know Elaine the cactus. She introduced us. Elaine's a hoot. You gotta' meet her, Stan."

"I did meet Elaine, Larry."

"Oh," Thigpen said, his look of disappointment indicating he felt he should have been the one to introduce us.

"Edgar the rock said Gary the pine tree is lying about his name," I said. "His real name is Martin. What about that?"

Thigpen looked at me with a serious expression. "If you believed Edgar the rock, it's no wonder you got hoodwinked by Gan the Salabian." I couldn't stand any more of this deranged conversation. I wanted to think Thigpen was joking with me, however, from the sincerity of his voice I concluded that he actually considered a pine tree and a cactus to be his friends. I was getting ready to leave but, as usual, I wasn't fast enough. With my escape cut off, I found myself in the middle of yet another drama.

At the next table sat the five ever present black clad geriatric gunslingers. The recent addition to their outlaw table, Nhoame, alias "Crazy Eddie," was sitting with them. Tonight, they seemed to be glaring more menacingly than I'd ever seen them glare before. Obviously there was some kind of problem they were itching to resolve. "Crazy Eddie" was trying to calm them but not having any luck.

That I was the source of their consternation was immediately evident. Black Bart put down the cards he was holding and stared at me in silence. Then he slowly pushed his chair back and stood up, his eyes glaring directly into mine. Things didn't appear to be going well this evening. Black Bart looked dark and evil, just as one would expect a man to look if he had a thick, full moustache, was dressed completely in black, and had a huge six gun hanging from his waist. And he was walking toward me.

Luckily the waitress, the smart-alecky one, walked up on my left to take my order just as Black Bart arrived to stand next to me on my right side. I had never been claustrophobic, but I was now. It also had become very warm. I ordered a beer then changed my order to two beers. I assumed that the black clad gunslinger to my right, operating under some ancient code of the west, figured it was his ongoing job to make things mighty unpleasant for somebody, that being me.

I pretended not to notice him standing next to me. Everyone else at the table couldn't help but notice him. They looked at him, then at me. Then they looked back at him and then at me. This could go on forever. I turned to face my unwanted visitor.

"Hello, Black Bart," I said smiling. It was not the greeting he wanted to hear.

"Don't hello Black Bart me, Pardner." That he called me Pardner was not good either. (For some unknown reason, in the West they say Pardner as opposed to Partner.) "What does he expect? I couldn't say "Hello Black Bart" to anyone else in the saloon because I was certain no one else in the saloon was named Black Bart. After thinking about that for a moment, I remembered anything was possible in Empyrean. Not only was there undoubtedly someone else in the saloon named Black Bart, I shouldn't be surprised if it happened to be the petite blond sitting just three tables from ours who also shared that moniker.

"Okay, what's wrong, Black Bart?" I asked.

"You, Pardner. You're wrong. You're all wrong."

There it was, that pardner thing again. This was definitely not good. When a man with a six gun calls you pardner, it means he's about to kill you.

"What's wrong?" I asked again. For once, I thought I was completely innocent, but Black Bart didn't share that opinion.

"Where's our friends Herby and Rock?"

I looked over at Crazy Eddie (Nhoame), but he just shrugged his shoulders. He gave me a sympathetic look, but I was on my own. I never realized that Herby and Rock were good friends of the ancient outlaw gang. The gunslingers missed these guys and wanted to know what happened to them.

"Herby and Rock are being held captive by Gan the Salabian at the Chinese compound. The Chinese eunuch vampire warriors kidnapped them a couple of days ago."

"Yeah, I know all that," Black Bart replied, "but I thought you were going to get them back today. Then I saw you walk in here without Rock and Herby, and now Rhonda's missing too."

I thought he was getting ready to call a lynch mob together

because I failed to rescue Herby and Rock. Surprisingly, he didn't.

"Let me tell you something, Pardner," he continued, "you figure out what you're gonna do next. We're mighty unhappy about our friends being kidnapped and we want to get them back. When you figure things out, you come and see us. You got five of the fastest guns in the west sitting ten feet from you. We'll help you go get them. You savvy, Pardner?"

He said "partner" and "savvy." Those were two no-nonsense words if I ever heard two no-nonsense words. But that was good news. I knew we would have to go to the Chinese compound and take on Yao Wie, Gan and thirty-nine other warriors. We would need all the help we could get.

"I'll tell you what, Black Bart, I'll do just as you say, pardner." I thought that by throwing in the pardner word it would somehow validate my machismo, let him know that I was united with them in masculinity and bravado.

"Yeah, sure you will, Chester Arthur" he said with a sarcastic smile. Then he turned and went back to his table.

"What is this fixation with obscure American presidents?" I asked Dog Mayor and the four people at my table.

"I'll answer that," Galen said.

"No you won't," Manfred said. And that was the end of it.

"Don't let Black Bart bother you," Thigpen said. "We'll figure this thing out."

It was Galen who now surprised everyone as he began his discourse. "Look people, the only way to handle this is to make a fail-proof plan. Is everyone up for that?" Of course, everyone was. "Before we start, everyone must agree to keep our plan totally secret. Our success in rescuing our friends depends on complete secrecy. "Does everyone agree to do that?" Yes, they all agreed to that, particularly since the rest of us had no other plan.

Galen continued. "We know that Rock, Rhonda and Herby are at the Chinese compound. Stan and Latisha think Nancy Nussbaum is there too. We have to go there and get them." He didn't wait for a response. "The only question is how we do that. I think I have an idea."

"What is it?" Dog Mayor asked.

"Yeah, what is it Galen?" Manfred followed up.

We all knew Manfred's silence was due to his usual strategy of not getting into especially crazy discussions. He was therefore silent most of the time due to the sheer number of off the menu dialogues.

Galen talked on. "Okay, number one, we know that we have a secret weapon, my genus siestacillus. Number two, the only thing we need to do is round up some men to go with us to raid the place. And the good thing is we don't need many men because the genus siestacillus will put the Chinese eunuch vampire warriors and Gan to sleep."

"Yeah, it will put us to sleep too," Manfred said. "The winner of the battle will be whoever wakes up first."

"There you go again, Manfred," Galen said. "My mind moves so fast you can never keep up with me." Manfred rolled his eyes as Galen continued. "I purchased special World War One Army surplus gas masks we will wear. The siestacillus mixture won't affect us."

"When Galen demonstrated his genus siestacillus the other day, we all ended up in the hospital," I said to Latisha, bringing her up to date on our progress.

"I apologize for putting everyone to sleep at my office," Galen quickly added. It was important to Galen to preserve his scholarly affectation in front of Latisha. "I got a little overzealous in my demonstration. Before I released the compound into the air, I should have had everyone put on the special gas masks instead of merely holding their noses."

"No kidding," Thigpen said.

"As I was saying," Galen continued, "we will secretly gather a group of men tomorrow. There will be the five of us, the five outlaw guys plus Nhoame, and maybe the sheriff could round up an impromptu posse."

"Galen," I said, "the sheriff won't let us raid the Chinese compound, let alone go with us when we do. He's not authorized to act against them because it has 'embassy status.'"

Galen, as expected, had an answer. "Stan, if someone witnessed a U.S. citizen being kidnapped and taken into an embassy, the sheriff is authorized to search the place. I got hold of the special agreement the Chinese compound has with the government. The sheriff not only can, but must go in and rescue the U.S. citizen. You witnessed Rhonda being kidnapped. That's all he needs. That agreement was signed back in 1853?"

"Good job, Galen," I said. "I didn't realize the agreement was signed in 1853 but, of course, I didn't care. But I did care and was embarrassed to see that he had gotten far more done than me.

"Okay," Galen said. "We won't tell anyone what we're going to do. We'll sleep on it tonight. Tomorrow, we'll go with the plan unless someone comes up with a better one. We'll meet at your office first thing in the morning, Stan. Then, in a lightning fast move, we'll round up all our men and Desert Chickadee. I know she'll want to go. Stan, I see that Virgil has your UFO Tour Van repaired. It holds eight people I believe. Manfred will have to drive too. The five gunslingers will ride in Stan's van with Thigpen and Latisha. That's the eight for your car."

"I'll ride with Manfred, Desert Chickadee and Nhoame. "The sheriff and his posse will follow behind us in another car. I'll have enough genus siestacillus masks for everyone. Is that agreed?"

"What about me?" Dog Mayor asked. "I should go too since I'm the mayor of the ...." A bark slipped out and then another. "Since I'm the mayor of the town, I meant to say. Besides, I need to get my human body back."

"Dog Mayor's right," Manfred said. "He needs to get his human body back so he can run the town. The town needs him."

"Mayor, you can ride with me if you can you stay out of the way?" I said. "No offense meant but, at ten pounds, you're not the most formidable of fighting machines."

"I'll stay out of the way," Dog Mayor said, "but, I intend to get Gan, one way or the other."

26

Commandos in High Heels and other Formidable Warriors

By eight a.m. everyone was in the office. Dog Mayor slept in the office overnight as had Thigpen and I. Galen and Manfred arrived together in Manfred's car, unusual because they never cared much for each other even though they were brothers-in-law. I got the coffee brewing and Galen, who had taken the temporary leadership role to everyone's amazement, began the meeting.

"Okay everybody, did anyone come up with a better idea than the one we agreed on last night?"

No one volunteered a better plan so by default Galen's plan was in operation.

"Well, I made up a fresh Zuyglyphen genus siestacillus grenade. That will put everyone in the compound to sleep without any trouble. I have a burlap bag outside with twenty-five anti-genus siestacillus masks, including a cute little pink one for you, your honor."

"Thanks Galen. If you weren't doing such a good job I'd probably have more to say about that."

"I'm sure you would, Mayor," Galen said.

"Okay, the only other thing we have to do is get our commandos together. We'll do that in a few minutes, at nine o'clock exactly. Remember, we have to keep everything totally secret until the last minute. Everything from here on will be done on an impromptu basis and taking everyone by surprise. We'll head over to the saloon and get the outlaw gentlemen and Nhoame. Then we'll get the sheriff and whatever kind of a posse he can muster. Everything must be spur of the moment. It's very hard to keep a secret in Empyrean."

Galen was right about that. Nothing happened here that the entire town didn't know about in less than an hour. That made for a lot of very embarrassing moments depending on what might have occurred you didn't want everyone else to know about. Say you secretly began---on second thought, let's not go with that. Anyway, you couldn't get away with much around here.

"Stan, do you have your van ready to go?"

"Right on, Galen. I checked it out last night and it runs great.

Virgil even cleaned it up."

"Okay," Galen continued, "Manfred's car is ready to go too. Here's how to put on the Zuyglyphen anti-genus siestacillus masks." Galen pulled an antique-looking device out of his coat pocket to demonstrate. What he was showing us was a modified World War One gas mask, not the latest in technology, but sufficient, Galen assured us. To say the thing was bizarre looking would be an understatement.

"The black rubber device is worn over the face and held on by straps in back of one's head," Galen said. "It is essentially a mask with two large, glass covered oval eye features and a protruding, snout-like, round metal mouth feature with a circular ring of twenty small breathing holes around its outer rim. The small snout-like flap extends from the center of the mask and rests on the nose."

I put on my mask and stared at the masks the others had put on. When looking directly at the wearer of the mask, it appears one is looking into the face of a giant insect. The mask is hot and has a pungent, unpleasant odor.

It was time to gather our commandoes for our surprise assault on the Chinese compound. Galen had his Zuyglyphen genus siestacillus grenade stowed in his heavy wool sport coat pocket. If it was Galen's intent to keep the grenade and himself warm, the wool coat would accomplish that objective. The temperature was going to soar to over one hundred degrees today.

However, Galen's only intent in wearing the absurd apparel was to maintain his professorial dignity, which would validate his righteousness in this nasty business we were about to undertake. The rest of us were dressed in shorts, tee shirts and sneakers. The Dog Mayor, of course, was not.

I pulled our Deluxe UFO Tour Company van up in front of the office to load our first group of commandos. Latisha, Thigpen and Dog Mayor climbed into the war wagon. With Manfred, Galen and Desert Chickadee following, we immediately headed for the saloon to pick up the five ancient outlaws and Nhoame from their usual table.

The Rio Malo Saloon was only three blocks away and we arrived in less than a minute. Galen told Desert Chickadee to wait in the car while he, Manfred, Dog Mayor and I walked into the saloon to alert our outlaw friends that an attack on the Chinese compound was underway. Bud scowled at us.

As luck would have it, the sheriff was also in the saloon. Judging by his attire however, he was not there on official business. Or maybe he was. Whichever, he had come to the saloon in order to practice some songs for next Friday night's karaoke competition. He intended to win once again. The sheriff was dressed in female attire including a blonde wig, gigantic purple pirate hat with a skull and crossbones emblem on its front, a bright, silky see through chartreuse blouse and a black bra showing from underneath. More horrific were the bright red silk short shorts and black fish net stockings. The six inch green rhinestone high heels completed the outfit. He wasn't especially ferocious looking, or maybe he was.

"Bud, give me a quick beer," I said, unable to handle the sight of a cross dressed commando with hairy legs that early in the morning. To be clear, I had no particular objection to cross dressing from an aesthetic perspective, however, from a military standpoint, combining a clumsy female costume with the role of "killing-machine commando" seemed a major disconnect. I was thinking the enemy would not be intimidated, although his outfit gave me a considerable scare.

Bud gave me the beer and I drank it. The sheriff didn't look any better. What the sheriff wore might have been flattering on a young woman, although I doubt it. It was nothing less than grotesque on a fifty-six year old man with a pot belly. He was just finishing his song.

"Hit me with another beer, Bud," I demanded. Knowing I was on my way to do battle with Chinese eunuch vampire warriors, Bud said, "this one's on the house."

"Thanks." I quaffed it down but the sheriff still didn't look any better. Sensing our lack of appreciation for his artistic efforts, the sheriff greeted us with something less than a warm welcome.

"What the hell do you people want? Can't you see that I'm busy?"

Galen, still relishing his temporary leadership role, replied, "Sheriff, we need your help. The Chinese people from the compound have kidnapped a U. S. citizen, Rhonda Wilkenshaver. We are requesting you put a posse together and help us get her back. Our outlaw friends over there will provide the back-up in case there's trouble."

At that moment Howard Winklethorpe, my would-be seductress who was actually a seductor, swooshed in the door of the saloon.

She, rather he, executed a three hundred and sixty degree turn so her, rather his, bright yellow skirt covered with orange polka dots would poof up to its widest expanse. It emphasized its wearer's entrance into the conversation of us unbalanced souls.

"Give me another Bud, beer," I pleaded, no longer caring about the order of my words.

He did. I drank it. Things were looking a little better, but not the sheriff. Howard pulled off the female impersonation best. What else could I say? He fooled me. That's all I'll ever say about it again.

The fact that Howard was here, complete with a blonde wig and six inch high heels, sort of balanced things out, but not especially for the better. Even Howard's bright red sequins didn't help. Ever the equestrienne, Howard had on his best Kentucky Derby outfit that included a bright red "Derby-Day" hat. Howard, too, intended to compete in the karaoke competition. He had spent the last two days rehearsing "My Old Kentucky Home."

"Howard, you're in the posse," the sheriff ordered. "By the way, you look lovely today."

Yes, things actually did seem balanced out for the better. It was the beer talking.

"Howard, did you bring your car?" the sheriff asked. "Deputy Nostradamus has my squad car over at the car wash."

"He has a deputy named Nostradamus?" I asked myself. I don't know why I asked myself. I didn't know the answer to the question.

"I need Bud another beer," I said, grasping for the proper word sequence.

He gave it to me. I drank it. For some reason, he gave me a can of beer instead of a glass this time. I didn't ask him why, assuming the explanation would inevitably morph into some transcendental analysis of why his mother still spanked him when he was twenty-three years old. Was this really my fourth beer? Things actually were looking better with each successive drink. I poured it into my empty glass, "to add a little class," I told myself.

"Beer, give me another, Bud," I demanded.

He gave it to me. I drank it. Even Bar the budtender was lookin' good. My level of concern about speaking properly had completely vanished. As long as I said all the words, it didn't matter what the hell order I said them in.

"Sheriff," Galen said, "can't you find more men? We need all the help we can get."

The sheriff pulled his cell phone out of the holster attached to his red silk short shorts. "René," he yelled, "get your tail over to the saloon right away!" There was a pause. "I don't care what you're wearing. Get over here immediately. We're getting ready to move out." There was another pause. "Well screw you too, René."

I was now drinking my fifth or maybe sixth glass of beer and found myself wandering off into another philosophical discourse. The question of whether a glass is half full or half empty still plagued me. But, how do we really know? I mean, from what point do we measure? Does a full glass mean full from the very top of the glass itself? It seems to me the most likely place to measure from would be the point on the glass at which the beer was at when it was initially served.

But if so, then the observation could legitimately be made that a full glass of beer down through the recorded history of the world was never really a full glass of beer at all. That's because all beers are served with a quarter to half inch gap between the top of the beer and the top of the glass.

In that case, billions of glasses of beer represented as full glasses of beer, but which were actually only ninety-five percent full, have been served to people all over the world from the beginning of time. That would mean a massive class action law suit, the likes of which has never been seen by the world-wide judicial community, is long overdue. That just goes to prove the point I made early on. True justice can always be found in a beer glass at a bar.

Government Agent René Orbostrowski arrived in a few minutes. It needn't be pointed out that as the commando invasion group increased in the number of people, the collective sanity level of the group decreased. Mathematically speaking, the increase in the aggregate quantity of the group was directly proportional to the decrease in the aggregate sanity of the group. René, also a cross dressing karaoke competitor, refused to be outdone. He was wearing bright red lipstick and a fluorescent green wig with a blue streak through its middle. This gave his head the appearance of an extraterrestrial skunk from the planet Strangero.

In a futile effort to be sexy, he wore the proverbial little black dress, which noticeably contrasted, with his big white body. The shoulder straps of the black dress were attached to its front by safety pins, indicating they had burst at some point earlier as he tried to slip the dress on his inconveniently large body. His black patent leather shoes worked nicely however. René planned to compete in the karaoke competition as a torch singer going by the stage name of Flame Amore.

I ordered my seventh, or was it fifth, or maybe sixth Bud, from Bar, the beertender. For some reason, just before Bud gave me the beer, he turned and faced the other direction for a moment. Then he handed me the beer. I didn't realize that when Bud turned his back on me, he shook the beer vigorously. Naturally, when I popped the top, the beer exploded from the can and shot all over everyone within five feet of me.

"I told you to never say, Hey Bud, give me a Bud. That ain't funny."

I didn't remember saying that, probably because I was too distracted worrying about the outlandish composition of our invasion force. Besides, Bud always thought everything was about him. Oh well, I didn't need to worry whether the can was half full or half empty because it was immediately empty when I chugged the few drops left in the can after the beerplosion. That was a new word I just made up.

Dog Mayor had rousted the five black clad outlaws and Crazy Eddie (Nhoame) from their table. They enthusiastically joined in and were ready to go. That was literally the case for Cole Younger and Jesse James who, like most elderly men, always have to use the restroom before they leave.

Suddenly, the saloon door burst open behind me. I was afraid to turn around to see what new calamity was now appearing on the scene. As it turned out I didn't need to. That gave me a precious moment to order my seventh beer, which Bud happily served me, disregarding the fact that I was the driver of the Deluxe UFO Tour Company war wagon. A shrill, grating voice rang out across the saloon like the synchronous wailing of a dozen cats in mid-fornication on the front porch at midnight. It was the unmistakable screeching of Desert Chickadee.

"What the hell are you people doing, Elliott?" she shrieked at Sheriff Landers. "My baby daughter is out there in the desert imprisoned by space aliens and you're here singing karaoke. Nice outfit by the way. Shave your damn legs, Elliott. I told you about that. Let's get going people."

That was the proverbial kick in the pants we all needed. I was too drunk to turn around and salute Desert Chickadee. Actually, I was too drunk just to turn around. As far as moving faster, I had already concluded the mission to rescue Rhonda, Rock and Herby would end in a total disaster so I just waved at her without looking. My seventh, or whatever number, beer was going down well. Even though the rescue mission was doomed to failure, at least I would get a good drunk out of it. We were ready to go.

The convoy was quickly assembled out in front of Bud's Rio Malo. Our Tour Bus would lead the way. Because I was much too drive to drunk, as I needn't have pointed out to anyone, Thgipen helped me get to the van and installed me in the right front seat to ride shotgun, even though I didn't actually have one. Thigpen would drive. Latisha and Dog Mayor would ride in the second seat, as would Cole Younger. Jesse, Billy, Black Bart, and Butch Cassidy would squeeze into the third seat. That was all we could carry.

Manfred drove his car, which carried Galen, Desert Chickadee and Nhoame.

The third assault vehicle, Howard Winklethorpe's pink Cadillac convertible, carried Sheriff Elliott Landers and Special Government Agent René Orbostrowski. All three men were dressed in their "karaoke competition duds," not having time to change into more "commando-like" attire. As I sat with my alcohol induced daze watching them struggle getting into the Cadillac, I wondered how they would fight the Chinese warriors. In addition to trying to keep their balance while wearing six inch heels, they would have to hold onto their wigs as they travelled in the convertible.

Other than the six-shooters the old outlaws carried, the only other weapon our commando group carried was Galen's siestacillus grenade. None of the lawmen brought a gun because guns were not suitable accessories. If the siestacillus grenade failed to roust the Chinese eunuch vampire warriors, the fight would end quickly.

Thigpen had wisely ordered three cups of black coffee for me. Then he confessed that, after my third beer, Bud was serving me some kind of non-alcoholic, lemon colored soda water. Instead of the seven beers I thought I consumed, I had, in fact, only drunk three, which is the most I can usually handle anyway. "We need you sober to lead this outfit, Stan," Thigpen said. "Don't blame Bud. I told him to do it."

"Thanks for taking care of me Larry," recalling that after my third beer Bud started serving me cans of what I mistakenly thought were beer. Instead, he was giving me cans of a special Mommy Drink he invented. "The Mommy Drink was invented by Bud as part of what was ultimately a colossal marketing disaster," Thigpen said. "Bud decided he wanted to expand his customer base and bring young mothers and their offspring into the saloon so he developed this drink for young mothers called Lemonagator.

Thigpen explained the Lemonagator" was a tasty enough drink, with the added benefit of having very few calories. However, in what was meant to be a clever tool for "mommies to keep their kids behaving good," as Bud phrased it, he designed special artwork for the side of the can. Ultimately, it was this artwork that undid the short-lived marketing campaign.

Displayed on every can was the name of the drink, Lemonagator, as well a picture of a bright yellow lemon with a large, open mouth filled with sharp teeth. The lemon monster had kangaroo-like legs, an alligator mouth, and was shown in the act of pouncing on a terrified child who was running for his life and screaming. This disturbing depiction was followed by the caption, "Shut up, Kid, or Mommy will throw you down the chute to Uncle Bud's basement and the Lemonagator will eat you."

Bud's logic was that the Mommies had to be able to relax and enjoy their drinks and they couldn't do so unless their kids behaved. Therefore, if the kid misbehaved, all Mommy had to do was show the 'bad kid" the side of the Lemonagator can. Then she could threaten him or her with being immediately gulped down by the monster in the basement if they didn't straighten out. This did not go well with the Mommies in the focus group. They gathered in the semblance of a lynch mob in front of the Rio Malo, ropes in hand and intent on hanging Bud. Bud concluded he would stick with his regular clientele and forget about trying to bring in disagreeable mommies as customers.

So Bud used the Lemonagator soda pop as beer substitutes for those who consumed too much and needed to be cut off. It was those four cans of soda that were having their own adverse effects. I had to stop several times to use the men's room in the guise of large saguaro cactuses. Now that I realized I hadn't actually consumed seven beers, I sobered up immediately.

During one of these stops, Manfred told me Galen didn't want to be the leader anymore. He was suddenly getting fearful, as were we all. He was sure he could handle the siestacillus grenade but, the leadership role was just too much for him.

"Tell Galen it's okay," I replied. I had already planned to take over when we got to the compound. I let Galen have a free hand in the planning because I've never been a detail man. However, I am pretty good at being able to get things done. We're going to rescue our friends Rhonda, Rock and Herby and my ex-wife. "We're going to win!"

27

Mutiny Aboard a UFO

When the evil Gan kidnapped Rhonda at Devil's Point he drove her back to the Chinese compound to show off his prize to Yao Wie. Yao Wie, however, wanted no part of this nasty business, fearing it would stir up trouble with the local population of Empyrean. That, of course, is exactly what happened when I returned to town after cleverly extricating myself from Gan's kite hostage trick. However, as Gan stood talking with Yao Wie, he had to make a decision as to where he would imprison Rhonda.

"You keep her here for awhile, Yao Wie," he ordered. "I've got other problems to handle and I'm too busy to deal with her right now."

"Oh no you don't, Wall Street guy," he replied. "She your problem. You Wall Street guys make problem then want somebody fix for you. You get her out of here before locals make trouble too."

Being called a Wall Street guy was the worst name anyone could be called. Gan had no choice other than take Rhonda to his space ship. To arrange his and Rhonda's beam-up to the oval shaped craft hovering overhead, he dialed Commander Zwie on his "Buzzy the Space Guy" secret transmitter. Incredibly, what had been a child's toy in the 1950's, was in reality a totally functional Inter-galactic communicator capable of contacting other Buzzy the Space Guy secret transmitters over millions of light years away. Even after all this time, it was by far the most reliable communicator in operation.

Kids who used the Buzzy transmitter in the 1950's were not aware that when they spoke into their transmitters, the voices answering them were real space aliens who didn't realize there was life on planet Earth. The kids thought the hollow voice sounds coming from the transmitters were recorded and part of the toy itself.

Of course, the fallout from the 1950's invention of Buzzy the Space Guy secret transmitter was the 1950's Flying Saucer epidemic. It was no coincidence that within sixty days of Buzzy the Space Guy secret transmitters being introduced in toy stores across the country, flying saucers were first spotted. Children using the transmitters inadvertently notified space aliens from thousands of galaxies that planet Earth was inhabited. "Come on down," was the implicit invitation.

Incredibly, national security was very lax in those days and the government didn't monitor technology being shipped out of the country let alone, off the planet. So, when one million of the Buzzy-the Space Guy secret transmitters were ordered by a Mr. John Doe in Hays, Kansas in early 1950, no red flags went up. Even when Mr. John Doe paid for the shipment of the one million-Buzzy the Space Guy-secret transmitters with a box of diamonds whose value was far greater than the price of the "Buzzies," as they are affectionately known, no alarms went off. But that's another story and I am digressing from the crisis at hand.

Gan's space ship was manned by the same four aliens who allowed Rhonda to escape with the neutron gun over two years earlier. In an effort to promote diversity, Gan had appointed male aliens from two different galaxies to be members of his space ship's crew. His diversity initiative did not include women. From the beginning, things did not go well. The two crewmen from Galaxy Andromeda III absolutely despised the two crewmen from Galaxy Centaurus A. However, the Centaurus A crewmen thought the Andromeda III crewmen looked funny. And, of course, Andromeda III crewmen did look funny, but not any funnier than Centaurus A crewmen.

Adding to the galactic discord, Andromeda III crewmen spoke with a deep drawl because they were from southern galaxies. Centaurus A crewmen could not understand Andromeda III crewmen when they spoke because of their accent. The problems were endless and Gan, not being the most empathetic of bosses, was completely incapable of finding some middle ground and promoting harmony.

Commander Zwie arranged for the immediate beam-up of Gan and Rhonda. Once on board, Gan had Rhonda tied to a chair and called a crew meeting. Normally a typical space ship would be manned by an eight person crew. The size of space ships had been decreased considerably to save on fuel. Because of cut backs in the Inter-galactic Conquest Departmental budget, the number of crew was also reduced by fifty percent. Even with the space ship's diminished size, the smaller crew meant an increased workload on each man causing a great deal of complaining and bickering.

Before Gan could get into his own agenda, which was the incarceration procedure for prisoners such as Rhonda, Commander Zwie requested to speak before the group. He detailed the crew complaints and the difficulty of operating the space ship with a four man crew. Of course, there was no way to resolve this manpower problem because the personnel office was two million light years away.

This was, Gan pointed out, similar to the location of personnel departments of American companies. In fact, he further revealed, all personnel departments of every organization in the Universe are actually located together on one planet at a secret location in the far reaches of space. Oh yeah, they're hidden behind a huge curtain of dark matter and a galaxy sized moat of black holes. That prevents anyone from ever contacting them.

But all that was actually irrelevant because Gan already knew that no additional crew would be authorized because of the strict manning levels dictated by said personnel people. Unfortunately, the nearly five hour meeting ended with absolutely nothing being accomplished. This meeting was exactly the same as meetings on Earth. Other than the main speaker becoming self-orgasmic as he or she spewed forth pseudo-wisdom, nothing productive ever comes out of any meeting. However, because of the constant bitching of the greatly dissatisfied crew members, Gan not only didn't get his chance to experience self-induced verbal orgasm, he never got a chance to outline his revised incarceration procedures. This would work to Rhonda's advantage.

When Rhonda was abducted two years earlier she was held captive for several days. While going through the usual examinations conducted by aliens aboard the UFO's, Rhonda made it a point to study her captors. She learned their routines, their inter-personal relationships, and she looked for an opening, an opportunity to escape. What Rhonda realized early on was that these aliens were highly sophisticated, almost to a fault. While they had advanced to a point where they were attuned to the very complex aspects of life in the universe and the highly technical, they had long ago discarded very simple concepts and contrivances from their consciousness. In other words, while they would immediately recognize very elaborate, complicated pranks or ruses, they could be fooled by very basic tricks.

Once Rhonda figured out that weakness, she made her move. In fact, it was Commander Zwie himself whom Rhonda tricked. Rhonda had waited until only Commander Zwie was in the compartment with her. She then asked him if she could be untied in order to use the ladies' room, even though there was not a ladies' room per se on board the space ship.

"Why don't you have a ladies' room on the space ship?" she asked.

"We only have a ladies' room on the mother ship," Commander Zwie replied.

Commander Zwie untied Rhonda immediately, recognizing an emergency when he saw one. As Rhonda stood up however, she screamed, "Who's that behind you?" When he turned around to look, Rhonda grabbed the neutron gun hanging on the wall and pointed it at Commander Zwie. She was now in control and forced the crew to land the space ship in Desert Chickadee's back yard. Rhonda exited the ship, keeping the neutron gun for any future needs.

Now, two years later, Rhonda was once again pondering her escape strategy when Gan got an emergency call from Yao Wie. Gan had given Yao Wie his own personal Buzzy the Space Guy secret transmitter and Yao Wie was presently screaming into it.

"You Wall Street dumb guy. Locals at compound gate now. Ask about Rhonda just like I tell you. You come and get them out here. I no talk them. Having lunch and go play golf. No time handle your mess."

"Settle down, Yao Wie. I will be there in a few minutes. Don't worry. I'll take care of them."

Gan figured he had some time before he had to leave. Several years ago he had purchased a set of motivational management DVD's entitled "Dealing with a Disgruntled Team." He called the crew together and told them they must spend at least three hours a day watching the DVD's until they finished all thirty-six of them. That would mean there would be one hundred and eight hours of training for each man that would more than satisfy the total annual individual training hours required by the personnel department. Commander Zwie then beamed Gan down to the Chinese compound.

Rhonda, in the meantime, had decided on the strategy for her escape. She would once again wait until Gan left the space ship. Then she would watch for the moment when she could somehow dupe the four aliens into a distraction. Several minutes later, Gan made his exit and she was now alone in the compartment with the four aliens who were sitting at the conference table attentively watching their training DVD's. Rhonda heard the pleasant female voice say "Empower yourself to make sure your co-workers have a nice day. Their happiness is your responsibility. Likewise, your own happiness is your co-workers' responsibility. If you make them happy they will pay you back tenfold."

"I already try to make everybody happy all the time," alien number one said. Nobody ever tries to make me happy."

"You never try to make anybody happy," alien number two replied. "And you never do your share of the work."

Rhonda decided now was the time to make her move. As alien number two was facing her, she addressed her comment to him. "He said you never do your share of the work," Rhonda blurted, nodding her head in incrimination toward alien number three.

"I never said that," replied alien number three.

Rhonda shook her head up and down at alien number two, indicating that alien number three did too say that and he was lying.

"Stop arguing right now," Commander Zwie ordered.

"You order people around too much," alien number three replied.

Suddenly, alien number three punched alien number two, while simultaneously proclaiming that everybody from the Centaurus A galaxy was stupid.

"You're a galactic racist!" alien number two shouted back. "That's worse than a Wall Street guy." Calling someone worse than a Wall Street guy was so disgraceful and insulting that all four aliens suddenly froze in mid-motion and became completely silent.

Commander Zwie, still shaken by alien number two's caustic insult, suddenly threw the glass of blue liquid he had been drinking into alien number two's face and all four men began wrestling on the floor and pounding each other with strange looking fists formed by their elongated fingers.

Rhonda managed to slip her hands out of the ropes tied around her wrists. Strangely, she was in the same compartment of the ship and tied to exactly the same chair to which she had been tied two years earlier. Conveniently, the same neutron gun was mounted on the wall less than three feet from her chair. Now free, she stood up and grabbed the familiar neutron gun.

"Stop right now," Rhonda ordered the brawling aliens. "I'm in control of the ship. You, Commander Zwie, tie up your friends, that is, those who used to be your friends. You know the drill."

A horrified Commander Zwie did indeed know the drill. He also knew Gan would be furious, but that was all secondary at this point. Right now, he had to worry about the unhappy blond sumo wrestler pointing a neutron gun at him.

"Bring the Chinese compound up on your surveillance screens, now!" Rhonda ordered.

Commander Zwie quickly followed Rhonda's command. For some reason, he suddenly remembered the motivational DVD's to which he and his crew had been listening. "Your co-worker's happiness is your responsibility," he remembered the lady's voice saying. Under the present circumstances, he thought, that was extremely good advice.

Rhonda tied Commander Zwie to the same chair to which she had been tied. She had learned how to operate the ship by closely observing the aliens. It was relatively simple and there were few controls. One stick controlled the ship's direction and speed. There was a laser gun operated by a point and click mouse-like device. That's all she needed to know. She was now watching events unfold inside the compound.

28

Day of the Mole People

Hellfire and damnation were headed toward the Chinese compound shortly before Rhonda had taken over the space ship. The three formidable assault vehicles hauling our fearless attack force were racing southeast across the desert to confront the evil residing at the compound. The Deluxe UFO Tour Company van led the way. Its military insignias, which also served as advertising in peacetime, were the alien heads painted on its sides. This was very intimidating to any would-be enemies of righteousness and justice. An extra element of fear was achieved by Virgil's forgetting to remove the moustache and vampire teeth graffiti added by mischievous teenagers.

Following closely was Howard Winklethorpe's pink Cadillac convertible. Because the top was down, wind blasted through the open car forcing its three lethal, female impersonator occupants to hold their wigs in place with their right hands. Surely no Chinese army ever faced a force such as ours. We would soon arrive and the Chinese eunuch vampire warriors' worst nightmare would become reality.

I was feeling guilty at this point because, in a moment of pre-battle jitters, I had consumed three beers and four sodas I mistook for beers. What initially motivated my flight into alcoholic escapism was the state of our own attack force. What could a force such as ours, force being used very loosely here, do against powerful armed warriors?

I feigned confidence and assured everyone we would conquer the enemy. In reality, victory was hopeless unless Galen could score an early, overwhelming defeat with his Zuyglyphen grenade of genus siestacillus and put them all to sleep. That was the key to the success of the mission. Let's face it, the Chinese eunuch vampire warriors are professionals. They each weighed at least two hundred pounds and carried big swords.

Although I tried to maintain a glass half full attitude, I realized our commando force of un-trained, non-professionals might have some serious Achilles' heels type issues, un-trained and nonprofessional being two of them.

"Hey Stan," Billy the Kid yelled, "can we stop for a minute? I gotta go." We pulled over to the side of the road and Billy got out, followed by Cole, Butch, Bart and Jesse. I got out too, wondering if my three beers and four sodas were a more justifiable excuse for stopping than were the five outlaws' ancient bladders. In a few minutes we were on our way again.

Then there were the three karaoke competitors outlandishly cross-dressed for maximum impact on the "Karaoke Star Stage." How could they fight two hundred pound, sword wielding Chinese warriors when they were fighting to keep their balance in their six inch high heels? The sheriff hadn't even brought his gun as his holster didn't match his purse.

Actually, the most formidable warrior we could put on the field was Desert Chickadee. She had already proved her mettle by defeating the Chinese warriors who invaded her house. For all I knew, she might be able to defeat all thirty-nine Chinese warriors herself.

We had pulled up and stopped at the closed wooden gate of the compound. I got out and walked over to the gate and knocked. It opened slowly, but only a crack.

"A red robed Chinese warrior type stuck his head out and looked me over.

"What you want, fella?" he asked.

"We would like to see Yao Wie," I replied.

"Yao Wie not home now. He at........," the warrior paused, turning to look back at whoever was prompting him. "He at school picking up his kid."

Being the perceptive detective that I am, I sensed his story was full of holes. First of all, it was Saturday. There was no school. Second, how can a eunuch have a kid? He has no, a, well, a, no equipment to make that happen.

At this point, Special Government René Orbostrowski, who had been struggling to walk in his six inch heels, had managed to reach the gate and our conversation. He introduced himself and stated that he, as a duly appointed special agent for the government, was authorized to search the compound for a kidnapped U.S. citizen named Rhonda Wilkenshaver.

"She not here," the warrior said. "You go way. That nice dress you wear but you too fat. You break dress," he said, pointing to the burst straps held in place by safety pins.

René again insisted that we be admitted to the compound. Apparently, his little black dress and patent leather heels projected a greater level of authority than I had been able to achieve dressed in my shorts and tee shirt.

"You wait here," the Chinese warrior said. "I go check Yao Wie."

"You said Yao Wie was not here," I reminded him.

"He come back now," the warrior replied. With that, he closed the gate.

We waited in the hot sun for approximately five minutes. The gate again opened slowly and the same warrior appeared. "Yao Wie say you go to hell," he said. He began to close the gate.

Anticipating there might be a problem, we were ready for action. Our small army of commandoes had donned their antique gas masks and was poised to attack. I jumped forward, throwing myself into the narrow space between the closing gate and the wall. I was pushing the gate backward as hard as I could, but the Chinese warrior was definitely stronger. However, René was now pushing with me and the gate suddenly flew open as the Chinese warrior turned it loose and retreated across the courtyard screaming for reinforcements in his little girl voice.

Thirty-eight other red robed Chinese eunuch vampire warriors poured into the courtyard and formed a defensive line across its south side. Our assault vehicles were now inside the gate however, and our commandoes were lining up on the north side of the courtyard. This would be a fight to the death. René and I quickly donned our gas masks.

The only commandoes among us that had any weapons were Galen Withersby carrying the Zuyglyphen grenade, the five geriatric gunslingers with their six shooters, and Desert Chickadee with her baseball bat. They formed the front line of our attack force. Manfred, Thigpen and I, along with Dog Mayor and Latisha, were in the second line of attack along with Sheriff Landers, Special Agent Orbostrowski, and Howard Winklethorpe.

While we knew we were out-muscled by the group of Chinese warriors, as we stood facing them in our antiquated gas masks, I sensed apprehension on their faces. They had, after all, come from the fifteenth century. They had never seen gas masks before. They seemed to think the masks were our actual faces. As such, they wondered what kind of creatures they were fighting. Perhaps we were aliens from another planet. Or, maybe we were strange monsters come to destroy them. The large eyes and long thick snout of the gas masks were frightening them.

Yao Wie came out of his office and moved to the center of the rigid straight line of Chinese warriors and was now in a position to lead them forward. They began advancing slowly with their swords drawn. We held our ground, waiting to see what the warriors would do next. As they walked, I noticed their line was wavering as various warriors slowed their pace and lagged behind the others. Some stopped moving altogether and stood staring at us. Then, what remained of their line stopped when they were within twenty yards of us, leaving only Yao Wie still marching forward to engage our fighting force.

Yao Wie, not realizing his group of warriors was no longer marching behind him, now stopped approximately five yards from our front line. The thirty-eight warriors had stopped at various points along the direction of march and were now scattered in back of Yao Wie. He stared menacingly at us for a few moments, but then sensed that all was not as it should be in back of him. He turned his head slightly to his right and then left, hoping his peripheral vision would reveal what was going on behind him. There was an empty space where before there were warriors. He turned around, only then realizing that all of his warriors had stopped in their tracks at random points along the march forward. Many of them were shaking, unable to move. Five or six dropped their swords and ran back to their barracks screaming hysterically in their little girl voices.

As they had gotten closer to our commando force they got a much better view of the hideous gas masks they assumed were our faces. What they only suspected before was now very clear fact. They were under attack by an alien force from outer space or some sort of giant insects out of a 1950's "B" movie.

What we did not know was that there exists a terrifying Chinese legend about evil mole people who left the surface of the earth many centuries ago. At an unknown time in the future, these evil mole people would once again rise up out of the earth and kill humans that lived on the surface. The Chinese warriors concluded the "day of the mole people" was at hand and the monsters now stood before them ready to kill them all.

Galen saw his chance. He pulled his genus siestacillus grenade out of the pocket of his wool sport coat and stepped forward, slightly lifting the bottom of his gas mask. In true dramatic flair taken straight from the pages of a GI Joe comic book, he raised the grenade to his mouth and took the circular metal pin between his teeth. He yanked the grenade forward anticipating the pin would slide easily from the handle thus allowing it to fly off when he threw the armed grenade at the enemy. That was how GI Joe did it, he recalled.

Galen's painful yell informed everyone that the stubborn pin had not cooperated in being pulled out, the result being that he had instead broken two of his teeth. His shriek also caused another half a dozen more warriors to run screaming to their barracks. But Galen recovered quickly, and decided pulling the grenade's pin with his index finger would be a better idea. He did exactly that as the remaining Chinese warriors stood frozen where they had stopped, trying to decide if they were terrified, dumbfounded or both.

Galen threw the grenade toward the Chinese warriors and it landed in front of Yao Wie who had fallen back to join the fragmented group of warriors. The terrified warriors were curious and moved closer to the grenade lying on the ground. Suddenly, there was a soft popping sound and a puff of white smoke shot out of the grenade. The Chinese warriors simultaneously screeched in alarm and jumped back several paces. Another four warriors ran squealing toward their barracks.

"Forward, men," Galen commanded. We now began marching, confident that the grenade, which had been perfectly thrown, would do its work. In a tactical oversight, however, none of us had checked the direction of the wind. The Chinese warriors were lined up to the southeast, which is the direction from which the wind was blowing. The wind was therefore blowing the Zuyglyphen grenade's potent genus siestacillus to the northeast, in the opposite direction of the Chinese warriors, and toward us. The invisible gas was no problem as it blew past because we were wearing our protective masks. We didn't give it a second thought that the gas was also blowing toward the town of Empyrean.

The remaining twenty or so Chinese warriors, seeing the group of evil mole people was advancing toward them, decided to make a desperate last stand. Yao Wie rallied his troops and they reformed into a line, their swords once again raised.

At that point, there was no choice. Billy the Kid drew his six gun and began blasting away at the advancing line of red robed warriors.

Cole Younger, Black Bart, Jesse James and Butch Cassidy immediately followed suit and joined in with their guns blazing. The line of warriors broke again, with red robes running in all directions screaming in their shrill voices. Yao Wie, yelling directions to everyone but no one in particular, stood in the middle of the blazing guns, gun smoke, and screaming warriors running crazily back and forth to nowhere.

The courtyard was in total chaos with bullets flying and ricocheting off every surface and breaking windows in the buildings around the compound. Every window in our parked assault vehicles was broken, as were the headlights. This strange phenomenon occurred even though the parked vehicles were in back of us and the five gunslingers were shooting in the opposite direction of the vehicles. Oddly, no Chinese warriors or anyone else appeared to have been hit. The vehicles however, were "shot all to hell" as Black Bart later described them.

The gunslingers, who had received no prior notice about the attack on the Chinese compound, only carried a few spare rounds of ammunition and they immediately ran out of bullets. The Chinese however, did not know that. When the shooting stopped, they quickly surrendered assuming that since none of them had been injured, the purpose of the loud weapons had only been to warn them. They figured that if they quit now, they would be spared the really bad things that would soon happen. Yes, it was definitely best to quit now, they decided. All thirty-eight red-robed Chinese eunuch vampire warriors gathered into a circle in the middle of the courtyard, throwing down their swords and raising their hands high in the air.

Suddenly, out of nowhere, Gan appeared, and was now standing next to Yao Wie.

"What are you doing, Yao Wie?" he screamed.

"We quit now while ahead," Yao Wie replied. "Where you been Wall Street guy?"

"I've been on the space ship, but I have good news. My space ship is coming and the Mother ship just called me on my "Buzzy "and it will also be here soon with reinforcements."

"No need Wall Street guy. We quit now, go back to Emperor in fifteenth century. We no do this no more. Bad for health."

"Oh no you don't" replied Gan. "You must stay here with me and lock those people up. We will take them to the planet Rhostugasht.

Ha, ha. That will take care of them."

"They got bad weapons, Wall Street vermin," Yao Wie replied. "No want men to get hurt. We lose one man already because of you."

"Well I have a bigger gun than they do, little yellow guy," Gan replied.

"I told you not call me yellow guy," screamed Yao Wie.

"When you see what I do to them you won't care about that," replied Gan, as he pulled out a strange looking pistol from the holster on his belt.

He pointed the weird gun in the direction of our commando force and took aim.

"Watch this, Yao Wie!" Gan yelled, as he prepared to blast us commandos into infinity.

Abruptly, a four foot wide hole near Gan's right foot was ripped open as a white laser ray blasted into the dry desert ground.

"Put down your weapon, Gan," someone commanded from above.

Everyone looked upward to see a large oval disc, a real UFO, quietly hovering over the battlefield. Desert Chickadee immediately recognized Rhonda's voice.

"I have taken command of your space ship, Gan." Rhonda's voice boomed. "Put down your weapon or I will blast you next."

Gan had no choice but to drop the weapon immediately. I ran over and picked it up.

"Fly any kites lately?" I asked. Gan didn't smile.

"You idiots," he screamed at the hovering space ship. "You are idiots. They're idiots," Gan screamed as he shook his fist skyward at the UFO. "I'm gone for thirty seconds and they let her take over the ship. They're idiots." Dog Mayor ran over to where Gan and I were standing.

"Remember me?" Dog Mayor screamed, accidentally barking several times between words.

Gan did remember him, and definitely understood the gist of what Dog Mayor had said. In case clarification was needed, Dog Mayor was now making his point ever more clearly as he stood with his right hind leg held high and urinating all over Gan's pants leg and shoe.

"Remember me, now?" Dog Mayor screamed at the cowering Gan. "You species altering pervert, you recidivist, you deviate, you apostate, you fiend, you, you........"

Dog Mayor had temporarily run out of words. That was a good thing because I didn't know the meanings of at least two or three words, actually, everything after pervert.

"Gan," I said, pointing the gun at him, "change the Chihuahua back into his human form."

Gan reached into his pocket.

"No tricks," I sternly warned him. "You're not exactly the most popular guy here and I wouldn't mind doing you in, as they say."

Actually, I didn't like violence and had no intention of "doing him in," but it's what they always say in the movies and I thought it would make an impression.

"No, no," he nervously replied with his hands slightly raised to show he was not about to try any tricks.

Gan reached back into his pocket and pulled out a small, black rectangular object. "This is a species permutator device," he said. He moved some tiny dials on it, pointed it at the Dog Mayor and said, "Get ready!"

In an instant, a naked man was now standing where the Chihuahua stood a moment before.

"Thanks Stan," ex-Dog Mayor now naked man said. "Excuse me. I have to get some clothes."

He was no longer the Dog Mayor now. He was just the mayor.

"My god," we've won!" Manfred exclaimed, although I could tell by the way he was continuously scratching his head that he was having much trouble accepting that most unlikely outcome.

"Stan, we won!" said Thigpen. "It is Stan, right Stan?"

"Yeah, Larry, it is. I know we've won." I stood shaking Galen's hand. "Was there ever any doubt in your mind?" I asked.

Latisha was also very excited and hugging Nhoame, as difficult as that was with his skinny little body. Then she hugged me. However, I could tell she was anxious to rescue her partner Nancy Nussbaum.

Rhonda landed Gan's space ship in the middle of the compound and marched the four person crew down the walkway and put them into a cell. We quickly rounded up the entire group of thirty-eight Chinese eunuch vampire warriors and put them in cells that had no windows so they couldn't change into their bat forms and escape. Nhoame was an immediate hero when he freed the ninety-nine captive aliens. We also freed Rock and Herby. Unfortunately, Nancy Nussbaum was nowhere to be seen. Latisha was visibly disappointed.

"Don't worry, Latisha," I reassured her. "We'll find Nancy, I promise." Although I was more confident about saying things like that now, I had no idea where to look for Nancy if she wasn't in the compound.

Before I put Gan into a cell with a visibly upset Yao Wie, I took his species permutator device so he wouldn't be tempted to change anyone into some other species such as he had done to the Dog Mayor.

I looked over at Manfred. He was still scratching his head trying to understand how we had defeated the formidable Chinese eunuch vampire warriors and captured the aliens' space ship. I understood Manfred's bewilderment. I'm not really sure how we did it either. But we could sort all that out later at Bud's Rio Malo over a beer.

The three cross dressed karaoke contestants were holding hands and dancing around in a circle, obviously giving themselves most of the credit for the victory. And I suppose if shock and awe had anything to do with our conquest, the grotesque appearance of the three overweight transvestites in their mole-like gas masks provided a great deal of both.

The five outlaws were engulfed in a self-congratulatory hand shaking frenzy, not remembering whose hand they had or hadn't already shaken. They were also trying to figure out why approximately one hundred and fifty bullet holes were in our assault vehicles.

Everyone knew that righteousness and justice had prevailed. The day was ours. At least that's what we thought. But suddenly, a massive dark shadow blanketed the compound and surrounding area. We looked up to see a huge UFO directly above us. It was of such large size that it extended to the horizon in every direction. It was well over a mile in diameter. We knew we had troubles now. There was no way we could hope to defeat this monstrosity of high technology.

"Everyone stay where you are," boomed a familiar and unsettling voice from above.

"I know that voice," I said.

"Stan, don't you recognize who that is?" Latisha asked.

"I know the voice, but who is it?"

"That's Nancy."

"What?"

A portal on the underside of the UFO opened and a blue, mist-like transparent cylinder projected downward. Two people descended through the tube to the ground. As they stepped out of the bluish tube and walked toward us, I recognized my ex-wife, Nancy. Just as surprising, however, walking beside her was my sort of girlfriend, Jean Monaghan.

To say that everyone was overwhelmed would be an understatement. We all anxiously waited, wondering what was going to happen next. Thigpen, Nhoame, Rhonda and our entire commando group gathered around Latisha and me. Manfred, Galen, the five ancient outlaws, Desert Chickadee, Sheriff Landers, Howard Winklethorpe, René Orbostrowski, Manfred and Galen were prepared to make a last stand. It was touching. I was not thinking last stand, however, taking the glass half full approach. Dog Mayor, unable to find any clothes other than a red Chinese robe, rejoined us. "It's all I could find," he said.

Nancy, wearing a silver jump suit adorned with medals and insignia indicating a high military rank, stopped in front of us. Jean Monaghan stood next to her. Nancy greeted Latisha and me as we stood dumbfounded. She winked at Latisha and Jean nodded at me and smiled, lessening the formality of the situation.

"Hello, Stan," Nancy said. "I hope you don't mind my checking up on your love life. I strongly approve of Jean. She said you came to Arizona to rescue me because I was kidnapped. That's very sweet of you. I didn't think you had it in you to do something like that."

"It seemed like the right thing to do, Nancy," I said.

"I do appreciate it."

Then she looked at Nhoame. "You will be happy to know the Salabians will no longer be raiding your planet and killing your people." She turned to Latisha. "The night you thought I was kidnapped, I was really leaving on my own accord with Chinese warrior spies. The emperor heard that Gan was using his Chinese warriors to create misery and death. He didn't like that. We have a good working relationship with him and we want to preserve it. Gan had no right to enslave other people and then use them as gladiators to ultimately be killed. By the way, where is Gan?"

"I'll get that no-good bully for you," Rhonda said in a firm voice.

Rhonda retrieved Gan, and holding him by his right ear, pulled him toward Nancy and our commando group.

"I heard you had trouble with Gan, Rhonda. What punishment do you recommend for him?"

"That's easy," replied Rhonda. "Make him a eunuch and send him back to the fifteenth century with the rest of the Chinese eunuch vampire warriors."

"Done," said Nancy. Rhonda hauled the squealing Gan back to his cell.

"Latisha, you and I are leaving together," Nancy said. There are a lot of places in the Universe I'd like you to see. Nhoame, you can have the small space ship to take your people back to your planet."

Then Nancy moved toward me. "You're all right, Stan," she said. "Because of your helping Latisha, we'll close this compound down and you can have it for whatever purpose you wish to use it. Nhoame can drop the Chinese eunuch vampire warriors and Gan off in the fifteenth century on the way to his planet."

With that, Nancy and Latisha walked arm in arm to the bluish tube protruding from the large craft. They turned and smiled before they ascended upward through the misty tube and into the mother ship. The massive flying machine instantly shot skyward without a sound and disappeared.

"I bet they have ladies' rooms on that baby," said Rhonda.

29

The Deluxe UFO Tour Company

Our group of commandoes headed back to Empyrean in our bullet riddled assault vehicles. It was noteworthy that no one had fired any guns except our five outlaw friends. They didn't manage to hit anything except our own vehicles. The mayor, in his restored human body, was leading the way, riding alone in the truck he borrowed from the Chinese compound. Our Deluxe UFO Tour Company van was next, carrying Jean Monaghan, Thigpen, our five gunslinger sidekicks and Nhoame. Nhoame opted to stay on Planet Earth and work at the Deluxe UFO Tour Company.

Manfred's car was next, carrying Galen, Desert Chickadee, Rock, Rhonda and Herby. They were followed by Howard Winklethorpe and his pink Cadillac with its passengers Sheriff Landers and Special Agent Orbostrowski.

Everyone was finally happy. Dog Mayor had been transformed back into a human. Rhonda had gotten her revenge on Gan by stealing his space ship and sending him to the fifteenth century as a eunuch. And Nhoame's ninety-nine friends had been freed. Oh yeah, and I rescued my ex-wife Nancy, in a manner of speaking. But, Latisha was happy and that made me happy. Of course, Jean Monaghan's being there also made me happy.

Before we left the Chinese compound we turned the space ship over to Nhoame's ninety-nine friends so they could return to their planet. Along the way, Nhoame's friends would accelerate to hyper-warp speed, which allowed time travel. By so doing, they would be able to deliver Yao Wie, his Chinese eunuch vampire warriors, and Gan back into the fifteenth century. Six of the Chinese eunuch vampire warriors stayed behind to form a choir. Their being allowed to stay was conditioned on signing a pledge to confine their blood-sucking to Phoenix bars. I mean, like anyone really cares about those mindless revelers in Phoenix.

As a side note, the Emperor was delighted to have the vampire eunuch warriors come back to the fifteenth century as he was very short of eunuch personnel. His Public Relations Staff just couldn't spin the positive advantages of a career path that began with having one's testicles hacked off. It was "so American company" the potential recruits would say. Besides, women were forcing their way into the Eunuch Vampire Warrior field that confused the testicle hacking thing even further. Change is a bitch, literally, the older eunuchs thought. They were later sued by the women who wanted their jobs.

We were just approaching the city limits on the south side of town. As on the north side, a faded yellow welcome sign displaying two silver UFO's informed travelers they were entering Empyrean. In bold letters, the first two lines of the sign proclaimed, "Welcome to Empyrean, Home of the Most UFO Landing Sites on the Planet Earth." The third line provided the additional bona fides, "They landed here before they crashed in Roswell." The final line was the town motto, "I found myself in Empyrean, Arizona." For some strange reason, I was comforted by the sign, even though its peeling paint made it barely readable in some spots.

"I like the sign," Jean said. "It makes it sound like a person can find out who they really are in Empyrean, Arizona."

I smiled. "I think you're right."

But when we entered the city limits there was trouble. It was as if the town was frozen in time. Everything was stopped. Cars were parked in the middle of the street with their drivers sleeping and people were lying on the sidewalk, also asleep. I drove the Deluxe UFO Tour van over to the curb and Manfred pulled up behind me. Manfred, Galen and I got out of our vehicles to talk.

"Oh no," Galen said. "We never checked the wind direction before I set off my Zuyglyphen genus siestacillus grenade. The wind blew the gas into Empyrean."

"You'd think it would have dissipated before it got to town," Galen absently-remarked remarked in true scholarly fashion. He sounded like a frightened school kid who did a bad thing. When I thought about it, he was a school kid since he'd been in his Ph. D. program for thirty years. And he did a bad thing. He put the entire town to sleep.

Manfred was not impressed. "Galen, you have to stop doing these crazy things. You'll get kicked out of town if you don't."

I turned to Manfred and reminded him that it was Galen who had saved the day. "Look we'll blame the sleeping gas thing on Gan the Salabian and the UFO's. That will keep Galen out of hot water. We owe him that, don't you think?" Manfred agreed and that was the end of it.

Rather, it was almost the end of it. All the emergency services were located on the far north side of Empyrean and they apparently had not been affected by the genus siestacillus gas. As we drove further, it was clear that every EMS person, ambulance, fire truck and police car were on Main Street waking people up and giving them coffee. They were working their way through the town and making very good progress. On second thought, I had no way to really judge their progress as I had never before been in a town where everyone abruptly fell asleep in the middle of the day.

Manfred, Galen, Thigpen and I were trying to look as innocent as possible as our Deluxe UFO Tour Company vehicle with its shattered windows and bullet holes rolled past the drowsy citizenry.

"Remember, we blame it on UFO's," I said. Our shot up vehicles didn't provide added credibility however.

It took about a month before things got back to normal, as if normal was even a remote possibility for Empyrean. On this particular day I was holding a meeting with the Tour Committee, which included Rhonda, Herby, Nhoame and Thigpen. We were going to have our grand opening tomorrow and we wanted to go over the final route and the events that would happen along the way. We would also do a dry run today after the meeting.

We had installed a paved waiting area outside with benches and a roof to protect customers from the sun. Tours would run every two hours and twenty-four people could go on each tour. Herby Titsmore would drive our new bus to and from the tour area.

The tour route originally set up by Larry Thigpen included ten stops. However, we decided to have two levels of tours, Platinum and Regular. The difference between the two was that the Platinum Level Tour, which only ran once each day, included an extra stop at Desert Chickadee's house to enjoy her "Sun Welcoming Ceremonial Dance." While Desert Chickadee insisted that it was an authentic American Indian ritual, my research did not uncover any such ceremony or dance in the Native American repertory. That's not to say that I didn't miss something because I'm not a detail man. At any rate, that tour was by necessity an early morning tour.

Since Desert Chickadee collected fifty dollars from Deluxe UFO Tour Company for every dance, she was also trying to talk us into an evening "Farewell to the Sun Ceremonial Dance." While she insisted this too an authentic American Indian dance, once again my research could not find any references to this particular rite in the Native American inventory.

The committee decided that the "Sun Welcoming Ceremonial Dance" included with the Platinum Level Tour would be sufficient. If it proved successful, we might later adopt Desert Chickadee's evening dance.

In our original planning, the Regular Level Tour had all ten stops located in the desert. While all the stops were scenic, they basically looked the same. Each stop had red rocks, mountains, cactuses and other desert vegetation. It was all beautiful and adults might enjoy the scenery for a few stops, but seeing the same thing over and over would not keep anyone's attention for long.

We decided to enhance each of the stops with some kind of surprise or unusual happening. That would break up the tour a little bit and add some interest and suspense. Thigpen made a series of recordings and installed miniature sound systems at certain stops on the UFO landing spot tour. The miniature sound systems in the brush were activated by the tour driver pushing a button on his steering wheel. On stops where there was no sound system, he left little clues that aliens had recently been there.

For stop number one, Thigpen recorded the sound of a vacuum cleaner followed by the take-off roar of a jet plane. This made the people on the tour think that a UFO was taking off from behind the big rocks.

On Stop number two, Thigpen recorded two Chinese eunuch vampire warriors speaking to each other very rapidly in Chinese, as if two aliens from outer space were having a conversation behind the rocks. Of course, we realized that if any Chinese people took the tour, they might recognize the language. On the other hand, who knows? Aliens from outer space might speak Chinese since China is claiming it not only owns the planet Earth but the entire Universe. Maybe they do.

On Stop number three, Thigpen made little alien markings at the base of one of the large rocks. The tour bus driver luckily had the translation of these symbols. "Greetings people of Earth."

On Stop number four, there were again alien symbols on a rock. "Turn back, people of Earth. Do not proceed."

And, the same for Stop number five. "People of Earth. You have been warned!"

On Stop number six, Nhoame jumped out from behind a rock and put his hands in the air and then ran back behind the rock. The tourists had no idea this was an actual extraterrestrial.

On Stop number seven, one of Manfred Starshine's apprentices sat at a small table dressed in a "celestial robe." We disembark here for a rest room stop, optional palm reading, and an invitation to visit Manfred's store on Main Street.

Stop number eight is one of the most interesting. Virgil Tarsenberg built an oval disc UFO looking contraption. He pretends he is working on it. This stop is called "UFO Repair Station."

Stop number nine features the six eunuch Chinese choir. They sing several songs in their beautiful high pitched voices. It doesn't have anything to do with UFO's landing, but it is definitely a weird experience to see six Chinese men in red robes vocalizing in the middle of the desert.

The last stop, number ten, features a bright metal sign with a philosophical message: "The truth is out there. So stay at home."

The committee decided we were ready to go. Everything was set up for the dry run so we headed out to the UFO landing sites. Rhonda actually had all scheduled tours booked for tomorrow. Things were looking up for the Deluxe UFO Tour Company, as well as me. Jean Monaghan found an apartment and a job as a teacher in Empyrean. Our romance was going well.

Mayor Bobby Jeperson was once again firmly in control at City Hall. He also set up his new campaign headquarters in order to run for governor. Being a cautious politician, he had never taken a stand on the immigration issue however his experience with UFO aliens emboldened him. In a daring move, his platform included a firm position that all aliens from outer space must have citizenship papers. He did not say how that law would be enforced. Not surprisingly, he had also become a leading animal rights advocate.

Sheriff Elliott Landers, Special Agent René Orbostrowski and Howard Winklethorpe set up a university at the Chinese compound. (Landers received an unexpected financial windfall when Gan the Salabian purchased his Ida LaBelle torch singer outfit and gave him several large diamonds.) The three men, passionate about higher education, renovated the compound and established Karaoke University. The university, which has the distinction of being the only institution of its kind in the United States, was fully accredited immediately.

While the three men kept their day jobs, except for Howard

Winklethorpe who was independently wealthy and had no day job, they devoted all their spare time to Karaoke University and even taught several of the classes. The course schedule lists the following classes taught by the three adjunct professors.

"The Art and Philosophy of Karaoke" - taught by Professor Elliott Landers

"Negotiation Skills" - taught by Professor René Orbostrowski

"Equestrian Singing for Cowgirls" - taught by Professor Howard Winklethorpe

Galen Withersby was appointed president of the University, which was its only full time position. He also awarded himself a Ph.D. from Karaoke University even though the school was only accredited as a four year university. Galen also appointed himself as head of the Zuyglyphen Studies Department, which offers one hundred and forty six different classes, the most of any department in Karaoke University or any other university for that matter. To date, no one has signed up for any of the classes.

The following courses are taught by other adjunct professors at Karaoke University. Obviously, the greatest intellectual burden falls to Professor Manfred Starshine.

"Interaction with Non-visible Worlds" - taught by Professor Manfred Starshine

"As so Here, Also so There" - taught by Professor Manfred Starshine

"Past Lives in Spheres Floating Around Us" - taught by Professor Manfred Starshine

"Self Esteem Through Tiny Breasts" - taught by Professor Nurse Fluckenberger

"Assertiveness Training" - taught by Professor Rock Wilkenshaver

"Olympic Target Shooting" - taught by Professors Billy the Kid,

Black Bart, Jesse James, Cole Younger, Butch Cassidy.

As said, Herby Titsmore drives the Deluxe UFO Tour Company tour bus. We upgraded to a small bus because our original tour van had two hundred thousand miles, shot out windows and was riddled with bullet holes. It fell short of the professionalism we desired in our now thriving operation. The government's generous monthly subsidy allowed for the extravagance of a new bus.

Rock Wilkenshaver's full time job is working at Bud's Rio Malo as a greeter. He dresses in a black cowboy outfit and carries a pretend six shooter. He describes the gunfight at the Chinese compound as if he was a participant. We actually found him hiding under his bed when we freed him from his jail cell.

Rhonda is the office manager for Deluxe UFO Tour Company and also responsible for ticket sales.

Lawrence Thigpen, the former owner of Deluxe UFO Tours, is now the general manager of the operation. He still has trouble remembering my name sometimes but his memory seems to be improving.

There was one incident however, which gave me pause. I walked into Bud's Rio Malo one night and sat down at Thigpen's table. "Who are you, Mister?" he asked.

"I'm Stan, Larry. My name is Stan."

"Oh, it's you, Stan. I couldn't see you. My contact lenses fell into my beer and I drank them."

Nhoame works for Deluxe UFO Tour Company as a "tour enhancer specialist." His job involves jumping out from behind rocks and scaring tourists riding in the Deluxe UFO Tour bus.

"Grand Opening of the Deluxe UFO Tour Company" signs were all over town. Tomorrow was the big day and I had to be at work early in the morning. Today had been a long day and I was tired. I wanted to go back to my new apartment and rest but Larry Thigpen insisted I go with him to Bud's Rio Malo Saloon for one beer.

"Okay," I said. "I'll have one beer with you Larry."

While I had experienced many shocks at Bud's Rio Malo, I was completely unprepared for what greeted me as I walked through the front door with Thigpen. Bud was smiling at me, which caught me totally by surprise. But everyone in the room was also smiling at me and cheering. "Good luck, Stan" signs were all over Bud's saloon.

Everybody wanted to buy me a beer. Even Bud was giving me

free beer. As I sat there on the bar stool, Wang, the naked bottomed Chinese gentleman whose seat I mistakenly occupied several weeks before, came up to me and shook my hand. I looked straight into his eyes as I didn't dare look down. As I shook his hand, curiosity finally got the best of me and I did check to see if he had on pants. I was shocked. He did.

He found the surprise on my face highly amusing and began laughing, as did everyone else who also somehow magically guessed what had happened. I began laughing myself. Then he asked me for a job at the Deluxe UFO Tour Company. He promised to wear pants so I hired him. Why not?

It was just two months ago that I arrived in Empyrean, Arizona, home of the most UFO landing sites on the Planet Earth. When I first got here, I had enough baggage to fill the luggage compartment of a 747 airplane. But now, life was starting to look pretty good. Everybody I knew was happy, including me. And I had a new business, which I now owned one hundred percent because the mayor sold me his half. It couldn't help but make money because of the ridiculous monthly government subsidy. I was also in a new apartment. I had some good friends for the first time I can remember. How could so many good things have happened in such a short time?

The answer was simple, yet profound. Somehow, I had discovered that place of universal truth and enlightenment for which I had searched at the bottom of so many beer glasses for so many years. My faith in mankind had been restored. And the crazy thing was, when I drove into Empyrean that very first day, the answer was right in front of me on a faded yellow sign. It was the town motto and it had proven to be so very true.

"I found myself in Empyrean, Arizona."

###

About the Author

James Wharton's books include:

Delirium
Deluxe UFO Tour Company.
Strange Breakfast and Other Humorous Morsels
The Destiny Project
The Jaguar Queen
Invasion of the Moon Women
Ghosts of the Grand Canyon Country,
Ghosts of Arizona's Tonto National Forest
Detour
Voyeurs
Ghost Pets

His coming books may be seen on his web site:

http://www.jameswharton.net

24304546R00112

Made in the USA
San Bernardino, CA
20 September 2015